UNDER A BLUE MOON

A.J. DOWNEY

BOOK NINE

COPYRIGHT

~

Editing & book design by Maggie Kern @ Ms.K Edits

Cover art and Indigo Knights logo by Dar Albert at Wicked Smart Designs

DEDICATION

To David, for pulling it out in the clutch and being fabulous with your time and music knowledge. I owe you one. I'm sure you'll find a way for me to repay you at some point. Love you, bitch.

*P*oe...

"Car thirty-two, we have a report of a carjacking at the corner of 153rd and Cash Street. Respond."

I picked up the radio handset as my partner, Brody, flipped the switch for the lights, holding off on the siren until I completed the call.

"Dispatch, this is car thirty-two, go ahead and mark us en route."

"Copy, car thirty-two. Report of one female victim and two witnesses. All three are waiting on the corner to make contact."

"Thank you, dispatch."

I hung up the radio.

"Amateur night back there," my partner grumbled.

"Right?" I asked.

Unnecessary information to trade over the airwaves always tended to annoy us. Everything that we needed to know was already coming up on the laptop screen, the airwaves needed to stay clear for priority-one traffic. It was crazy out there tonight. A Blue Moon. Somehow, the gods had seen fit to curse our asses with a second full moon in the same month.

"Victim's described as a blonde in a jean jacket and hoodie," I said, reading off the screen.

"Got a name?"

"Mmm – no."

"Seriously, they get a description but not a name? Jesus Christ." My partner made a noise of disgust that I wholeheartedly agreed with as we rounded the corner onto 153rd and slowed down on the approach to Cash Street.

A mixed-race dude jumped off the curb a block ahead and waved us down. We double parked and we got out.

"My girlfriend and I saw the whole thing!" he called out. "Dude, he shoved a gun in her face and *everything*. Scared the shit out of us, man. I thought he was going to shoot her!"

"Where is she?" I asked and he waved me along.

"She's over here with my girlfriend."

I followed the guy who couldn't have been older than nineteen over to the curb. Brody was already asking him questions. A pretty young black girl was crouched down and huddled next to a blonde woman who sat on the curb, her stylish but sturdy brown boots had their heels planted in the gutter, her head bowed, her forearms propped on her knees, her hands shaking. She wore a pair of jeans with the knees torn out and a jean jacket over a gray hoodie. Our victim by the description provided.

"Ma'am, are you okay? Are you hurt?" She looked up at me and I was rocked to my core. Nearly put back on my ass by a pair of eyes that belonged on a fairy princess out of some fairy tale, not set in a human face. Especially one as ethereal and as pretty as hers.

She had one deep bronze eye edged in green except for one wedge of blue that matched the other eye which was a startling blue that seemed too blue to be real.

"I'm not hurt, I'm okay," she said and yet her voice betrayed her some. It was exceedingly brittle but still with an undercurrent of steel to it. She'd been shaken up. *Hard*. But she was holding it together. The adrenaline crash hadn't come yet.

"Okay, you got your ID?" I asked her, trying to get ahead of it and the information I needed before the potential hysterics and inevitable waterworks.

She pulled her small utilitarian purse around from behind her hip, and I was glad she at least had that on her. That the perp hadn't gotten away with her complete identity. Bad enough he got her car, and maybe her phone. At least she was spared from having to cancel all her credit cards, etc. I took the laminated rectangle from her fingers that was her identification and frowned at the unfamiliar license image and setup.

"Washington State?" I asked. "A little far from home, aren't you?"

"This was supposed to be my new home," she said miserably and the harsh sigh that fell from her lips sent out some bad vibes.

I was writing down her info, Saylor Grace Dresden, last known address some place called Olympia in Washington State, which was clear across the country and *almost* then some it was so far west from here. Depending on the route she took, she had a couple of mountain ranges between her and Indigo City.

"Supposed to be?" I asked absently.

"My boyfriend and I have been together in a long distance relationship for close to five years – or, well, we *were* together. The plan was that I was going to join him out here. I thought everything was fine and that he was as excited as I was. Except, when I got here and knocked on his apartment door, he didn't look happy to see me. He said he had cold feet and that this was a really bad idea and he was sorry and just shut the door in my face. I was trying to find a place to park for the night and figure out what to do next when – *welcome to the city* – this guy ripped open my door, shoved a gun in my face, and told me to get out of my car."

"I'm so sorry, Ms. Dresden. That's not how I want to hear someone's been welcomed to Indigo City. Can you tell me what kind of car you drive?"

"Uh, yeah, it's a 1994 maroon-ish Volkswagen Golf and has one black fender and two black doors on the driver's side. Um, it's pretty banged up and has literally all my stuff in it."

She wouldn't look at me, her voice starting to wobble a little as she stared up the night-dark street. Her eyes misting over, she sniffed and looked at the ground so I wouldn't see her cry and my heart went out to her – it really did.

"Can you tell me what your assailant looked like?"

"Ah, yeah. Um, he was black. I know that sounds awful, but it's the truth."

"No need to apologize," I told her. "Anything else you can remember about him?"

"The gun was, um, black and a lot like yours, I guess."

"What about clothing? Did you see what he was wearing?"

While I talked with Saylor, my partner was saddled with the other two witnesses over by our patrol car. I took down her description of the guy and radioed in the details about both the perp and her car to dispatch to put out as an all-points bulletin.

"I'm really sorry this happened to you," I reiterated and I meant it. It was a shitty position to be in.

"I honestly don't even really care about the car or any of the clothes –

it's just my granddad's guitar was in the back seat and I really want it back," she said and wiped at her face.

"Okay, is there anything else you can tell me about the car?" I asked. "Do you happen to know the plate number or anything?"

"Oh, yeah, it's Washington plates." She rolled those spectacular eyes of hers and added sardonically, "Obviously." She blew out an unhappy breath and rattled off the number, peeking around my arm at my notepad to make sure I got it right. "Five-zero-four dash the letters *W, D,* and *E.*"

I got on the radio and called it in, reiterating the make, model, and adding the detail of the plate number for dispatch to add to the APB out on the car.

There was no telling what the guy was running from but most times a carjacking like that? The perp was trying to make a getaway from something much worse, more violent, and I couldn't exactly say I was surprised about that, especially in this neighborhood. A lot of shit went down in this part of the city, unfortunately. It was one of the poorer neighborhoods full of drugs with a bunch of robberies going down weekly.

"Can I get you a ride somewhere?" I asked her, and she shook her head, miserably thrusting her hands into her jacket pockets.

"Even if you could, it's not like I have any money for a hotel or anyplace to go. I had about forty bucks left to my name and that was in my guitar case."

"Wow. You literally put everything on this guy, huh?" I asked and tried to keep any hint of accusation or derision out of my tone. She didn't need judgment right now. It was probably the last thing she needed to be honest – I was pretty sure she knew exactly how stupid it was to have come all the way across the country for a guy. I felt my jaw tighten. Fucking scumbag to do her like that.

"You really trusted him, didn't you?" I asked softly and she looked up at me sharply.

"Yeah," she said quietly and tears slipped over her bottom lashes and coursed down her pale cheeks. There was something so raw and beautiful about it. The hurt radiating from her face, the ache in her heart represented in her eyes. She looked so tired, washed out by the lights strobing from the top of my car – her hair kissed by the light of the blue moon hanging low in the sky overhead.

For some reason, her pain and her fear was resonating with me unlike any other call I'd taken thus far. I didn't quite know what I was thinking but there was something brewing in the back of my mind. I was just waiting for it to hit the front of my consciousness so I knew what it was.

Before any thoughts were fully formed, my radio crackled to life at my shoulder. Both my partner and I looked at each other.

"What?" Saylor asked nervously. "What is it?"

"Might have found your car, honey. Come on and get in." My partner opened the back door of our patrol car and Saylor hesitated. She didn't look *nervous* but there was something there. Maybe a bad memory when it came to the cops back where she was from. She looked up at me and I smiled and gave her a nod.

"We'll take you to it," I said, and put a light hand on the back of her shoulder. She stared me in the eyes for a long moment before giving a light nod and letting me guide her to the back of the car. I put my hand on her head absently to protect it from the roof and she settled into the hard plastic seat.

Brody and I traded a look over the patrol car and I felt a grim expression settle on my face.

Her car wasn't even a mile away and was wrapped around a light pole. The suspect driving the car had tried dodging another unit and had zigged when he should have zagged. He'd popped off rounds and had thankfully missed, but the unit chasing him hadn't missed him. It was still coming out over the radio how bad it was.

"What's happened?" Saylor asked from the back seat and I turned in mine.

"Suspect was in an accident with your car," I told her, and she slumped back, turning to look out the window, the color draining from her already colorless face.

I glanced at my partner who was eyes forward, watching the road and studied his expression which was neutral, bordering on… bored.

Just another day at the office, I thought to myself. *Shitty things happen to good people every day.*

So why the fuck was this one bothering me so much? I read what was coming across the laptop screen and turned in my seat to steal another look at Saylor Dresden.

She stared out the window, huddled in on herself, her beautiful eyes vacant and her expression defeated and it made my heart twist almost to the point of pain. Still, it wasn't unlike any other call I'd ever been on. Nothing about this was outside my usual routine of shittiness I dealt with on a daily or nightly basis. Swing shift saw it all, and this really was no different.

Except for the fact that there might have been a little magic something or other in the air because of the blue moon. I was a cop, though; and cops weren't supposed to believe in magic.

2

*S*aylor...

I was so fucked. I was so fucked. *I was so fucked!* And it was way more than usual this time. I got out of the back of the police car, the cop who had been talking with me, working with me, held open the door for me and what I got out to look at had my heart sinking into the bottom of my boots.

My car was a total loss. The front end smashed in and wrapped around a light pole. Sparks occasionally showered down from the busted fixture, steam rose in a pissed off hiss from my fucked up engine compartment.

"Hold on." The cop's hand fell onto my shoulder, gripping it lightly when I went to move forward and go to my car.

I looked up at him and hated how my eyes felt too wide as I stared up at his handsome face. He gave me a crooked smile that held an edge of sadness and said, "It's a crime scene. Let me see if I can get anything out of it for you. Might not be able to for a while though."

"Okay," I said swallowing hard, not trusting my voice to say anything else without cracking on me. It was sort of how I felt. Cracked in two, all the important things and feelings leaking out. Like I had a hole in my soul and no way to stem the flow.

I have to remember that, I thought. *Write that down.* I hoped I would remember. My journal and notebooks were in my backpack which was with my granddad's guitar, which was currently in my smashed-up stolen car, which was currently police evidence and *oh, my God, I was so fucked!*

"Hey."

The cop who was trying to help me stepped between me and my smoking smashed-up car, as a firefighter let loose with a fire extin-guisher beneath the crumpled hood, drowning out any potential flames before they could start. I looked up into the officer's eyes which were gravely concerned, the color indiscernible in the dark, whatever color they boasted leeched away by the strobing red and blue lights flashing and overwhelming the purer light of the moon. His hand fell lightly onto my shoulder and gave it a squeeze and I took the strength that was being offered.

"You're going to be okay," he said evenly – and surprise, surprise I actually *believed him,* which was strange in and of itself. I didn't believe anyone anymore. Nothing was ever what it seemed and people were always fishing for an angle to come out on top. It just was the way the world was. It was a miracle I wasn't more cynical than I already was.

"What do I do now?" I asked softly, breaking down just a little. It'd been a long time since I was in a situation that I just didn't know how to get out of or fix myself.

"You wait here. I'm going to try and get you some of your stuff out of your car. I need to talk to the detective in charge to see if that's possi-ble. Aside from your boyfriend –"

"Ex," I cut him off sharply.

"Aside from your ex," he amended, "do you know *anyone else* in or around the city?"

"No," I said firmly.

"Okay." He nodded, pursing his lips together and staring back over his shoulder, eyes narrowed. I could see the wheels turning in his head and finally his hand fell from my shoulder and he said, "Wait right here. Don't move a muscle."

"Okay," I muttered and watched him move across the cracked and worn asphalt of the street, nearer to the corner and the curb that my car had jumped to a man standing with a notepad open in his hand, writing things down.

I watched him talk to who must have been the detective in charge and I could also see it was about as effective as ice skating uphill.

"Just take her to the homeless shelter on third for tonight! She can sort shit out at impound later!"

The cop who was helping me shook his head adamantly and spoke in a tone too quiet for me to hear, the expression on his face was clear, though. He was angry. Righteously so and on my behalf and he was fighting it out with this guy to get me at least some of my belongings. I gazed past him, longingly, at my guitar case sitting on top of the rest of my worldly goods in the back seat of my car.

It was *right there,* and I knew they wouldn't let me anywhere *near* my car in the impound yard without paying up first. At least, not if they were anything like the cops back in Washington. That'd been a nightmare the one and only time I'd managed to get towed, and I had done more than a few things I wasn't proud of to get my car out before the fees got so high I couldn't.

The officer helping me now swore, spit on the ground in his fury and stalked back over to me, and I felt my heart sink.

"Thanks for trying," I said faintly, defeated.

"Come on, I'm going to take you to a shelter for tonight," he said and gently took my elbow. His partner was standing in the street directing traffic and he called out to him.

His partner turned and I was numb and indifferent as he told him he was taking me to some homeless shelter on Third Avenue and that he'd come back to get him. His partner nodded and waved a random car through the intersection. It was busier on this street than it had been on Cody's. God, just the thought of his name sent a bitterness roiling in my mouth enough I wanted to spit.

He opened the back door of his patrol car for me and I got in. I was so angry at life literally kicking me in the balls once again, my eyes were growing misty with hot tears. I wanted to scream, I wanted to cry, and I wanted to rage for all the good it would do – but I couldn't. It wasn't seemly. That and I didn't want to be admitted on a psych hold for being crazy when I wasn't.

He closed the door behind me and I was grateful for the fact that the hard plastic seat felt heated. Likely as a byproduct of being over the car's exhaust system, but I would take it. It was a brisk fall evening heading into winter out there and the only good thing was the sky was clear. I would take dry cold over wet cold any day of the week. Washington had *always* been a wet sort of cold that had seeped in around your edges until you were frozen to your very soul.

In other words, not very pleasant.

"Okay," he said, getting into the driver's seat with an exhaled groan. "Away we go."

"Thanks," I said dully.

"For? I'm afraid I couldn't do much back there."

"You tried," I said honestly. "That's a lot more than I can say about most people when it comes to me."

"Tough life, I take it," he said.

"Kind of," I agreed. "Mostly went downhill after fifteen."

"How old are you now?" he asked.

"Old enough to know that it could suck worse," I said and sighed.

"It could *always* be worse no matter how hard it sucks," he said. "Don't discount the fact that what happened to you tonight was beyond a shitty situation."

"Trust me, I don't," I said. "Still, there's nothing I can really do about it. I just need to let it go and figure out where to go from here."

"I see," he said and we lapsed into a silence. I was okay with that. I didn't want to talk anyway. In fact, I was actually kind of grateful he hadn't pried about my past. I was a firm believer everyone had one and that in a lot of cases it should stay right behind them where it belonged. The journey was about the road ahead, not the one you'd already traveled.

"Out of everything in your car," he said suddenly, snapping me out of my inner monologue, "name three things you can't live without."

"My guitar in the back seat, my backpack on the front passenger floorboard, and the small carryon suitcase in the back seat under the guitar, in that order – why?"

"Just curious," he said and blew out a breath, pulling up to the curb in front of an odd little building.

It looked like an old roadside motel, except it'd been modified to an extent and *really* wasn't that big. The bottom floor was all solid garage doors, three of them in a row, and the second floor had a staircase leading up from one side of the building along an open-air walkway with a spindly metal railing bent in some places. There were three doors that faced the street, but it looked like the doors went around all four sides of the building.

"Come on, we're here."

"This doesn't look like a homeless shelter," I said and he got out of the car.

He opened up the back door to let me out and said, "That's because it's not. I just told the rest of them that to keep me out of trouble."

"Trouble?" I asked curiously. "Where are we?"

"Someplace safe," he said, shutting the door behind me as I stood in front of the building gazing up at the cracked and flaking blue-white paint between and above the garage doors.

"Follow me," he said and I fell in to step just behind him as he went around the side of the building, along a narrow alley to the stairs leading up to that second floor.

"This isn't a homeless shelter," I said nervously and he sighed and paused midway up the steps. He looked over the railing down at me and I bit my bottom lip and looked up. Though the neighborhood was rundown and poor, the streetlights were intact and the moon hung low in the sky illuminating things quite well. I stared up into a sincere pair of green eyes the color of new spring and he stared back searching my face.

"This is my place," he said finally. "And I could get into *a lot* of trouble for even considering this, but I can tell you've been through a lot and I just really want you to be safe tonight."

"You brought me to your apartment?" I asked and blinked one long slow blink of an amalgamation of shock, confusion, and yeah – even a little fear.

"Hey, whoa, nothing like *that*, I promise you. I really am one of the good guys. If you want to go to the shelter, I completely understand I mean – shit… I'm fucking this up, aren't I?"

"Yeah, kinda," I said a little hollowly. "First things first, um, *what is your name?*"

"Oh, shit – are you serious? I didn't tell you?" He looked like he'd sucked on a lemon and I laughed lightly.

"You might have," I said, coming around to the bottom of the stairs and starting my way up. "I honestly can't remember everything. Is that weird?"

"Shock," he said. "It's not weird. Look, I've never done anything like this in my life, and it's all up to you on what you want to do but my name is Jeremy. Jeremy Poe, but everyone just calls me Poe."

"Hi, Poe. I'm Saylor."

"Saylor Grace, yeah. I know. I read it on your license."

I nodded faintly and sighed, leaning a hip against the metal rail, suddenly feeling like I had a thousand pound boulder sitting between my shoulder blades, weighing me down.

"Look, I can let you in. You can take a hot shower, scrounge through my drawers, find something, and sleep for the rest of my shift. When I get home in a few hours, we can figure out what to do from there… what do you say?"

I bit my bottom lip and honestly, I was out of ideas and I *really* didn't want to crash in a shelter tonight. This wasn't like back home. I didn't know anybody here and so far? Indigo City had not been kind… except for this man.

I rolled the dice and took the risk.

"I'll stay."

"You're sure? Because I mean it, I'll take you wherever you want to go."

"I'll stay," I said, my voice a little stronger. "Thank you, Poe."

He gave a nod, his expression thoughtful as he turned and led me the rest of the way up the staircase and to the middle apartment door in the front of the building overlooking the street. He keyed open the lock on the front door, both the deadbolt and the doorknob and opened it.

"I'd say ladies first, but I don't want to creep you out any more than I probably already have," he said and went inside before me. He flipped a light switch just inside the door and stood aside for me to come in.

It was a cozy little studio. The kitchen straight ahead as you came in the front door, the bed and rest of the tiny apartment to the left with the bed taking up the majority of the main room. The kitchen was open on the side facing the room with a gap between the top cupboards and the countertop giving you a view of the bed.

He had a low dresser with a television on top of it beneath the kitchen counter, and the bed was a queen. I swallowed hard. I hadn't known what to expect, but a studio hadn't been it. I mean, I had at least expected a couch or something.

"I mean it. Make yourself at home. There's coffee and tea, maybe even some hot cocoa in the kitchen. Fresh towels are in the closet and everything in the dresser is clean. Help yourself to whatever you need."

"Thank you," I murmured not really knowing what to do with myself.

"I have three hours left on my shift. Maybe four with some extras. I'll be back probably no later than midnight but seriously – don't wait up. Get some rest."

"I will," I said gently and he nodded, searching my face.

"Come lock this door behind me," he said.

"You can trust me," I said. "I mean, I'm trusting you but you can trust me too. I won't rob you or narc you out. I'm not like that."

His shoulders lost some of their tightness and eased down slightly.

"I'm not going to get inappropriate with you," he vowed, "and I'm going to try and get you some of your stuff out of your car. Your guitar, backpack, and the carryon suitcase, right?"

"Yeah, but don't get yourself in trouble – please? You've already done way too much with this." I waved my hand around me by way of emphasis.

"Make you a deal," he said. "I won't worry about you if you don't worry about me." He gave me a wink and he was out the door, shutting it firmly behind him. I swallowed hard and went to it, turning the locks like he had asked.

I turned back to the room and watched his muted shadow pass along the closed blinds as he went between the window and the brightly illuminated streetlight outside. A few heartbeats later, the police cruiser started up and pulled away and I was alone in his home.

"Universe, you're giving me whiplash with my luck tonight," I murmured then belatedly added, "Thanks for this."

Of course, there wasn't any answer. There never was.

The first thing I noticed about Jeremy Poe was that he was extremely neat and orderly. His kitchen clean and barely used, everything in his main room which was also his bedroom was in its place. The only sign of remote disorder was the fact the bed wasn't made, but *God* did it look inviting.

I was telling the truth when I said I wouldn't rip him off, but that didn't stop me from being a horrible snoop – opening drawers and touching fabrics, peeking in cupboards and checking behind the little space's two doors. One was the closet with shelves in the back and neatly pressed uniforms hanging in their dry-cleaning plastic. I pulled down a towel, thought about it and eying the stack, pulled down a second one.

The bathroom was spotless, and I intended to keep it that way. I still did my due diligence and looked through the medicine cabinet, though. You could tell a lot about a person depending on the meds in their cabinet.

Jeremy Poe only had a couple of bottles of cold and flu medicine; one daytime formula, and one nighttime formula – a bottle of ibuprofen, a bottle of opioid painkillers that was over a year old and still had a majority of the ten prescribed tablets in its little orange cylinder. That was a relief. He definitely wasn't an addict. At least not to painkillers.

The rest of his medicine cabinet held tooth care and shaving needs. All in all, so far, Poe was ordinary and a little boring and that I could most definitely handle.

I didn't want or need any more excitement in my life at the moment, I'd had quite enough tonight alone, thank you very much.

I set my two pilfered towels down on the closed lid of the toilet and opened the glass shower door. It was just a shower, no bathtub, which I had to take a second and pout about. There was honestly nothing I loved more than to take a long hot soak, but a shower would have to do.

I locked the bathroom door and hung my denim jacket on the peg on the back, setting the rest of my clothes on the closed lid of the small stacked washer, peeking in the dryer above it. It was empty, and with a peek under the washer lid, I discovered that it was empty too. I decided that after almost a week of driving and sleeping in my car? I deserved this shower and clean clothes would be a mighty fine bonus. After all, this was just for tonight – who knew when I would have the opportunity to have either of those things again.

I emptied my pockets, shoved everything into the washer, and unlocking the bathroom door, darted across the 'hall' and fetched down some of the laundry pods off the shelf.

I didn't start the washing machine until I was out of the shower, grateful that wherever the water heater was, it was up to the job and apparently wasn't micro-sized like the rest of this placc was. I nicked one of Jeremy Poe's white wifebeater tank tops out of their drawer and a pair of his boxers out of another and made do with them until my clothes were out of the wash.

I settled cross-legged on his bed and breathed out, intending to stay awake until my laundry was out of the dryer. I made it all the way through the wash cycle. Got them into the dryer and started, but I was so tired by that point that I don't even remember crawling into his bed and stretching out. I certainly don't remember falling asleep all cozy in his underwear.

3

oe...

"Hey, Benny."

"Poe. How you doin' man? What brings you out my way?"

I stopped at the gatehouse to the impound lot and huddled in my leather jacket. Benny was a stone's throw from retirement and manned the gate at impound on his way out. He was getting too old to be pounding the pavement with us young bucks and hadn't been shy about telling me so when I was a rookie.

Albert Benny had been my field training officer and he was old-school. Something I was counting on, because while he wasn't *crooked* by any shape of the imagination, he was *old-school* and wouldn't have hesitated to give Saylor some of her essentials out of her car back at the scene.

Somehow, in the right applications, Benny had maintained his compassion and humanity even after thirty-five years of service.

He was the kind of cop I hoped to be at the end of my long bid.

"I wish it was a social call Benny, but there was a situation earlier tonight. Something I was hoping you could help me with."

"Aw, yeah? What's up, man? What happened?"

I explained Saylor's situation and Benny heard me out, sucking his teeth every once in a while, looking thoughtful. When I was through, he looked up at me and reached into the guard shack and flipped the switch to the cameras.

"Aw, damn. Not again! That's the third time this week," he declared and made a sweeping gesture with his hand to proceed.

"They really oughtta fix this old system," I declared, slipping around the arm leading in and out of the gate and hustling my way through the yard.

"Southwest corner!" he called after me and I waved over my shoulder.

I got all three items – backpack, guitar, and small suitcase – and took stock of the rest of the interior of the car by what I could see in the darkened corner of the lot. She had trash bags of clothes and blankets in the back seat, and boxes in the rear cargo area.

Her whole life was in this car and visually, it didn't amount to a whole lot. Especially when you boiled it down even further to just these three items.

I was hella tempted to snoop through them, but I resisted – just barely.

I got the hell out of the impound yard with a nod and some thanks to Benny on the way out. Back at my bike, I had to figure out how to strap and pack this shit on to get it back to my place.

It wasn't pretty, but I managed to make it happen. I was glad it was late. Getting on toward midnight on a weeknight meant that there weren't many people out. It meant there wasn't much traffic on the streets. I made it home, glancing up to the light glowing from around the blinds in my window as I waited for the garage door down here to open. I pulled in and parked. Turning out my headlamp plunged the rows of water heaters against the back wall into darkness. They all sat squat and hunched back there reminding me of a line of soldiers in the dark.

I took my time getting my spoils off the bike, coiling the paracord I'd used to tie everything down to the back of my seat and the back of *me* to get it home around one hand. I stashed it back in the compartment under my seat and stretched.

I was beat, but like the old poem said – I had miles to go before I could sleep. Not physically, but figuratively. Right now, I had a strange girl chillin' upstairs in my place and I had to talk to her and figure sleeping arrangements out. Likely, I would be making up a pallet on my floor on the side of my own bed and surprisingly? The thought didn't bother me one bit.

I let myself in my front door and set her suitcase just inside the door so I could transfer her guitar case into my other hand. She was lying on her stomach in my bed, *out cold.* I knew she'd been exhausted. There wasn't any way around it. I had also known once the adrenaline had worn off, she would need a safe space to decompress and there wasn't any place safer than completely alone behind locked doors.

I set her guitar on the floor and leaned it up against the kitchen counter but the damn thing slid and hit the floor with a bang.

I cursed, but damage done. I heard her suck in a breath and push herself up from her prone position.

I fought not to smirk, thinking to myself that even though it was out of pocket to think so, Saylor Grace Dresden looked damn good in my underwear.

"Oh, God," she groaned, hauling blankets to her chest to cover the stiff peaks of her nipples beneath the thin material of the undershirt she'd borrowed out of my drawer. "I meant to stay up and get dressed. My clothes are in your dryer. I hope you don't mind…"

"Nope. I told you to help yourself. I'm glad you did."

"Oh, my *God*! Is that my guitar?" She scrambled off the end of the bed, smoothing back her wild mane of just-past chin-length hair, hanging it up on her cute little ears as she forgot all about the fact she was wearing just my underwear in her excitement to get to the instrument.

I laughed. "Uh, yeah. I said I would do my best to get some of your things. I got lucky and pulled through."

She kneeled at my feet in the narrow space and opened the hard black faux-leather case with all of its random colorful stickers to reveal the old acoustic guitar inside.

It was a beautiful piece, even with its sunburst finish starting to flake in places. I couldn't tell you what brand it was or how old, but it was definitely a traveled and storied piece. She sat down right there on the floor and put it in her lap, playing a few chords, her fingers walking expertly up and down the frets, fingertips of her opposite hand plucking along the strings.

A neighbor banged on the wall of the kitchen and she looked up startled.

"Shit, sorry! I guess it's a little late."

"Ah, yeah, I get it though. It must be important to you."

"Very. It's one of the only things I have left of my granddad."

"I'm glad I could get it for you, then," I said and she set it back in its cradle of crushed blue velvet. She closed up the case and set it reverently against the end of my dresser where there was just enough wall sticking out behind it to keep it from sliding and crashing again.

"Thank you, seriously. I mean, you have no idea how much it means to me that you got it."

"I got this too," I said, shrugging out of her old-school olive drab military backpack full of patches of places traveled. The thing had to be nineteen seventies, probably found at a thrift or surplus store somewhere.

"Jesus! You got it all, didn't you?" she asked, taking it from me.

"Mm, just the things you asked for," I said, wheeling her suitcase from around the kitchen counter.

"Please tell me you aren't going to get in trouble for this," she said, looking up at me with those wide, dual-colored eyes of hers. I smiled and shook my head. They were even more beautiful in the dedicated light of my apartment lamp.

"I shouldn't, no," I said.

"Thank God. I seriously don't know what I would have done without you, tonight."

"This is definitely not something I've ever done before," I said.

"Well I'm grateful you saw fit to trust me, even though I'm not sure why you do," she said quietly.

"Me either, to be completely honest. I guess I just get a certain kind of good vibe off of you. After being a cop, you get a certain read on people, I guess."

She backed off and sat back down on the bed, hugging her backpack to her chest.

"Anything I can do to repay you, seriously, just name it."

"It's been a long night," I told her. "I honestly just want a shower and to get some sleep. I have work tomorrow."

"Sure. Um, I've had a nap – obviously. I can get dressed and go."

I shook my head and tried not to chuckle. I mean, there really wasn't anything funny about it. Instead, I stepped carefully around her guitar and toward my closet shrugging out of my leather jacket and cut and said, "How about this? I'm going to get in the shower and when I get out, you tell me how you want to handle the sleeping arrangements – what would make *you* the most comfortable, and that's what we'll do."

She chewed her bottom lip thoughtfully, those dual-colored eyes of hers roving my face and finally she asked, "Why are you being so nice to me?"

I shrugged and said, "Seems to me that you're overdue for some kindness. I mean, correct me if I'm wrong."

She shook her head and I raised my eyebrows.

"You're not wrong," she said softly.

"Kind of figured," I said kindly and went to my dresser, picking up my flannel pajama bottoms and plain white tee that were folded on top of it.

"See you in a few, I guess," she murmured after I pulled a towel down off the closet shelf. I gave her a nod and shut myself into my bathroom.

I sighed out and stripped down, kicking my boots into the corner by the door and tossing my clothes directly into the basin of my stacked washer and drier. I took a luxurious long and hot shower and half expected that when I did get out, that she would be gone. I was a little surprised to find that the thought vaguely hurt – but I would understand.

When I got out, I toweled off and got dressed pretty quickly. It wasn't quite cold enough to warrant turning on the heat yet, but it wasn't exactly warm out of the shower, either.

When I opened up the bathroom door and rounded the corner, she was still there. Sitting up in my bed, closest to the window and door, a pillow shoved behind her back and a leather-bound, thick journal open on her lap. She absently chewed the end of her pen as her eyes roved the page in front of her and she sighed out, a frustrated sound, and struck something through and scribbled something else below it.

"You make up your mind on how we're going to do this, then?" I asked.

She looked up at me and asked, "How old are you?"

"Just turned thirty, why?"

"I'm twenty-five."

"So?"

"So we're both adults past the age of consent and while I'm not consenting to sex, I think we're both old enough and mature enough to sleep in the same bed, if that's okay with you."

I smiled and nodded. "As long as you're good, that's all that matters."

"That hardly seems fair," she said.

I raised my eyebrows and asked, "How's that?" She considered me a moment as I rubbed my towel over my wet hair to get it from 'wet' to just damp.

"Consent goes both ways. I'm a firm believer in that. Women are just as predatory in their own way as men – it's just showcased differently."

"I can see your point and believe me – I've done a lot worse for myself than just sleep next to a pretty woman I've just met. I think we all have at some point or another."

Her lips crooked up into a one-sided smile and she asked, "So you think I'm pretty?"

"Shit," I said. "I did say that, didn't I? I'm sorry if I've made you uncomfortable."

Her smile took over the other side of her mouth and soon she was grinning, her nose wrinkling impishly. The look was adorable and I felt my heart do this skip-a-beat thing in my chest. I mean, if I were a dog, not a man, I would be panting and it was ridiculous.

"You're adorable, you know that Jeremy Poe?"

I laughed and felt myself blush slightly and asked, "Adorable? I don't think anyone's called me that since my memaw."

Her smile grew, as if that were possible and she got up out of bed and went to her backpack. She tucked her journal and pen away and came up with a toothbrush and a mostly used tube of toothpaste out of one of the side pockets.

"Just let me brush my teeth," she murmured and I stepped aside, between the bed and the wall to let her pass. She went into the bathroom and I tossed my towel into the dirty-laundry hamper in the bottom of my closet. There were a couple more in there and I was glad she'd felt comfortable enough to shower. Of course, why wouldn't she? She'd certainly felt comfortable enough to help herself to my underwear drawer. The thought pleased me, and every time I thought of it, I suppressed a chuckle. I went back out and switched out the light before heading to bed and climbing in on the side she'd left for me.

The water shut off a second later in the bathroom and she switched off the bathroom light.

"Oh!"

"Sorry, you good?" I asked, figuring she was taken aback by the dark of the room.

"Um, yeah."

She sounded uncertain and I frowned slightly.

"You sure? You don't sound like it."

"It's stupid," she declared and the bed dipped, her silhouette disrupting the faint lines of streetlight coming through the slats of the blinds over my window. She sank down on the edge of the bed, the mattress dipping slightly under her weight as she slid under the covers.

"I promise it's not," I said, genuinely curious by now.

"Twenty-five years old and I'm still afraid of the dark," she said quietly and I fought not to laugh. I succeeded but only by a slim margin.

"Why's that?" I asked.

"Why's what?"

"Why are you afraid of the dark?"

The bed shifted slightly as she shrugged.

"Bad things happen in the dark," she whispered.

"Good things happen in the dark, too."

She laughed and I was glad for it. I mean, I really wasn't trying to come off as totally creepy but it seemed like despite my best intentions, when it came right down to it I was suffering from foot-in-mouth disease tonight.

"That has to be one of the sweetest, yet cheesiest things that's ever been said to me." She giggled and I couldn't help but smile in the close dark. I turned from my back to my side and propped my head on my hand.

"What exactly is your story, Saylor Grace?"

She hummed out and turned onto her stomach, hugging her pillow to her chest.

"Well, I was born in California and when I was three, my mom and dad moved back to my mom's hometown; where my mom grew up in Washington. By the time I was five, my grandma was dying of cancer and my dad was drinking a lot. He would beat my mom. I don't remember much. I think I blocked it out or whatever, but he ended up killing my mom and himself and I ended up with my granddad."

"Shit," I said softly.

"Yeah. My granddad was awesome. The best thing ever. I mean, my grandma had died, so it was just me and him. Then, when I was fifteen, he had a heart attack and died in his sleep. I was put into foster care after that."

"Wow." I didn't know what else to say. I mean, she'd had it *rough*.

"I ended up sleeping under a bridge for the most part. The foster family was shit and I didn't want to be there. I didn't graduate but, I did eventually get my GED. I spent a lot of time couch surfing – the indie music scene was great in Seattle, but it was *so expensive* to live there, so I eventually went through my granddad's and my stuff in storage and pitched everything but the essentials. Took the car and made my way here to meet up with my now ex-boyfriend, Cody. *God, what a joke.*"

"Hey, it's not your fault, his actions are no reflection on *you*." Too many times I'd heard the victims of a given scenario blame themselves, or blamed by others for the pile of shit they'd landed in. It was a tough and bitter pill to swallow. Society had it all wrong in that regard. Yes, there were preventative measures a person could take when it came to being victimized, but there was never a one-hundred-percent foolproof way to avoid being victimized. It happened to the best of us. It happened all the time. It was a hard truth and a fact of life.

"I've heard that one before," she said with an edge of bitter laughter to her voice.

"Yeah, from who?" I asked and felt a little steel creep into my tone.

"Cops like yourself," she said a little more softly. The vulnerability in her voice at the confession made my heart brittle.

"Not like me. Cops, maybe, but not like me. Not like a lot of my brothers, either," I said.

"Brothers?" she echoed. "How many you got?" I could see her attempt at changing the subject but…

"Biologically, I have one sister. An older one. I'm talking about my club."

"Club?"

"Yeah, I belong to an MC or motorcycle club. We're all first responder and law enforcement types. They're my brothers in every which way but blood."

"Yeah?"

"Yeah." I heaved in a big sigh and let it out. "Cops are people, too," I said. "Flawed, imperfect. We got a lot of assholes on the force. Some of 'em jaded from too long on the front lines. Some of 'em have no business being cops – never have and never will, but it's tough when the whole department is judged by the actions of a few."

"You know what they say," she murmured, "one bad apple spoils the bunch."

"Yeah," I said unhappily, but I couldn't argue.

"You're one of the good ones, Jeremy Poe," she whispered after a long silence and I was riding that fine edge of sleep.

"Yeah?" I murmured, fighting to stay awake.

"Yeah," she whispered.

"Glad somebody thinks so, Saylor Grace."

She let out a little puff of air, stifling her giggle and said, "I'll let you go to sleep."

I don't know if I said it out loud but I certainly thought it, *I'm glad that somebody is you.*

4

___

*S*aylor...

I left a note and slipped out the next morning, promising to return for the rest of my things but itching to explore the city some. I mean, I was stuck here. I might as well make the best of it, right?

I walked until things became more populated and I found a pretty stable bus line, waiting for the next coach with my guitar in hand and my backpack perched on my back with a pocketful of change.

The bus fare was hella cheap here! Back in Seattle, it was pushing three bucks a ride, here it was just a little over half that. Yes, I had a car, but it wasn't always feasible driving it everywhere back in Washington. Olympia was sixty miles south of Seattle, but Seattle had the best spots for busking – er playing on a street corner, in the region. If I could score me a good spot at Pike's Place Market or on Capitol Hill, I could really rake it in. The best way to get around was, by far, walking or the bus system inside city limits, so I usually found a Park & Ride along the light-rail line or outside the city and rode mass transit in.

I sometimes spent weeks couch surfing, which is how I learned the hard way that I needed to go move my car every few days. I almost lost it after it got impounded for sitting too long. That was the first time. The second and last time it'd gotten impounded was when I had been pulled over for a taillight out, got caught driving without insurance and when I refused to blow the cop that'd pulled me over? Yup. Impounded again and left stranded on the side of the road.

I sat up front on the bus and made small talk with the bus driver, trying to get the lay of the land, eking out the best spots for us artsy types. Where the best busking in the city could be found – where the best tourist traps could be found.

I'd carefully written down the address number and apartment number of Poe's place and had walked to the end of the block and gotten the street name so I could find my way back. It was a pain in the ass without having a map of the city at my fingertips, but my phone had long since been shut off and the only way I could look anything up on it, get or return messages, or otherwise use it was when I could rob a Wi-Fi signal.

A map would be reeeeally handy. Even if it was a half-assed tourist map. Something was better than nothing.

"Awright, this is you, honey," the bus driver said, pulling up to a stop.

"Thanks, Bernard!" I got up from my seat.

"Well now, that would be my pleasure. You be safe out there now, y'hear?" He tipped his bus driver's cap in my direction and I smiled at him.

"Always am!"

"Welcome to Indigo City, now!"

"Thanks!" I called over my shoulder.

I looked up and down the street and let out a long slow breath. It was a beautiful waterfront area, the buildings old and reminiscent of Seattle's Pioneer Square except maybe a few of them were *older*. It made me feel right at home. Across the street were wide concrete steps leading down to a broad waterfront park.

Bernard hadn't steered me wrong. This looked like a prime location to set up shop, so-to-speak.

First order of business was coffee. I set off up the street, looking in the windows of little boutiques and peering down the steps into a flower shop just starting to set up for the day.

"Coffee?" I called out to the guy rolling out the display from inside.

"About half a block up there's a place," he called back without looking up.

I soldiered on, thinking about Poe and a few more doors down it was just a matter of following my nose.

"Oh, yes!" I whispered to myself in triumph as I came up on the source of the coffee and baked goods smell.

It was a little French bakery that was almost *exactly* like Le Panier at Pike's Place, back home.

Rich, buttery, flaky croissants were *just* coming out of the ovens and I recounted my money that I'd relocated from my guitar case to my front jeans pocket this morning, hoping that it'd somehow magically multiplied.

No such luck, of course, but this place was reasonably priced and for less than seven bucks I scored a cup of rich dark coffee lightened with heavy cream and a chocolate croissant.

This place was authentic as fuck! The rich, flakey pastry with its paper thin layers wasn't in a crescent shape meaning it had been made with real butter. I took my culinary prize to a table in the corner and called out to the hipster barista, "Hey, would you mind if I played outside your door for a little while?"

"Uh, it depends," he called back. "Are you on drugs?" I shook my head and pushed back my sleeves, rotating my arms so he could see.

"Do you suck?"

I laughed and said, "I think I do, but nobody else has ever complained."

"What's your name?" he asked.

"Saylor. You?"

"Josh. Where you from, Saylor?"

"Olympia, Washington, technically."

"Where?"

"Olympia. It's in Washington State."

"Never heard of it."

"It's the capital," I said.

"Don't care," he shot back. "Sure you can play for a while. Might want to suck that down and get started. The morning rush is about to start."

"Thanks for the tip, Josh!"

"No problem, and you better have a permit!" he called as I stood up. "If you don't have one, watch for the cops. The fine is twice as much as getting one."

"Where do I even get one and how much is it?"

"City center, the courthouse and it's only twenty-five bucks for the whole year."

I chewed my bottom lip and thought about it. "And the fine is fifty?" I finally asked.

"Yup, plus they can deny you a permit for up to a year if they really want to be assholes about it."

I heaved a sigh. "You are totally saving my life right now," I said.

"You must be *fresh* off the bus into town," he said and I went over and leaned a hip against the counter while he went around doing whatever needed doing behind it.

"Just got in last night, actually."

"Oh, yeah?"

"Mm-hm."

"Well," he winked a deep brown eye at me and blew a stray dark curl off his forehead that had escaped his man bun, "welcome to Indigo City, Saylor Moon."

I rolled my eyes. "Like I haven't heard *that* one before."

He laughed and I sipped my breve, and asked, "How far is it to the courthouse to get this permit?"

"You got enough for one?" he asked.

"Barely. It's going to probably wipe me out and leave me enough for a few bus rides, but I'm literally stuck here until I get some capital built up and I would really rather not blow it and be looking over my shoulder every twenty seconds for a cop. Do it right the first time and you never have to do it again, am I right?"

"That's using your head for something other than a hat rack," he said, playing the lip ring in the corner of his bottom lip back and forth with his top lip. His teeth were very white in his dark beard as he grinned at me and I smiled back from behind my coffee cup.

It actually felt kind of good to flirt, even if it was harmless and wasn't likely to go anywhere.

"Here." He reached into the tip jar on the counter and pulled out a five-dollar bill. "Consider this my contribution to a most worthy cause. You have to promise to come back and sing for me. Now you better fly little nightingale." He set the bill on the counter and walked backwards toward the kitchen.

"Fly, fly, fly!" He waved his hands as if winging away and I laughed and shook my head.

"Thank you, and I'll be back. One last thing, you know where I might be able to find a map?"

"Now *that*, I don't know."

"Thanks again, Josh!" I said, picking up the rumpled bill.

I backed out of the coffee shop, croissant in my mouth, coffee in one hand and guitar in the other and went to find the nearest bus stop.

My thoughts went back to Poe. I wondered and worried a little about my stuff, but I knew it was all in my head. Poe *really* was one of the good ones, like Josh had been just now, but different at the same time.

I knew that I would eventually have to do *something* for that five he'd just given me. Likely it was an opener to ask me out, and I had to put way too much brain power into a gentle letdown, but I would be lying if I said that five-dollar bill wouldn't make a huge difference in my day.

I needed to get to the courthouse, I would easily drop twenty-five plus a couple dollars or more in fees on the permit I needed, then I would need to get *back* to this part of town and risk only pulling in a few bounced nickels the rest of the day. Then it would be bus fare back to Poe's... *and then what?*

That was the problem. I didn't know. I didn't know where I would go or where I would be staying tonight and I didn't know enough locals or have any inroads to the local artist's scene... it was a *superprecarious* position to be in.

At least back in Seattle, I knew which homeless camps were safe-ish and which ones to avoid. I knew which overpasses provided the best shelter and which ones leaked or were too loud to sleep let alone hear yourself think.

Here I knew no one. Here I really had nothing.

Damn you, Cody.

I waited for the next bus to come and asked the driver which routes went to the courthouse and which one I should catch to connect to what and scribbled it all down in my journal.

Turns out, I was *back* on Bernard's bus for the first leg and thankfully, he wouldn't hear of collecting fare from me. Instead, he chatted with me the whole way as the bus filled up with people bussing to the center of the city for work and the like.

"Okay," he said pulling up to a stop. "This is you. You get on the two fifty-four and tell the driver you need the courthouse, but I promise you – you can't miss it. It looks just like a courthouse should."

"Thanks again, Bernard. You're a lifesaver," I said.

"You just gots to let me hear you sing some time, girl!"

"As soon as I get that permit, I promise."

"Atta girl!" he called after me as I stepped off the bus and waited for the two fifty-four.

By the time I made it to the courthouse, the morning commute was so over and I had missed my window. I still had the lunch rush and the evening commute, depending on how long it took to get this damn permit.

I asked directions and put my backpack and guitar through the x-ray machine, ditching all my change in the little dish. The officers manning the machine were gruff and of absolutely no help, pointing me in the direction of some random clerk's office.

The clerk was rude, but helpful – barking at me that I was in the wrong place and I needed room whatever on the second basement level.

I went to the elevator, found the second basement level and eyed the directory for something that sounded even vaguely familiar to what she'd said to me but that I hadn't quite caught. I found something promising and went in that direction.

Poking my head in the door, I asked the lady behind the desk meekly, "Performing arts permit?"

"Yes! You've found the right place. A busker, are you?"

"Um, yes."

"Got your ID?" the bubbly and buxom blonde asked. She had to be in her forties, but she was super nice. I didn't let my guard down, though. I had met plenty of clerks that were nice on the surface and the second you forgot to call them ma'am or became too familiar they'd turn into a real Karen or Susan. Stuck up and unbearable.

"I literally *just* moved here *yesterday*," I said, scrabbling around my wallet looking for my ID. "Will an out-of-state one do?"

"As long as you have the current address of where you're living in the city or surrounding area, it should be fine."

"Um, yeah. That I *do* have," I hedged and fetched my journal out of my backpack. I rooted through its pages looking for the one I'd scribbled Poe's broken address on.

"Okay, good." She was being patient, which I was grateful for. Usually when dealing with the civic types you could get your head bitten off for not having this info at the ready. She took all my information then sent me to the line of chairs against the wall to wait.

It took over two-and-a-half hours for my permit to be signed off on and the lady at the counter was nice enough to laminate the notarized square of paper.

"Okay, you're all set. Keep this on display in your guitar case and nobody should bother you. If something happens to it, we can make you another, but re-prints cost ten dollars plus a two dollar and fifty cent administration fee."

"Okay, thank you."

"Mm-hm, good luck out there," she said. "It can be a tough crowd from what I gather."

"Okay, that's good to know, thank you."

"You're welcome!"

God, I sagged with relief and got the hell out of there. Outside the courthouse I scanned up and down the block. There was a café down a couple of blocks and across the street that looked promising and if I were going to find a place to set up to take advantage of the lunch rush? I needed to do it *now*, so I made a break for the crosswalk and dashed across the street as soon as the little man appeared in the walk/don't walk signal.

"Hi!" I called out to a lady as I approached the café. She was in an apron clearing off one of the outdoor tables, so clearly, she worked there.

"Well, hi there!"

"Could I, maybe, set up outside your door and give things a try for the lunch rush?"

"Oh, you know, I'd really love that!" she cried. "We don't get many street musicians in this part of the city. I think it might be really nice."

"Thank you," I said. "I only just got my permit and I am dying to play," I said, stepping aside and opening my case.

"What's your name?" she asked me.

"Saylor. Saylor Grace," I said, my mind drifting back to Poe and how he always seemed to use my middle name along with my first.

"It's really nice to meet you, Saylor. My name is Millie and I'm the owner."

"Thank you for giving me a chance, Millie," I said and she smiled warmly at me and headed inside with her dishes.

I sighed and put a dollar and some change in my open guitar case at my feet, settled the strap over my body and against my backpack and strummed a few experimental notes, tuning things up.

I let my breath out slow like my granddad had taught me to do, drew a deep breath, and I mean *deep* all the way into the pit of my belly and started to play and to sing.

I only sang my own songs. Spared me the drama of unexpectedly having to shell out royalties to some big-name artist with more money than God, who had forgotten where they'd come from.

If I had to describe my style, I would call it somewhere in the realm of folksy, bluegrass, and seriously *old-world* folk. Like fairy folk kind of folk. Like *Green Sleeves* is something I would sing on occasion, and there were other super old fair-use songs I would do between my own to inject some little familiarities into things.

I sang my heart out in front of that little café for harried lawyers and clerks and smiled and hoped for the best, encouraged by the gentle clink of coins as handfuls of change landed in my case as they slipped out of the shop.

I finished probably a solid first set and stopped, trying to catch my breath. I turned and Millie held out a glass of water.

"That was just *beautiful*," she said, and I took the glass of water.

"Thank you," I said and sucked several gulps down. God, it was perfect, cool and sweet to my parched mouth.

"I'd say you pulled in quite the tidy sum," she said with a wink, taking the empty glass from me.

"I'll have to have a look and see," I said with a smile.

"Take your time, have a seat, and come back any time," she said, going back inside.

"Thank you!" I called after her.

I took a seat and sorted through my spoils, pulling out the paper bits, separating out the inevitable receipts that some people tossed in and setting them aside on the table. I pulled out the bills and shoved them in my jacket pocket, and guitar braced between my knees, swung my backpack off and found my purple Crown Royal bag where I kept all my loose change. I got the coins stored, put my guitar away and closed up my case. My bag went back on my back and I straightened up and stood my case up between my knees, wrapping my legs around it and crossing my ankles.

I checked my pocket and sorted the bills, making sure to keep the metal table between me and the street.

I halved the money, a cool *thirty bucks*, and put half of it in the top of my sock and the other half in my jean's pocket.

"How'd you do?" Millie asked, coming out to collect a coffee cup and saucer.

"I think I'm going to like Indigo City," I said laughing.

"Yeah?" she asked excitedly.

"Yeah," I said and grinned.

Another windfall like that during the evening commute and I would be one *very* happy girl.

5

*P*oe…

I woke up alone, stretching luxuriously and frowning at the piece of paper sliding off the pillow next to me getting trapped between my arm and the sheets. I pushed myself up and dragged the page from her journal in front of my face.

She had nice handwriting; the note read she had to get out there and figure things out, that she didn't want to wake me, but she was kind of begging forgiveness rather than asking permission to leave her stuff at my place for today – that she would be back tonight to get it.

I frowned and wondered where the hell she could be.

I worried about her. She hadn't exactly been welcomed to the city with open arms and it could be brutal out there. I lived it every day I wore the uniform. Frowning, I got up and went through my morning routine. I was hoping that somehow, by some miracle, I would run into her out there but there was no telling. It was a big city, and I had no idea where she'd gotten off to in it.

Damn.

I couldn't believe I hadn't woken up, that I'd slept right through her moving around my place. Getting dressed, leaving. I didn't hear the door open or shut – *what the hell?*

I stewed about it all damn day. Through my workout at the Blue Line, through muster, briefing, and all through my shift. Looking down side streets and in alleyways for that flash of blonde hair, the spark of her blue and green eyes.

No such luck.

I dragged my ass home, the nagging worry chewing me up from the inside as I pulled into my garage. My heart did a fucking barrel roll in my chest when I rounded the corner, keys in my hand, to find her sitting outside my front door. I still have no idea how I hadn't seen her from down below when I'd pulled in.

"Jesus! Saylor. I've been worried about you all fuckin' day!"

She looked up from her journal perched on her knees, her guitar case laying beneath her legs as she scribbled on its pages, her backpack pressed between her and the wall behind her.

She smiled up at me and said with a wink, "I can take care of myself, Officer Friendly. How was your shift?"

I hung my head, hands on my hips and snorted a laugh.

"Same shit, different night – we were talking about *you*, though."

"Mm, my day was a busy one. I went and got a permit so I could sing for my supper – that took most of the day. I made a killing, though. Indigo City is way more lucrative than Seattle and your bus fare is so *cheap!*"

"Sounds like you had a better day than you did last night," I said, holding down a hand to her. She flopped her journal closed and reached up. I hauled her to her feet and she tittered a laugh.

"A much better day, for sure. I made enough that I can just afford this cheap motel I heard about on the other side of the city. I can be out of your hair tonight if you want."

I eyed her in my peripheral vision as I keyed open the locks on my front door.

"You eat today?" I asked.

"Mm, I had coffee and a croissant this morning."

"What time this morning?" I asked.

"Sometime around six or seven."

"Saylor, it's almost midnight," I said shoving in the door. She bent and picked up her guitar and smiled when she said, "I know."

I held the door for her and she slipped past me.

"So, have dinner with me," I said, "and let's talk about this."

"I will never pass up free food," she said, setting her guitar aside and sighing, "But I've already soaked up way more of your hospitality than I should and I feel guilty."

"Guilty?" I asked.

"Yeah. I mean, if anyone found out about any of what you're doing for me you could be in a lot of trouble, right?"

I went to my closet and shrugged out of my jacket and cut, hanging them up.

"Not as much as you'd think," I lied. "You gonna tell on me?"

"What? No! I may be a bitch sometimes, but I'm not *that* kind of a bitch."

I chuckled and said, "Good to know."

"Seriously, though... I made just enough to cover my ass for a roof tonight and maybe a meal tomorrow, so I'm all good."

"Are you for real?" I asked and fixed her with a look as I tried to pull some of the tension riding my neck and shoulders. It'd been present all day, tightening up the more I wondered where she was at or what she was doing and that bothered me. I found myself asking myself what was up with that – worried I was acting all possessive and crazy over this girl I barely knew.

"What?" she asked, and her expression was startled, like she couldn't really comprehend what the big deal was.

"Look, I know we barely know each other," I said, "but I've been thinking about you *all day*."

A wrinkle formed between her eyebrows as she swept the loose gray beanie slouched on her head off her hair and shoved it in her back pocket.

"Really?" she asked.

"Really. I work these streets every damn day and you up and disappearing like that this morning? I don't know why, but it scared the shit out of me. I was wondering and worrying about what happened to you all day – and believe me – I know that's weird."

"Wow," she breathed, her mouth lingering in this adorable little 'o' of surprise. "You're really for real right now, aren't you? Like, you're really serious."

"Yeah, Saylor. I am."

She leaned her butt against my dresser and crossed her arms over her narrow chest, sort of just huddling in her jean jacket and white hippy blouse underneath it. She stared down at the toes of her brown boots, her jeans rolled up at the cuff to just above the tops of those same boots.

"I don't understand…" she said finally. "I've only known you like *a day*, that's it."

"If it makes you feel any better, I don't understand it either but some things? It just is what it is, you know?"

She nodded slowly and twisted her lips back and forth.

"So what are you saying? You want me to stay?"

"For now, yeah… until you got a better plan than some fleabag, junky den, hotel in one of the worst parts of the city."

Her stomach growled audibly and I sighed.

"Look, you don't have to make a decision right this minute. Let me just fix us something to eat, we can talk about whatever you'd like, and then you can just let me know what you wanna do."

"Okay," she murmured, visibly shook.

"What's wrong?" I asked.

"Nothing!" she said quickly and my bullshit detector pegged in the red. I gave her a flat look. She scraped her peeling bottom lip between her teeth and finally said, "I just don't think anybody's cared about what happens to me like that since…" she trailed off and went mute.

"Since when?" I asked.

"Since my granddad died. I mean, it's been a long time, okay? Plus, you don't even really know me so I guess I just don't get why, you know? Like, why you would."

"Maybe I just got a good feeling about you," I said with a shrug, moving past her around the dresser and kitchen counter into the kitchen itself. I had a giant ass T-bone steak in the fridge I'd planned on doing up with some instant mashed potatoes. It was more than enough for two and should go pretty quick cooking-wise, too.

"You're serious about me staying here tonight?" she asked softly, following me and standing in the kitchen entryway, leaning a shoulder against the wall, arms still crossed defensively over her chest.

I straightened with the steak in my hand and turned, swinging the fridge door shut.

"Yeah, I'd like to help you get back on your feet – at least here, I *know* you're safe."

She gave me an almost shy smile and timidly tried some dry humor on me when she said, "This is all so *highly* irregular."

"It is," I agreed, "and I must be some kind of nuts putting it on offer, but it's out there now and I don't ever go back on my word."

She lost that smile of hers and got real serious.

"You're one of the good ones," she said and there wasn't a question at all in there so I didn't try to answer one. I didn't argue, either – even though I didn't feel like I was anything special. I mean, I was just a guy standing in front of a girl who had it way worse than I ever had. I just wanted to help. I didn't know why, and sometimes you just didn't question things like that.

I wasn't particularly religious, even though I'd been raised with religion. My parents had dragged me to church every Sunday and I'd admittedly hated it. They'd stopped taking me when I was eleven after Pastor Steve got caught diddling a bunch of Sunday schoolers. Mostly boys. While I'd been groomed, he hadn't sealed the deal with me. Probably because my dad was a cop.

Still, even though now I could appreciate how lucky I'd been to not be one of the pastor's chosen ones – I didn't exactly escape without issues from the experience. I'd gone through therapy as a teen, had been pretty mistrustful when it came to sports and had, unfortunately, been on the receiving end of *a lot* of fucking high school bullying.

Even so, I was one of the lucky ones with no real lasting effects from my brush with evil – except knowing that evil was out there and wolves really did wear sheep's clothing.

Anyway, even though I wasn't religious, I had to maybe think I'd been put in Saylor's path for a reason. Maybe I was some good karma finally coming her way and maybe my history was what was really rubbing me the wrong way where Saylor's situation was concerned. She was petite, pretty, and a prime target for traffickers. Indigo City had a seedy underside like most urban centers and I don't want to say that where she'd come from didn't too, but there she'd found her way and had people she could trust.

Here, not so much. Clearly, if what'd happened with her boyfriend was any indication.

"I'm just a kid who followed in his dad's footsteps," I said. "Not good, or bad. I'm just a dude trying to find his way as much as anyone else," I finally told her.

"Your dad was a cop?" she asked.

"Yeah."

"My dad was a drunk, but I already told you about that."

"Yeah, you did, and I'm sorry that happened to you. Just like I'm sorry you got all the way out here and the one you were supposed to be able to trust, shut you out so completely. I feel like you were fed to the wolves, so-to-speak."

"Yeah, maybe," she said with a shrug. "That doesn't make me your responsibility, though."

"No, true, it doesn't," I said, melting a pat of butter in my cast-iron skillet and getting some water started in a pot on a separate eye of the stovetop.

"I don't want to seem ungrateful," she said, shifting uncomfortably on her feet. "What I mean to say is *'thank you'* but I'm notoriously bad at accepting help."

"Why do you think that is?" I asked.

Her eyebrows shot up. "Adding amateur shrink to your repertoire?" she asked lightly, amusement coloring her voice.

I chuckled and said, "Touché, touché. To be fair, you kind of have to be as a cop. You have to be a human lie detector at the very least."

"I bet," she said. She sighed and shook her head slightly and went on with, "In all seriousness, that part of me is all my granddad's doing. He raised me to be smart and to stand on my own two feet. He raised me to breathe fire if I needed to and taught me self-reliance like no other."

"Sounds like a stand-up guy."

"Oh, totally! He was. He had some adventures leading up to meeting my gran. I think he went a little overboard with me and the 'you can't depend on anybody but yourself' because of what happened with my mom. He didn't want me to be like that, you know? Dependent on a man, or whatever. I think he felt like he made some kind of mistake with the way he raised her, you know? He wasn't the kind of man to make the same mistake twice."

"Is he the one who taught you how to play?" I asked as the meat sizzled in the pan.

"Yeah, actually. He did. I've been playing music since the time I went to live with him. Started when I was five or six."

"Bet you're pretty good by now," I said absently, stabbing the steak with a fork to flip it in the pan, spooning melted butter and runoff over it.

She chuckled and nodded a little. "I'd play for you, but I think your neighbor might have something to say about that after last night."

"Ah, yeah."

"I guess that brings me to *my* next question."

"Aw yeah? What's that?" I asked.

"What're the rules? If I'm going to be staying here for a few more days or whatever..." She shifted again and I smiled, flipping off the burner for the potatoes and looking up.

"I know it's tight quarters," I said, "and because it's tight quarters, I insist things be kept neat and orderly. I like a clean space, obviously."

"That's easy enough," she said. "Is there, uh, anything under the bed?"

"You didn't look?" I asked amused.

"Probably the only place I didn't," she said and blushed a faint scarlet. I laughed.

"A few low, flat, plastic storage bins," I said. "I think there's enough room for your guitar at the foot of the bed. Your suitcase can be tucked in the bottom of the closet, and your backpack can fit in the cubby under the end table on your side of the bed."

"My side of the bed, huh?" she asked amused.

"You picked it," I said, plating half the steak and dishing up mashed potatoes beside it. "It's yours," I smiled and held the plate out to her.

"Thank you," she murmured.

"You're welcome."

"So, uh, where do you eat?"

"Sometimes standing here at the counter, for the most part on the bed with the TV on."

"God, I haven't watched TV in so long."

"What do you watch when you do?" I asked, plating up the rest of the food for myself.

"You know, it's honestly been so long I don't even remember. What do you watch?"

"Honestly, I watch a lot of war documentaries."

"Seriously?"

I laughed and we went over to the bed which I'd made that morning. She carefully sat on her side with her plate and silverware and I sat on mine, picking up the remote on my way over from where it was chillin' by the television on my dresser.

I switched it on, whatever was on the History channel playing through. We surfed channels for a while and finally landed on one of the *Harry Potter* movies.

She smiled and I could see the nostalgia in her eyes, her features softening. We ate and enjoyed the movie but I had info we needed to trade, so as soon as it hit a commercial break I started the process before I had the chance to forget.

"How long were you out there before I got home?" I asked.

"Couple of hours," she answered, taking another bite of meat.

"Okay, see, that's not cool. You got a phone?"

"Yeah, but it doesn't work as a phone. I mean, it's not hooked up."

"How do you make calls and what the hell do you use it for then?"

"Wi-Fi, and I make calls through messenger and that." She shrugged. "It works."

"Okay, we got to work something out for tomorrow so I can get you a key."

"Um, I played outside this café a couple of blocks down and across the street from the courthouse at lunch time today. It was a good spot. Made close to thirty dollars in an hour."

"You plan on playing there tomorrow?" I asked.

"That's the thing, playing the same spot like that multiple days in a row can be dicey." She made a wincing face and got up, taking her plate to the kitchen, scraping it into the trash underneath the sink and running the water to wash her plate.

"How so?" I asked. "You did good today, why wouldn't you tomorrow?"

"People get too used to seeing you in one spot and they stop tipping," she said.

"I have a buddy in the prosecutor's office across the street from that café," I said, a plan forming. "If I can get him a key to my place before lunch tomorrow, do you think you could be there for him to give it to you?"

"Yeah, sure. That works. You're sure you trust me with a key though? I mean, I could wait out front like I did today – it's no big deal."

"It's not the best neighborhood," I told her honestly.

"Really? But you live here."

I laughed and got up, joining her in the kitchen. She automatically took my plate and utensils from me and I murmured thanks before letting her in a little bit more.

"I live here because it's a dirt-floor poor neighborhood which means the rent is dirt cheap. I'm saving my ass off to buy a house with the biggest down payment I can put together so that I don't have a mortgage hanging over my head for thirty years."

"Oh, that's really smart…" she said trailing off and then she took a breath and asked me something that had me cracking the hell up. "So, you're going to tell your girlfriend that I'm staying with you – right?"

I laughed until my sides hurt and tears gathered at the corners of my eyes.

"I don't have a girlfriend," I said when I got my shit together. "If I did, as much as it would have pained me, I would have taken you to the shelter last night."

She was blushing pretty hard and wouldn't look at me.

"I just figured you *had* to be taken," she stammered awkwardly.

"Yeah? Why's that?" I asked, leaning back against the counter, crossing my arms and tucking my hands under my armpits, a habit I'd had since forever.

"Never mind," she said. "Just forget it." I chuckled and she changed the subject with the speed of light. "Were you going to take a shower?"

"Yeah, I was planning on it, but if you wanted to –"

"Oh! No. I was just thinking it was getting pretty late."

I nodded slow and smiled. "Yeah. Good lookin' out, you're right it is. Be out in a snap."

"I'm happy to finish the dishes. You cook I clean, I cook you clean?"

"Sounds fair to me," I said. I grabbed my things to take them into the bathroom.

"I promise I'll get back on my feet as soon as I can and you can have your space back," she rushed out just before I shut the door.

I looked back out at her, peering into the kitchen over the dresser, between the cupboards and the counter and said, "Seriously. No rush."

When I got out of the shower, she was curled on the far edge of the bed, the lights out, the television off, the silence cloying where I had already grown fond of hearing her light and lyrical voice. I silently slipped into bed behind her and laid on my side, staring at her back. She wore a girl's tank top. One of the fitted kind. Her hair was shorter in the back, and I let my gaze travel over the knobs of her spine that showed under her delicate skin.

She was too thin, fragile looking, and I turned over and over in my head just *why* I had taken such a special interest. I didn't know. I couldn't fathom, but *something* was there just beyond our conscious reality telling me that I was absolutely doing the right thing.

One thing was for sure, I knew she was grateful. By the time I'd gotten done with my shower that could have only lasted five minutes, all of her things were stowed where I'd suggested.

I closed my eyes and fell asleep to the deep and even cadence of her breathing in the dark.

6

*S*aylor...

A small man in a well-tailored suit stopped to listen to me outside the café near the courthouse the next afternoon. His dark eyes were lovely but cynical as they roved me from head to toe and I made it my mission to make him smile, his stern look off-putting. I made eye contact and smiled as I sang. It was one of my original songs with sea shanty like overtones. The beat was happy.

He stood still and watched me, hands buried in the pockets of his slacks, mouth a thin line nearly hidden by his perfectly trimmed dark beard.

It was a solid two minutes of my singing and his standing in silent witness before the song came to an end and I could still my playing. There was a smattering of applause and the clink of coin in my guitar case but the tailored man made no move... that is until he asked, "Are you Saylor Grace, then?"

"I am. Are you Jeremy Poe's friend?"

A *slight* smile edged its way onto his lips and I returned it freely.

"I'm Yale." He held out his hand. "I'm one of Poe's brothers. It's nice to meet you."

"Ahhhh." I transferred my pick into my other hand and held out my right to shake his. His grip was firm, but kind. Gentlemanly.

"It's nice to meet you, Yale."

"Likewise," he said, cocking his head slightly.

"You have something for me, then?" I asked after an awkward silence.

"I do." He reached into his pocket and withdrew a key on a metal ring, the key chain reminiscent of a dog tag in shape, only a little longer, a little wider, and shiny.

"Thanks," I murmured.

"I'm guessing you realize just how much trouble Poe could get into if anyone found out how you met," he said dryly.

"What? At the coffee shop?" I asked, recognizing the blatant lie of it by staring Yale right in the eyes. He smiled genuinely then.

"Exactly. At the coffee shop."

"The one by Bayside Park with the French pastries."

His smile grew and he looked at his shiny professional shoes.

"The one with the French pastries," he echoed.

"You really shouldn't worry," I said, smiling as kindly as I could manage to mask the vague hurt his questioning had wrought – I understood that he was worried for his friend and I also understood he didn't know me from Eve… but the vague hurt was there nonetheless. I finished my sentence, "I'm not that kind of girl."

"I'm starting to see that," he said with a wink. "A piece of unsolicited advice?" he asked.

"I'm all ears."

"Try ten-thirteen Muller St. around the dinner rush. A restaurant called The Cormorant. They're always busy and you might have some luck there. Ask for Skids at the bar, tell him Yale sent you and I'm sure he'd be happy to let you play out front."

"Thanks," I said softly. "I'll try that tonight."

"Be safe, Saylor Grace."

I smiled. "I will."

He tipped his chin down in a graceful nod, turned and went into the café behind me. I looked at the tag on the single key ring and smiled. Embossed on it in full color was the logo that was on the back of Poe's leather jacket.

I pocketed the key in the breast pocket of my leather jacket, switched my pick back into my right hand and launched into my next song.

LUNCH WAS STILL PRETTY LUCRATIVE, but not as much as the day before. Still, that was okay – especially for only two hours of work. It beat working minimum wage plus tips in some diner somewhere. Not that waitressing wasn't good honest work. It was. It just wasn't for me.

I loved what I did. I had always been a free spirit, and rather than stifle that impulse, my granddad had nurtured it. Of course, they say it skips a generation and if that were true, then I had definitely gotten this way thanks to my granddad's genes. It was my grandma that'd given my granddad his roots. He always told me he'd had no desire whatsoever to settle down until he laid eyes on her.

He'd said she was what'd made working a regular nine-to-five bearable. He'd always told me he'd walk through fire for her and my mom. Then, at the mention of my mother, he would get so somber, so quiet, and would get this far away look in his eyes. Sometimes, his features would tighten with anger. Sometimes, it would simply go slack with despair. Every time he would blink the tears away, refocus on me, and he would *smile...* and it was like a rainbow on a cloudy day. Every time he'd looked at me like that, I felt invincible – like nothing bad could ever happen to me again.

Of course, reality was always there lurking around the nearest corner waiting to hoof me right in the front butt.

I stood on the edge of Bayside Park hours later, the sky darkening, the wind cold off the water and breathed the salt and thought to myself that it was so weird how the Chesapeake smelled so much the same as Elliot Bay back home.

Except it didn't feel like home. It never really had, which is why the adventure of coming here had been so appealing. Nothing and nowhere had felt like home after my granddad passed and I struggled with that.

"Maybe someday," I sighed and turned around. Muller Street was a block past the boulevard in front of Bayside. I'd found a waterfront tourist map today marking out 'Old Town' or Indigo City's version of Seattle's Pioneer Square. The historical district, I guess you could call it.

I set off in the direction of the boulevard and crossed at the corner. I kept walking, found Muller which was a one-way, and looked for the nearest building number. I started walking, completely lost on which way was north versus south or east versus west. *Everything is backward here,* I reminded myself. Water was east. Always east. You hit water and the next stop was jolly old England.

I rolled my eyes when the numbers were climbing rather than declining and turned around and retraced my steps, looking for *ten-thirteen.*

I found it. The gilded shingle hanging outside, the diving sea bird painted on it. I waited for traffic to clear and dashed across in the middle of the block, squaring my shoulders before I went inside.

It wasn't noisy yet, but it was getting busy. The hostess smiled at me and asked if I needed a table for one.

"Ah, no… I was told to look for someone named Skids?"

"Oh, yeah. He's behind the bar. Are you twenty-one?"

"Twenty-five, actually," I said with a laugh. I knew I didn't look a day over seventeen sometimes.

"Go on up," she said and waved me past into the bar area.

I went to the bar and leaned my guitar underneath in front of one of the stools and slipped up onto it, waiting for the bartender to work his way to me. It wasn't *super* busy in here, as I said, but there were a few patrons and it was certainly picking up.

"What can I get you?" he asked, sliding a bar napkin down on the rich wood in front of me.

"Oh, I'm not here to drink. Uh, Yale sent me? He said I should ask you if it would be alright if I played out front."

"Yale? You Saylor Grace?"

I blushed faintly and said, "I am."

"So you're staying with Poe, huh?"

"How'd you know?" I asked and he chuckled.

"I'm his chief – I'm supposed to know these things," he said with a wink and a crooked grin and even though his words could be construed as creepy or arrogant, everything about his expression and body language changed the tone to playful and kind.

"Seriously, though, I'm the president of the Indigo Knights, his club. We don't keep things from each other. Especially not important things."

"Things like," and I leaned in close and dropped my voice to avoid being overheard, "moving strange girls into your shoebox of an apartment on a whim?"

He laughed. "Yeah, things like that." He looked me up and down and sighed. "Be lying if I said we weren't all worried about him. Poe just doesn't do things like that."

I chewed my bottom lip. "Yeah?"

"Yeah. He must really be getting a good vibe off of you."

"I'm not a trash human being, I promise." I said. "Maybe a trash *panda* in that I'm cute, I like to stay up all night, and I will fight you sometimes for the rest of an apple or something – but definitely not a bad person."

He laughed and asked me, "When was the last time you had something to eat?"

"I had a coffee this morning."

"A coffee? That's it?"

"Yeah and don't think I'm begging because I'm not. I work for my money and my meals."

"Ah-huh." He eyed me up and down and whipped out a menu from behind the bar. "Either you pick something, or Reflash is going to do it for you. Now what're you having?"

"I can't really afford –" I stammered.

"I ain't asking you to. Now what are you having?" He braced his hands wide on the inside edge of the bar and leaned heavily on them waiting on me. I pursed my lips and looked over the menu and settled on the cheapest yet most filling looking thing I could spot.

He gave a nod at my selection and took the menu and asked, "Now what are you drinkin'?"

I smiled and said, "Water?" and he raised an eyebrow.

"Brandy in some hot tea?" I guessed again.

His expression smoothed out into something more genial. "Right answer, you get a gold star."

I laughed and he moved off and it was only then that I realized he hadn't given me an answer on whether I could busk outside his establishment. I mean, I didn't technically need his permission. I had a permit and it was a public sidewalk – but I always found politeness could and would take you miles and miles so I always tried to go the *extra* mile – *and I need to write that down.*

I pulled my backpack around into my lap and brought out my journal and pen and turned to the page where I was keeping scraps of lines and penned that one in among the rest, staring at them all, letting my eyes follow the curves of all the letters, doodling flowering vines around the borders, a moon and stars at the top of the page, willing the scraps and snippets to fall into order and for the notes to come together for a song to form.

It was remaining stubbornly elusive and was driving me nuts as a result, but I didn't have time to think about it really, because a plate of food was set in front of me and I looked up – not at the bartender but at who could only be the cook himself.

"Hi," I murmured.

"Hi," he echoed in his thick New York accent. "You must be the mystery girl Poe's got himself involved with. Skids said you were here."

"We're not *involved*," I said, "but he's helping me, yeah."

"That's not like him." The cook leaned on the bar heavily and eyed me.

"So I keep hearing," I said. I frowned slightly. "It's starting to feel like I have to keep defending myself. I can fuck off if it would make you all feel better. I mean, I know you care about him and that's good and I know the world sucks and I'm new and –"

He put a hand over mine where it rested on the bar to stop me and his standoffish posture eased. A teasing twinkle entered his eyes and his smile broke the ice.

"Relax, sweetheart. Ain't nobody leveling any accusations. Yeah, we care about Poe but Poe's a big boy. You're all good. Skids seems to like you and Yale wouldn't have sent yah here if he didn't. Eat up, and you can go on out and play for as long as you like.

I felt the stiffness in my shoulders melt a little and said, "Thank you."

"Lotta stigma around street people," he said and took a deep breath letting it out slow, heaving a sigh that was weighted with a lot of things. I could tell he felt bad for having approached me with his preconceived notions and I pursed my lips.

"To be fair, stereotypes become stereotypes for a reason."

He looked at me and nodded, looking a little chagrinned and took the forgiveness I extended like an olive branch. If these people were important to Poe, who was going so far out of his way and to his own personal detriment to help me? Well, I really wanted his people to like me. I didn't want to make waves. I seriously wanted nothing but smooth sailing here.

He shut his mouth and nodded once and said, "That they do, doesn't mean it's fair to apply them liberally to people that don't deserve it. I'm sorry if we made you feel like we did that to you."

I smiled, nodded and said, "That's okay."

He wrapped his knuckles against the bar top and said, "Eat your food before it gets cold, and it's on the house – we mean it."

"Certainly do," the bartender said setting my tea made with brandy on the napkin he'd placed earlier. "Sorry this took so long. Honey?"

"Yes, please."

"Sure thing. I'll be right back. Gonna grab my secret stash."

"You have a secret stash of honey?" I asked, raising an eyebrow.

"Yeah, girl we know cultivates honey bees. She gives us several jars at the harvest. We keep it in reserve for special guests and if you're a guest of Poe's you're a guest of ours," The chef waved over his shoulder and disappeared around the corner and back into the kitchen.

"That's Reflash," Skids said with a wink and went down the bar, returning with a mason jar of honey and doled some out with a spoon into my cup. He left the spoon with me and disappeared down the bar and I started in on my chicken fettucine with broccoli and Alfredo sauce.

It was amazing and it took everything in me not to eat to the point that I didn't have a sizeable portion of leftovers for another meal later on.

I waved down Skids and asked, "Could I please have a box?"

"Sure! You want me to keep it behind the bar here for you while you play?"

"Uh, yeah, that would actually be really great."

"Was it good?"

"Oh, my God." I rolled my eyes skyward. "It was heavenly!"

"Glad you liked it."

"I'm going to finish my tea and get out there."

"I got you covered, just don't tell anyone there's brandy in it." He winked at me, and produced a paper cup and coffee lid from under the bar, poured the remaining contents of my mug into the cup, slapped the lid on and handed it over.

"Free refills on the hot water and as many fresh tea bags as you want. You just come find me."

"Oh, thank you!"

"It's no worries, it's getting colder out there. Especially nearer the water like we are."

"Oh, I know, it was the same on Elliot Bay."

"Seattle's a fun town," he said.

"Oh yeah? You've been?"

"A few times back in my younger days." He was summoned down the bar. "Whelp, got to go!"

I smiled and got up, shoving my journal back into my pack and my arms through the straps. I picked up my guitar case by the handle and my spiked tea in the other hand and with a satisfied and full belly went outside. There was enough of a ledge at the bottom of the window about a foot and a half off the ground to set my tea, saving me from having to reach down all the way. I opened up my guitar case and reverently brought out the instrument, putting the strap over my head and jimmying it back and forth to get it to slip down over my backpack.

I kept the strap on my guitar intentionally long to do this. I learned pretty fast as a street rat you *never* wanted to set down anything you didn't have to. You set it down, it almost instantly became fair game for any pack poachers or thieves that might be lurking. I had too many important photographs in my journal and in my pack to want to risk it, even though I never kept money or my ID in it. Those were either in my pocket or in my little purse which was also across my chest but kept cinched high against my ribs *under* my jacket.

I got settled and plucked out a few experimental notes, gave a tuning peg a slight twist here and there and satisfied, tapped my foot and launched into a song and honestly? This was the most relaxed and the happiest I could remember being while playing in a long time.

7

*P*oe...

"You did what and you want me to do what now?" Yale stared at me hard like I'd lost my fucking mind, and I honestly couldn't tell him I hadn't. I mean, what I was doing for Saylor *was* nuts and could cost me everything. I mean, the rip I would get wouldn't necessarily be a total career ender, but the trust it could damage with some of the other guys in the rest of the department? That was something you could never get back. You make a big enough questionable decision like this one and you could wind up having *every* decision questioned.

"Yale, I know –"

"I don't think you *do* know Poe!" He went to his office door and shut it and I stood there feeling three inches tall compared to the prosecutor's five-foot-five even though I was well over six feet. I looked down at him as his gaze smoldered in my direction and a muscle in his jaw ticked.

"Hey, none of you were really like this with Youngblood," I said with a nervous laugh and his eyes blazed.

"One, Youngblood *knew* Chrissy. Two, Chrissy was *gainfully employed* with a *degree*, and with a *roof over her head*. She wasn't some unknown street musician making poor life decisions driving across the country to live with some sight unseen internet boyfriend!"

"Okay, so maybe she was having a solid blonde moment – I mean, she *is* a blonde but I've already agreed to let her stay for a couple more nights." I was hedging on the timeline hard, but Yale was smokin' hot and acting more like my *dad* than my equal and brother. The only reason I wasn't telling him to go fuck himself right now was that I could see how *worried* he was and truthfully, I got that.

If my best friend Blaze had come at me with this shit, I probably would have blown a gasket of my own, *but there was just something about Saylor Grace* and it wasn't something I could explain. It was something that had to be experienced, and I thought that it was too damn convenient that she was parked outside Yale's office at lunch and I figured if I could get *Yale* on my side, the other brothers would follow.

Yale was, after all, one of the toughest nuts out of all of us to crack. That, and I knew, if he just met her – even for only a few minutes – Saylor Grace would have him on her side and she could use every ally she could get in this city on her new start.

"I'm just asking if you could drop this off to her at lunch. If I did it, I'm gonna be late for my shift."

He breathed in slow, in through his nose and out and grated out, "Fine, but only because I want to have a look at this girl so I can judge for myself and you had *better* be at church tonight."

"Whoa, hey," I said handing over the key on its key chain. "This isn't club business."

"Really?" he asked, holding up the fob with the key with the club crest on it. "You're part of this club, Poe, and being part of this club means we look out for you as much as you look out for the rest of us." He took a seat on the edge of his desk and I suddenly felt like I'd been called into the principal's office. I tried not to smirk at the mental image. Now was totally not the time.

"That means, when it looks like one of our members is about to go off the rails it's our duty and responsibility to get him back on track." He fixed me with a hard look.

"Look, Yale, I know it sounds completely batshit fucking crazy, but I swear. She's a good girl. She radiates it."

"You run a background on her?" he demanded.

I smiled and nodded. "Yeah. Might not be up to your exacting standards but she's got a couple of old charges in Seattle. Juvenile ones, so the records are sealed. I know she's been a street kid since she was fifteen. She told me. I imagine it was vagrancy, maybe marijuana possession. Seems to be the thing out there with the recent legalization."

"But you don't know."

"Not for sure, no – but I know her type, and I'm telling you, bro. She's good people."

"I really hope this doesn't end with an 'I told you so,'" he said with a reluctant sigh.

"Just hook me up, give her the key and judge for yourself. I swear to God, it will only take a couple of minutes."

"I already agreed, didn't I?" he asked, pinching the bridge of his nose.

"You did. Thank you."

"I'd better see you tonight."

"You will, I promise. As soon as my shift ends. Do not pass go, do not collect two hundred dollars. I'll get my ass directly to the *10-13*."

He looked calculating for a second.

"Fine. See you tonight."

"See you tonight," I echoed and left, I had to get to work.

I called up my best buddy, Blaze, first though. I didn't want him finding out from the rest of the guys about this sudden turn of events. Plus, I hadn't talked to him in a few days and didn't want to be that kind of a dick.

He answered on the second ring and was like, "Yo!"

"Hey, man. What's up?"

"I don't know, you're the one that called me."

"Yeah, about that… I kind of did a thing."

"A thing?" He laughed. "What'd you do, adopt a puppy?"

"Not exactly…" I filled him in and I swear the line went dead.

"You did *what* now?"

"Yeah."

"Are you fucking serious, bro?"

"I wouldn't joke about something like this."

"You two fucking?" he asked.

"Dude, no, it's not like that. I'm seriously not trying to be a creeper. I'm just trying to help her out."

"How long has this been going on?" he demanded.

"Two nights, that's it, I promise."

I shifted on the seat of my bike, the traffic going by on the street and Blaze said, "Man, you aren't even close to forty yet, its way too fucking early to be starting a mid-life crisis."

I laughed. "It's not a crisis man. I'm good, I swear. I honestly don't know how to explain it. She's… she's just different. A different kind of vibe, man."

"You smoking something?" he asked.

"Seriously?" I demanded.

"What? You're the one picking up stray homeless chicks off the street and moving them into your place without knowing a damn thing about them."

"Okay, true. Okay, fair – but I'm pretty much asking you to reserve judgment until you meet her."

Blaze let out a heavy sigh on the other end of the phone and said, "This isn't you, man. Are you *sure* you're okay?"

"Yeah, man. I mean, I think so."

"Not exactly a rousing endorsement, there, buddy."

"I know," I said. "I know this isn't like me and I'm not sure what made me do such a big thing on such a whim… I guess I'm just stuck in a rut. Sick of trying to help and not really making a difference, you know?"

"Ahhh, I think you might be onto something there, man."

I nodded slowly.

"I think so too. Thanks, brother."

"What the hell did I do?" he asked laughing.

"Dunno, but talking to you tends to get me out of knots like this one sometimes."

"Good deal. So when can I meet her, and what was her name again?"

"Uh, maybe this weekend? And her name is Saylor. Saylor Grace."

"Pretty name. Different," he mused.

"So is she, man. So is she."

"I look forward to meeting her."

"Cool. Cool."

We hung up after a couple more seconds of chitchat and I stowed my phone and looked up the street. I turned to look at the café, but Saylor wasn't there. Not yet. I had a couple hours before my shift, and I wanted to hit the grocery store and get some food in my place for the both of us.

It was going to be a long day.

WHEN I PULLED into the alley to park my bike at the *10-13*, the last thing I expected to see was Saylor standing out front, strumming her guitar, chin held high, smile slight, her breath pluming the air as she sang her heart out on the sidewalk.

I parked, shut off the bike, but I was still too far to hear. When I got up to the corner I paused and listened a moment.

You tear me up like no one can do
You carved a home in my soul.
Promised my heart to you, you cut me through
I'm wheeling out of control.

The tempo was upbeat, her voice clear as she sang,

If your love is poison, drink it down to the dregs
If your love's a knife, run me through
Whatever it costs me, no other I'd choose.
I cut myself to pieces for you

I walked around the corner and met her mismatched blue green eyes.

She smiled a little bigger, those eyes lighting up with surprise as she went into the refrain. I wiped suddenly sweating palms on the thighs of my jeans and with a nod to Saylor Grace, reached for the door into the *10-13*.

She smiled and I let a group of people out, holding the door for them as I stepped in and Saylor didn't miss a beat, just smiled a little bigger, made eye contact with me and kept right on belting out her song.

I don't know what I'd honestly expected, but she was good. Damn good. A lilting voice with just enough country in it. Not quite blue-grass-y... I didn't know what you would call it but 'folk' was the closest I could come. It was beautiful, and I was glad when one of the women leaving the *10-13* dropped a dollar or two into Saylor's open case.

I didn't want to distract her, so I just went in and threaded my way through the bar area to the fishbowl and found my seat at the table.

"The man of the hour," Skids drawled and I frowned at Yale who raised his eyebrows and looked completely unapologetic.

I looked to Blaze and said, "Looks like you get to meet Saylor Grace a little sooner than the weekend," I declared.

"Dude, not funny." Golden scowled and I scowled right back.

"Settle down, now," Skids said and Yale brought his fingers down from where he had them steepled in front of his chest.

He leaned forward and said, "Sorry, not sorry, Poe, but you were right. I met her, handed over your key and I have to admit... I like her. She doesn't set of any alarm bells and she truly does seem both grateful and protective of you. You were right, she's one of the good ones."

"That being said," Skids interjected, "I *really* fuckin' hope for your sake that this is a one-off thing."

"Totally is," I said, holding up my hands in surrender.

"That's why I engineered her being here," Yale said. "You were *also* right in saying she had to be met to understand where you were coming from. I figured that this way, everyone could and it would cause a lot less strife."

"Ain't nobody here upset with you, bro," Oz added. "We're just worried, that's all. This shit is *way* off your baseline."

Murmurs of agreement swept around the table and I realized – we were *all here*. It wasn't very often we got the dozen of us, butts in seats around this table. It was kind of a rude awakening for me.

"I didn't know you cared," I said, throwing a little sarcastic edge onto my tone. Except I guess I hadn't. I mean, not really. I was the quiet guy, sure – but often times I felt completely unnoticed. This shit, everybody being here like this because I'd done something even remotely out of character? While it was somewhat annoying because on one hand I felt like everyone was second guessing me, on the other hand, *shit,* these guys cared. Had my back in unexpected ways and *damn* I was grateful to be a part of this squad.

"Look man, I know we all get wrapped around the axle with our own shit – but hell fuckin' yeah we care," Driller said, leaning back in his seat.

"You ain't *ever* done anything like this. We know being a cop is all you've ever wanted and for you to risk that – are you *sure* you're okay, bro?" Golden searched out my face.

"I'm seriously *fine*, man. Just something about this particular case – I couldn't not do something this time."

"Wait, go back," Angel said. "Rewind back to what you just said."

I looked over at him and mulled it over.

"I guess I've been feeling frustrated lately," I said. "Like, I get out there and do my fuckin' job and shit but I've been feeling like it doesn't do a damn bit of good, you know?"

Church turned into a bit of a support group with the admission, and I was glad to hear I wasn't feeling alone. It was somehow freeing to be validated by my brothers and disheartening in the next breath to know that it was literally across the fucking board. That it didn't matter if we were cop, fire, medical, or even the fucking lawyers. We were *all* operating in this perpetual state of burnout.

"What's going on with getting you a house, man?" Narcos asked.

I sighed. "Got a real decent chunk saved," I confessed.

"Time to find a realtor?" Backdraft asked.

"Close."

"Maybe it is. Maybe to help you through this, you need something good to focus on. A project that won't blow up in your face and ruin your career," Golden said.

"You really have no faith in me, do you?" I asked him and he fixed me with a solid gaze and shook his head.

"Oh, I trust you. I just don't trust *her*. Not yet anyway."

"Have you talked to her?" I asked.

"Not yet."

"You maybe want to reserve judgment until you do?" I asked.

"No, not really," he said evenly.

Angel, his twin, rolled his eyes and fired off at G. in Spanish. Oz chuckled, and then full blown laughed at whatever G. shot back at his brother.

"English, motherfuckers!" Driller called, grinning. We were all smiling and laughing and the mood in the room was way improved by the time the meeting was called.

"Oh, hey, looks like a prime time to call your girl up here," Driller remarked.

I looked back over my shoulder and over to the bar where Saylor was smiling and accepting a paper coffee cup, her guitar back in its case, braced between her feet; trapped between her body and the bar.

"Shit, hold up," Skids said and went to the door and called out, "Hey, hold up, no charge for the tea, man."

The bartender manning the bar lifted his chin and waved Saylor off who smiled cheerfully in Skids' direction. Her smile growing when she caught me looking her way.

"Why don't you come on up here, Saylor?" Skids invited.

She nodded, picked up her guitar by the handle, and headed our way.

"Um, hi..." she said stepping into the fishbowl and we heard a peal of laughter from the ol' ladies table. Unfortunately, while all of the men of the Indigo Knights were in the house, not all of the women could make it. Probably a little over half of them were at their usual table as they played a round of darts.

"How's your night going?" I asked.

"Good!" she declared. "Not the most lucrative spot, but not awful, either. It'll get better here soon when it heads into the holidays. I make a killing at the really old carols."

"Come take my seat," Skids said. "You've been out there on your feet all day."

"Oh, I'm fine, really." She laughed him off and I smiled at her.

"Don't make him insist," I said. She took the seat then, and I added, "And don't any of you fuckers start grilling the woman, either." There was laughter and she blushed faintly.

"You know for a performer, I actually *hate* being the center of attention?"

There was laughter and I did my best to pull some of the attention off of her by introducing all of the guys in turn. She made it a point to get up and shake everyone's hand and the respect she showed everyone was genuine and real. A little while in her presence and anybody that had been hanging onto their doubts visibly started to let them go. Except Golden. He took a little extra work and a few minutes wasn't going to do it.

"You going out there for more?" Reflash asked.

"Oh, no. I think I'm done for tonight. I'm probably going to figure out the busses here soon and go get some sleep."

"I can give you a ride," I said. "You *are* going my way."

She laughed lightly and said, "This is true."

"Don't forget your food," Skids reminded her, and I felt a knot in my chest loosen, glad he'd taken care of that for her.

We stayed a little longer beyond that. Shot the shit with the guys and introduced Saylor to the ol' ladies of the squad.

Finally, it was definitely late enough, the place starting to close down, the only patrons left were club, and tired staff going through their closing routines.

"It was nice to meet you, Saylor," Coco said and Saylor smiled. "You too!"

Skids handed her a plastic grocery bag with her leftovers and a look of surprise crossed her face fleetingly at the heft of it. I didn't say anything, but knowing Reflash, he'd hooked her up with more of whatever she'd had.

"Ready to go?" I asked.

"Yeah."

We went out, Blaze coming with us, Narcos and Driller were standing in the alley near their bikes with Youngblood and Chrissy having a final chat.

"How are we supposed to do this?" Saylor asked, and I smiled at her.

"Paracord and a prayer," I said.

She blinked and said, "Oh, hell no."

I laughed. "I was only partially serious. I used paracord last time, but didn't have a passenger, so this could be just a little trickier.

"Mm, no it won't," she said eying the line of bikes, "but I'm going to need some help."

"You ever ride before?" I asked.

"A dirt bike, back home when I was like thirteen and never with a guitar. My granddad had liked to kill me when he found out about it, too."

I took her over near my bike and swore softly. "Anybody got a spare helmet I can borrow just for tonight? Mine's at home in the top of my closet."

"Yeah, I got you," Oz said, coming around the corner.

"Where's Ellie, anyway?" Backdraft asked.

"Wanted to stay home and paint, she hasn't gotten much time to herself to do her own thing. Big project came in at the museum and it's takin' like *all* of their restoration people to work on it."

"What the fuck she working on?" Narcos asked.

"Big fuckin' renaissance painting. Sucker's like twelve feet. She took me to see it and I was like *damn!*"

"Wow," Saylor murmured. "What's she doing with it?"

"Cleaning it and restoring some of it. Fixing tears in the canvas, that kind of shit."

"That sounds amazing," Saylor said and Oz grinned.

"That's my Ellie. I'm proud as hell of her. She's leading this project up."

We got Saylor set, and she sat on the back of my bike and took her backpack off while I held her guitar. She lengthened the straps as far as they could go and knotted them so they wouldn't slip through the metal slide things. She shrugged into one side and said, "Okay, set it up here?" I held the guitar to her back and Chrissy came forward and pulled the backpack strap left dangling around the guitar so Saylor could shrug into it on the other side. She pulled and tightened things as far as she could, trapping the instrument to her back and it was pretty secure.

"Not a bad idea," I said.

"Ain't you afraid that thing is gonna catch wind and rip right out the top and take you right over the back of the bike?" Driller asked.

"Not really, I've made this work on the back of a bicycle before, except I had trouble with it slipping out the bottom, then. With the wide seat stopping it, I think we'll make it."

"I'll go slow where I can," I promised her, dropping the borrowed lid Oz held out to me on her head. I helped cinch the chin strap.

"Alright you guys." I clasped hands and knocked shoulders with every- one. "I'll see you on the flip side."

"Later man," Youngblood called.

"The Blue Line?" Blaze asked when I got to him.

"Yeah," I said. "Maybe not tomorrow, day after?"

"Yeah." He nodded.

"Cool."

I got on, and Saylor hung on.

"You good back there?" I called over my engine after I started it.

"Yeah!" she called.

"Good, 'cause here we go!"

8

*S*aylor…

The ride was cold. I mean *really* cold, and it was already cold out here to begin with so that pretty much meant that by the time we pulled into the garage under Poe's apartment, I felt frozen to my very soul. My teeth chattering uncontrollably, I leaped up as soon as he shut the engine off.

"Ah, shit! Be careful of the pipes!"

"I'm fine," I said startled and he let out a breath pent up with worry.

"Pipes are *hot,* always dismount on this side to be safe, okay?"

"Okay, I'm sorry, I didn't know."

"It's cool," he said. "I'd just feel really bad if you got hurt."

I paused and considered him, hooking my thumbs in the straps of my backpack and holding them out, keeping my guitar tight to my back. It'd been an unwieldy ride and I kept feeling like it was trying to slip, but we made it just fine, laughing and giggling.

"Here, I got it." He grasped the top of my case and I shrugged out of

77

my backpack. It swung wide and tagged him in the stomach and he 'oofed.'

"I'm sorry!"

He grinned and laughed a little and said, "It's fine, I'm just yanking your chain."

"You got it?" I asked softly, worried.

"I got it, I'm right behind you," he said. I nodded and trusted him to carry up my most prized possession.

"You wanna try your key so I know it works?" he asked. "I didn't get to come back here and test it, but I'm pretty sure it's fine."

I fished out my key from my breast pocket and stared at it for a moment as the monumentality of it crashed into me and I teared up for a second.

I had a key. I had a roof over my head when I needed it and even though it was temporary, the added security of it? God, that was *huge*.

"Hey, Saylor Grace, what's wrong?" he asked and I sniffed.

"I don't think I can ever thank you enough for all of the things you've done for me. I mean, I haven't had a roof over my head in so long and even though it's temporary..."

He sighed softly and set my guitar against the railing, taking the bag of takeout off from around my wrist and setting it down.

"Come here," he ordered gently and wrapped me in a tight hug.

I let him, my gratitude multiplying as I wrapped my arms around his waist and it was like things just *clicked*... and I felt the safest that I think I had ever felt in my life, barring when my granddad had been alive.

I sniffed, silent tears dripping down my nose and put my ear to his chest and just listened to his steady heartbeat.

I don't know how long we stood there like that, him gently rocking me, twisting gently side to side, his leather creaking and sighing in the chill November night. Eventually, he broke the spell of calm ever so slightly by murmuring where my hair peeked out of my hat, "Let's get you inside and warmed up. K?"

"Okay," I whispered back, my voice stronger than I expected it to be.

I stepped back and all I wanted to do was rush back into his embrace. To feel that safety, that warmth that had nothing to do with the actual temperature.

I instantly felt guilty for wanting those things. I mean, hadn't he done more than enough for me already? Wasn't this supposed to be temporary, anyway?

The key fit perfectly, working like a charm. I unlocked the door and got emotional all over again.

I pushed my way into the warmer apartment and turned, Poe smiling down on me and gesturing for me to get in the rest of the way. I stepped into the kitchen and he handed me my food. I put it in the fridge and said, "I *know* I didn't have this much left."

He chuckled and said, "Knowing Reflash, he dumped another one of whatever you ordered right on top."

"I think he did." I turned and he straightened from sliding my guitar safe under the bed.

"How'd you do today?" he asked.

"Almost as good as yesterday. It all adds up. I have to find one of those coin machines tomorrow. My Crown bag is getting full." I shrugged out of my backpack and dug around in it, hefting out the Crown Royal bag full of coins. I had to use both hands otherwise I risked tearing it.

Poe let out a low whistle. "That's quite a haul for only two days, Saylor Grace."

I shrugged. "About thirty or forty bucks, I think. I've been trying to keep track, but I can't always. You don't want to be flashing too much green out there. That's how you get your bag ripped off."

"Here, let me tuck that away for you and get something hot to drink going. You're still shivering."

I nodded and went around him into the room, going to the closet and plucking my sleepwear off the top of my suitcase in the back. I hung up my jacket and slipped a towel down off the shelf.

"See you in a few," he said.

"I'll save you some hot water."

"No need, I took one back at the station. I do anytime we have church."

"Church?" I asked curiously.

"Club meeting."

"Ah, strange thing to call it."

"I guess so." He kneeled by my side of the bed and stuffed my backpack in the cubby in the front of the nightstand, the Crown bag, he set on top.

"Be right out."

I showered and soaked in the heat and it was wonderful. When I got out, I heard the sound of Poe shaking a packet of something back and forth in the kitchen. You could hear everything in this tiny space, and I couldn't say that was a bad thing. No surprises were definitely a good thing where I came from.

I ran my fingers through my hair to get it doing its natural beachy wave thing in the front and made a face at myself in the mirror. I tried to keep an A-line cut, short in the back, chin-length in the front, but it was starting to get a little long and I was glad for the colder weather that required I wear a hat. My slouchy beanies could hide a multitude of sins, from the frozen tops of my ears to my shaggy excuse of a haircut.

I hung my towel on the bar in the bathroom and shivered lightly when I opened the bathroom door, the air cooler out here than the bathroom in just my tank top and short sleep shorts.

"Almost done in here, get under the covers."

It sounded like he had water heating on the stove, but it wasn't quite boiling. I did as he'd gently ordered.

We didn't say anything. Rather, we lapsed into this cozy silence, the both of us tired, the wee hours of the morning catching up with us.

"You going to sleep in tomorrow?" he asked and I looked at the glowing clock on his cable box by the television.

It was three am.

"Uh, yeah. No way am I getting up to play for the morning commute. That would only let me sleep for like an hour."

He chuckled and said, "Usually I have tomorrow off, but I traded with another guy to help him out."

"I don't even know what day it is," I said with a heavy sigh, straightening the blankets in my lap.

"Well, it's technically Friday right this minute. I usually have Friday and Saturday off. What about you? What do you usually do on the weekends?"

"Holiday shoppers should be out; didn't Thanksgiving just happen?"

"A little over a week ago," he said, coming over to me. He handed down a steaming mug of fragrant cider. The kind made from the packet. I loved the stuff.

"You are a saint," I murmured and he laughed.

"You sing carols?" he asked.

"During the holidays? Absolutely."

"You religious much?" he asked, going around to his side of the bed and setting a steaming mug of his own on his nightstand.

I shook my head. "No, not really. I just like the carols."

"Which one is your favorite?" He stood for a while by the bed and stretched, twisting at the waist, bracing one arm behind the other and pulling it to him to get that extra deep stretch in his shoulder.

"Mm," I savored a careful sip of the hot liquid. "*Carol of the Bells.* It's not really a solo endeavor."

"I don't think I've ever heard it. Keep talking, I'm going to change." He went for the bathroom.

I chuckled and shook my head. "Oh, I promise you that you *have* heard it," I said, speaking up so he could hear me.

"How's it go?" he called back lightly, reappearing around the corner, pulling his plain white tee over his head, his blue plaid pajama bottoms hanging low on his hips showing off his lean stomach. Well, he wasn't exactly *showing off*, he had just grown comfortable around me, I guess.

"It's a choir piece, so it doesn't sound right just me singing it, but it goes..." I sang a little bit for him, the opening notes and he nodded rapidly.

"Okay, okay, I *have* heard it."

He sat on the bed carefully beside me and leaned back against the wall, shoving his pillow behind him. He twisted and picked up his own mug and asked, "So how you doing? Warmer?"

"Yeah, it got *icy* out there tonight."

"Only going to get worse. Snow is in the forecast."

"Shit," I swore softly. "I need to find some indoor spots and soon."

"I wonder what it's like," he said thoughtfully, looking at me.

"What?" I asked.

"A day in the life of Saylor Grace," he said with a charmed smile.

"When is your next weekday off?" I asked softly.

"Monday. Like I said, I switched days off with a dude to help him out. His wife left and he's got kids. Needed to take them to the doctors."

"Ah-huh. See, I told you so." I breathed transfixed by his soft green eyes and the way he looked at me.

"Told me what?" he asked amused.

"Saint Poe," I murmured.

"Patron saint of the lost?" he asked.

I nodded, mutely and he smiled, a wry amusement shading his expression.

"Somehow, I get the impression that no matter where you are, you're far from lost. You're a pretty capable woman, Saylor Grace."

"I was so screwed two nights ago," I breathed. "If it weren't for you, I don't know what I would have done. You kept me from losing literally *everything*… I don't know how I could ever thank you."

"You don't have to," he said and his voice had dropped low, too. I wanted to say we were just being considerate for the poor neighbors. I mean, it *was* close to four in the morning now… but I knew better. There was a sudden, not nearly awkward enough intimacy that'd just sprung up between us.

I was keenly aware that he was painfully attractive and that for the past two nights I'd managed to sleep mere inches from him. God, how had I not noticed? Better yet, how had I not embarrassed myself by now? I was a cuddler by nature and the fact I'd kept to myself in my sleep was a borderline miracle at this point.

"What are you thinking?" he asked softly.

"That I'm actually kind of amazed I've managed to keep to myself the past two nights. I'm an unconscious cuddler."

"Hey, worse things have happened then being snuggled by a beautiful woman."

I blushed and asked stupidly, "You think I'm beautiful?" I'd dropped my gaze to the amber liquid gently steaming in my cup that was warming my hands and he chuckled softly.

"I don't say it if I don't mean it, typically."

"You're not so bad to look at yourself," I mumbled absently, and he laughed.

"You're blushing," he pointed out.

"Shut up," I said, squeezing my eyes closed as I felt my face flame harder.

"You even do that beautifully," he said, and I could hear the smile in his voice and around the rim of his mug as he took a drink of his cider.

"Oh, God. So embarrassing," I muttered.

"Why?" he asked and laughed lightly. I giggled and couldn't help myself. I put a hand against my mouth to stifle it.

"This is all you, Saylor Grace. What you say goes," he said with a satisfied 'ah' after his next sip.

"Are you hoping I'll make a move?" I asked.

"Actually, yeah… kind of."

I laughed and said, "That's so backwards!"

"Maybe," he shrugged and I looked up at him. "But I want you to be comfortable – so to that end, you're in charge." The finality in the statement rendered me speechless for the moment.

"You're like, the total package!" I finally blurted. "How are you still single?"

He lifted one shoulder and let it drop.

"I guess maybe I was waiting for someone real. Like you."

Speechless again.

I took a swallow of my cider and stared at him. I took another swallow, thinking furiously in circles, asking myself, *just what do you want?*

The answer was that I *really* wanted him, but my head overrode my heart. At least for tonight. I sighed and told him the truth.

"I'm really tired."

"You've been up pretty close to twenty-four hours, you've been on your feet almost all fucking day, don't let me keep you up, Saylor Grace. Lay down and sleep if you're ready."

"Okay," I whispered, finishing off what was in my mug. I set it aside and scooted down.

He set his aside and got up to turn out the light. I bit my lips together and he went to the closet, rooting around in his leather jacket. He came back to my side of the bed and plugged in an honest-to-God nightlight for me. Something that beat back the dark without the harshness of leaving the light on.

I sat back up.

"When did you get that?" I asked.

"Today."

"For me?"

"You said you were scared of the dark," he reminded me gently.

"So, you bought me a nightlight?" I asked.

"Yeah, I saw it in a bodega and picked it up. An impulse buy."

He stood up and came back around the bed and I stared at the mermaid nightlight plugged into the wall, glowing softly.

I laid back down as he settled in and turned so I could face him. He smiled at me, lying on his side facing me, and I wanted so badly to close the space between us and kiss him with the swell of gratitude in my breast but I chickened out.

"What?" he asked me softly; searching my eyes in the dim lighting.

Wordlessly, I scooted closer and he simply opened his arms and just sort of naturally turned onto his back.

I cuddled into his side, his arms feeling incredibly good as they went around me. I laid my head on his chest and we both just sort of sighed out at the same time. A small peal of nervous laughter ensued and we settled.

"Goodnight, Saylor Grace," he whispered and kissed the top of my head.

I closed my eyes.

"Goodnight, Jeremy Poe."

9

P oe...

The feeling of waking up with Saylor still there, in my arms, was indescribable. I didn't know what to make of it, to be honest. I simply lay in the dim light seeping through around the closed slats of my blinds and relished the warmth and softness of the woman fetched up against me.

She slept deeply, her breathing deep and even and I realized that *damn*, I felt well rested. I couldn't remember the last time I had slept so deeply I hadn't freaking *moved* all night in my sleep. I closed my eyes and just listened to her soft draw of breath, the heavy exhale as her body autonomously kept itself running and wondered where her mind was.

Was she dreaming? If she was, what did she dream about? Was there happiness in her dreamworld right now?

Was I in it?

Was it stupid that I found myself hoping that I was?

She took a deeper, unsteady breath out of cadence with the previous

87

ones and let out a small *'mm'* sound. I couldn't tell if it was good, bad, or indifferent so I simply held still and let her come awake in her own time. She looked up at me and I looked down at her and she sucked in a soft breath, the look in her unique eyes slightly surprised.

"What time is it?" she asked.

"Don't know," I answered gently.

"Aren't you worried you might be late for work?" she asked.

I shook my head gently.

"No, not yet. My alarm hasn't gone off and I set it for eleven, so…"

"What time do you have to be into work?" she asked, sitting up a little, resting her chin on her hand which rested on my chest. I suddenly cursed my habit of wearing a tee to bed. I bet it would feel incredible, her soft skin against mine.

"Shift is from two to ten-thirty, usually."

"Oh," she whispered.

"Why, you have something in mind?" I asked.

Her smile was sweet yet held an edge of mischief.

"I'm not sure yet," she said and pushed up against the bed with her arm that was on the bottom. I breathed deep her light, feminine scent. A combination of her soap and deodorant – she didn't wear perfume that I noticed. She was, I guess, a natural beauty in that way and damn she smelled good. I don't know what it was. Something sweet, like cotton candy with a hint of extra vanilla.

It was subtly driving me crazy.

"Coffee?" she asked, stretching in front of the window, I cocked my head and nodded.

"Yeah, here or out there?" I asked.

"I can make it," she said and padded around into the kitchen.

I pushed myself up into a sitting position and put my back against the wall behind me to watch her.

She flitted throughout my kitchen like a fairy, going through drawers and various cupboards, plucking things down as she found them, or bringing them up from the drawers. She was graceful in her movements, deliberate, and I wondered briefly…

"You ever take any dance classes or martial arts?"

"What?" she asked, then laughed slightly as she filled the coffee maker's carafe with water at the sink, her back to me.

"I asked if you ever danced or took martial arts," I repeated.

"I know, just… Where did that question come from?" She laughed lightly.

"You just move with grace," I said. "Practiced, but not intentional, you know?"

She leaned against the counter, facing me, and smiled this flattered and charmed smile and shook her head.

"I fell in with some fire spinners and learned poi. Maybe that's where I get it?"

"Wait, what the hell is *poi?*" I asked.

I got a crash course in fire spinning, and I guess poi were fireballs at the end of a chain. Who knew? She told me all about the weekly practices at a place called 'Gas Works' back where she'd come from. How they went on all summer long, people taking turns to practice performing. How she would play for several, how others performed to an old boom box, and others to music from wireless Bluetooth speakers. How during the really special practices something called a drum circle would form.

It sounded kind of magical, if you asked me.

"I haven't really run into too many other performers here, yet," she said.

"They're around. All but the most diehard take the winter off, I guess. They don't in Seattle?"

"Don't get me wrong, it can get *cold* in Seattle, but it's not like out here. Seattle it's wet, and the cold is somehow milder. We get a lot of days in the thirties but it's the mid-to-high thirties and the coldest it usually gets is in January and February. Maybe the latter half of December. It rains *a lot* but we *maybe* get one or two days of snow per year. It's not your typical winter and it's shorter than just about any other place I've heard of."

"Huh."

"Yeah, it's actually pretty conducive to year-round outdoor perform-ing," she said as she finished moving around the kitchen, getting the coffee maker going.

She came back to the bed and sat down next to me.

"So, what are your big plans for today?" I asked.

"I was actually thinking about giving myself a day off. Maybe just stay here and compose a couple of new things. Go out tonight, or just hit the holiday shoppers up with some carols tomorrow. Get on the Wi-Fi and do a little internet research from my phone on popular spots for Christmas shopping – that kind of thing."

"Sounds good. Uh, you know, on the edge of my sector there's this old – and I mean *really old* building that was one of the first shop-ping malls back in like the 1800s or something. Now, they've converted the bottom floor into these little boutiques and shops while the two floors above them are these expensive-ass bougie micro-apartments."

"That sounds so cool!" she exclaimed and looked up at me with a sparkle in her eyes.

"I'll check it out and ask one of the business owners if it's cool you went in and did your thing."

"I'd like that, only to be fair, the bougie types are the most inclined to pinch their pennies so I don't know how well I would do."

"Won't know unless you try," I said with a shrug and she smiled big as the coffee maker gurgled its last in the kitchen.

"And at least I get to do the thing I love the most while trying, so there's always that."

"That's the way to look at it," I said and admired her positive outlook.

She got up and asked, "Creamer and sugar?"

"Oh, naw, the creamer in the fridge is sweet enough on its own. That's why I buy it."

"Okay."

She made us coffee and then rejoined me on the bed. We sat sipping and talking. Idle chitchat about her life as a street musician and mine as a city beat cop. Eventually we got into trading stories about the crazy shit we'd witnessed, respectively.

"I once saw a man hold up a convenience store with a samurai sword," she said as I ducked into the bathroom to get ready to head out to work.

"Oh, shit. Yeah, we haven't had one of those out here, yet. We did have a drunk guy walk up to a cooler in a convenience store, open the door, whip his dick out and start pissing on the milk. He was so drunk he thought it was a new type of urinal."

"Oh, God! That's so gross!" she cried laughing.

"Uh, yeah. Clerk was like 'I don't get paid enough, dude.' I think he quit that night."

"I know I would!" She shuddered and drank down the last of her coffee as I shrugged into my jacket and cut and brought down my helmet where I kept it on the top shelf.

I went over near her and said, "I'll be home by midnight."

"Okay," she said lightly, and it felt totally natural, comfortable, like slipping on your favorite sweatshirt when I bent at the waist and brushed my lips across hers.

I straightened quickly and said, "Holy shit. I don't know why I just did that."

She looked up at me, and the expression on her face was unreadable. I was seriously starting to panic on the inside when she finally said, "Me either, but come down here and do it again."

I smiled, my insides turning liquid with relief that I hadn't offended her and with a soft, "Yes, ma'am," I bent and touched my lips to hers again.

Her palm was soft and warm where it came up to caress the side of my face. She kissed me back, carefully, her lips moving lightly against mine, her tongue flickering tentatively out to taste my bottom lip.

I kept it light and drew away slowly, murmuring, "To be continued…"

"Okay," she said back carefully, her voice a bit strained with desire.

"See you around midnight."

She smiled. "Don't turn into a pumpkin on me."

"I won't. That's a promise," I said, slipping out the front door. I locked it behind me to keep her safe. The vision of her sitting there on my bed in her little boy shorts and thin tank top nearly did me in. My cock throbbing in my jeans, her faint, sweet, coffee-laden kiss more energizing than any of the caffeinated nectar I'd drunk that morning.

I wasn't even halfway down the walkway and I missed her.

Things were definitely not going according to plan – but considering

I'd only had a loose idea and no plan to begin with, I guess I was alright with that.

I looked up at my door one last time before wheeling my bike around to take off for work and thought to myself, *to be continued indeed.* Work tonight was going to be the longest commercial break ever.

10

*S*aylor...

I sat frozen on Poe's bed, my fingertips pressed to my lips as though I could push the feel of his soft lips against mine under the skin to hold on to it forever. I tingled in a glowing wash from head to toe, excitement and elation coursing through my veins.

He kissed me.

He was interested, and what was more, I was interested too. I mean, interested in *him*. Not his money, or the fact that he was putting a roof over my head for the time being. No, for those things I was grateful, but I didn't need those things. All I wanted, honestly, was someone just like Jeremy Poe. Someone who saw me as a person, dug me intellectually and not just for my looks.

Someone who when they touched me, my body came alive without my mind getting in the way and he'd definitely just accomplished that one.

In a flash, I re-prioritized my day. Getting up, I started all my clothes in a load to wash, settled in with my guitar and journal and worked on composition until that load was up, then swapped it into the dryer and put in the rest of Poe's things from the hamper in the closet. I was kind of grateful that he had just ditched some of his things directly into the washer. It made it so I would have a full enough load with my meager light belongings.

While the second load washed and the first load dried, I sat in my pajamas on the bed that I took the time to make and counted out all of my money, facing and organizing the bills in a fat stack, surprised when it came to a whole two hundred and thirteen dollars!

"Wow. Thank you, Indigo City." I sighed and went for my backpack and dragged it up here with me, dumping all of the contents onto the bed and sifting through it.

I smiled to myself and set my journal, pens, and my money off to one side, then sorted through the rest, putting them into smaller piles.

Things that needed to go back in the pack, things that needed more attention, and things I needed to find another home for temporarily. Some in my little suitcase, some in the cubby under the nightstand on what was quickly becoming 'my side of the bed.'

There was change *everywhere*, and I kept adding it to the Crown Royal bag which was straining to contain it all and had become heavier than a bowling ball. I couldn't even pull it up by the cloth or its strings anymore. If I did, I risked tearing it and I didn't want to do that.

I double-checked my guitar case, found a loose nickel and a couple of pennies then set about putting all of it back together again, going on to neaten the tiny apartment up to within an inch of its life.

My bathroom stuff I left out of my backpack and tingled with a low-level anxiety about it. I'd been lucky so far. I had never not had at the very least, the *basics* on being able to clean myself up. It was something I was as fastidious about as humanly possible. My hair and teeth brushed, at the very least I'd grab a whore's bath out of a gas station sink even if I was stuck wearing the same clothes for a week or more. Which only happened once by the way – when an ex-boyfriend held my shit hostage to try and get me back and I had to break into his loft when he was gone to get as much of it back as I could.

I sighed and tried not to go back to those particular memories. It wasn't worth it. It was hard to trust again after some of the run-ins and brushes with trouble I'd had but Poe? Poe made it so *easy*, and that in and of itself was pretty overwhelming for me but in a good way. At least, I think.

"Okay, Saylor – you're half way there," I mumbled to myself when I heard the washing machine quit. I went and checked the dryer. Not dry yet, but close. I checked the lint trap, cleaned it out and set it to keep going. I went through the apartment while I waited and gathered up the trash, put everything of mine away that I could, and stared at my flaccid, deflated backpack laying on the bed. The only thing in it – my big ol' bag of coins.

I went through my journal and found my recipes scattered throughout it. I loved the super thick book. The cover for it was leather that was dyed a deep brown and was unevenly cut so it could be folded over and tied with the leather thongs attached to the front cover. It protected the edges from the damp back home – which who knew if I would go back?

I couldn't do anything without my car, and it was pretty much gone forever. I still didn't know if I would ever be able to get the rest of my belongings out of it.

I tried to bravely thrust the 'what-ifs' out of my head for now. As soon as my clothes were dry, I set what I was going to wear aside on the bed, folded the rest of my things up and repacked my little suitcase and put it back in the closet.

Another shower where I took the time to shave everything with one of my precious razors and I felt like *brand new*. It was a good feeling. I dried my hair as completely as I could with a towel and dressed as warmly as I could with what I had in my bag. I put my guitar in its case and with an almost sick feeling, pushed it under the bed.

I wouldn't need it for what I was off to do. It was my mission to have Poe come home to a super nice dinner – that didn't mean I was about to go to the store hungry. I heated up half of what was my leftovers from the night before and ate before I went out.

I was glad when it was Bernard who pulled up in the next bus at the stop. The doors opened and he said, "Well, well, well! No music today, huh?"

"Not today," I said getting on.

"Where to?" he asked.

"Trying to find a good grocery store. One with one of those coin machines."

"Oh, yeah, yeah, yeah! Have a seat, I got you. I got one right on my route."

"Fabulous!" I declared and took a seat up front near him.

"Things get better for you?" he asked.

"Yeah! Actually, they have."

"Good deal!"

We made small talk and he pulled up to the curb at a stop and said, "Here you go! Just catch me on the other side of the street there, I'll get you home no worries."

"Thank you, Bernard! You want anything?"

"You get me one of them Kit Kat bars? I like them."

"One Kit Kat, made to order," I declared.

"Alright, now."

I intended to go shopping with whatever I got out of my bulk of change, and I can't tell you how good it felt when the coins weighing me down were out of my bag, sorted, and came to eighty-two bucks. It wildly exceeded my expectations and the machine gave me the option of either taking a hit on fees to take it in cash or to payout no fees in exchange for a gift card – and listed in the shops I could get a card from was the grocery store I was standing in.

I took the card option, went to the customer service desk and was free to load up on necessities!

I went and got a cart and thought about what Poe had at home in his fridge and freezer – which was honestly pretty meager.

I took a deep breath and let it out slow. When you were poor and living dollar to dollar rather than a steady paycheck to paycheck, you needed to make *every* dollar count and I was well aware there were certain necessities that *had* to be seen to while I had money. Whatever I had left after those were dealt with, I could get dinner out of.

First stop was the feminine care aisle. It was the *first* thing I always saw to – especially now since my last box of products was somewhere in my car in a cold and lonely impound yard. I wasn't due to start this week, or even next, that I could recall – to be honest, I'd lost track, but it was on my non-working phone. I had a tracker on there to help me that still worked, even without a signal.

I bought a variety box of tampons and went and found a bottle of Midol which was a *total* splurge. I warred with myself on the Midol between the bigger bottle which would last longer and the smaller bottle which was cheaper and went with the smaller one.

I picked up deodorant, skipped toothbrush and toothpaste, and skipped body wash – those could be gotten at the dollar store for *much* cheaper.

I took my time, going up and down the aisles, warring on cheap versus healthy, on if I *really* needed that now, or if I should hold off because if something were to go sideways, would I be able to carry it and where would I store it?

Being homeless was hard and *super* expensive. People didn't even realize. Having no place to store food, or wash your clothes meant paying for it on the regular and that could eat through your money so fast – especially the food part. Keeping yourself fed on-demand was a bitch when you couldn't cook for yourself or keep things cold or frozen.

I wound up splurging on salad and salad dressing. I got lucky and found the whole chickens, which were one of the cheapest cuts of meat out there, were buy one get one free today. Poe had a freezer, so that helped quite a bit. Still, I was limited in what I could carry. If I put the heaviest things in my backpack, which I had emptied for this, that would help with the load.

I puttered from aisle to aisle and tried to spend the most of my shopping energy on the outside edge where the healthy and fresh things lived.

I did cut down the baking aisle, loading up on the real MVPs of flour and sugar. I picked up packets of dry yeast and splurged on some cinnamon. I picked up butter, milk, and eggs looking into my cart with some serious trepidation. I started to really worry about weight, but I was a trouper. I would magically make it work somehow. I didn't know how, yet... but I would.

Peanut butter was another big splurge. I got two of the biggest containers I could. I didn't bother with buying bread when I could make it myself, and my final count had me still inside forty dollars before tax, so I snatched onions, celery, and carrots and grabbed some oatmeal and pasta from the bulk foods section.

I bought two big reusable grocery totes and the checker smiled at me and said, "Any particular way you would like this bagged?"

"If you could get the heavy items in my pack, I would really appreciate it. I'm afraid I may have overdone it."

"Nah, I think you can handle it. Want me to put the chickens into some plastic sacks just in case before I put them in here?"

"You're a lifesaver, seriously."

She told me the total and I frowned. I knew food wasn't taxable but… "Are you sure you didn't miss anything?" I asked.

"Yeah, why? What's wrong?" she asked.

"It just seems awfully *low*," I said.

She laughed slightly and tossed her long brown braid back over the shoulder of her green uniform vest and said, "Sounds like a good problem to have."

"What's your sales tax rate here?"

"Six percent, where are you from?"

"Holy shneikeis! I'm from a land where it's like ten percent, so that makes sense."

"Ten percent? Wow!"

"Um, where's your candy aisle?" I looked back past me.

"What do you need?" she asked.

"Hershey's Kisses, oh! And a Kit Kat."

"Hey Pete!" She called to another employee mopping up a spill behind us at the mouth of her checkstand.

"Yeah?"

"Grab this lady a bag of Kisses and a Kit Kat off the candy aisle?" she asked.

"Oh, yeah!" he turned and jogged down a few aisles, disappeared, and returned with one of the big bags of Kisses and a king-sized Kit Kat bar.

"That all?" she asked, swiping them across her scanner.

"Yeah." I handed her my gift card with a big smile and she ran it.

"Balance will be on your receipt, have a nice day!"

"Oh, I will, thanks!"

I turned and nearly ran smack dab into Josh from the coffee shop.

"Whoa, hey!" he laughed.

"Oh, God, I'm so sorry!"

"No worries. I was trying to see if it was you – hard to recognize without the guitar."

I laughed a little and hefted my backpack, shrugging into it and *oh boy,* it was heavy.

"Can I help you carry?" he asked.

"Oh, um, sure – I'm only going as far as the bus stop out front."

"No worries." He lifted the two totes which were heavy as well.

"Stocking up for the storm?" he asked.

"Storm?" I echoed.

"Yeah, the snowstorm that's supposed to –" He stopped and laughed as we stepped out into the cold falling white and I stood there like a landed fish, my mouth a little 'o' of surprise.

"Oh, shit."

"Come on, the busses are still running, which one you taking?"

"Um, the number thirty-two."

"Shit, you better hurry, that one comes in like three minutes."

"Oh, damn! I didn't think I was in there that long."

We hustled to the bus stop and he asked, "Can I see you home?"

"Oh, uh, that's probably not a good idea. I'm staying with a – a friend," I stuttered. I didn't know exactly what to call Poe.

I mean, he already felt like more than a friend and I honestly really wanted to be more than a friend which left me all sorts of confused… like I wondered, did that make me a bad person? I mean, Cody may have done me dirty, but I literally didn't feel any kind of way about it now and it was only what? Two? Three days ago that it happened?

Josh and I made it to the bus stop just in time, laughing slightly and out of breath from the cold and the weight.

"Hey there, Saylor!" Bernard called in greeting.

"That's me," I told Josh and he smiled and said, "To be continued, then, I guess."

It made me think of Poe. Of his angular jaw and sharp cheekbones, his green eyes like cut emeralds with candle flames behind them as he'd said the same thing to me that morning. Of how I couldn't wait for him to make good on the promise in his voice.

Poe.

He was literally *all* I could think about even with Josh looking at me hopefully right now.

I took my bags from him and smiled and said, "I'll come by the shop sometime soon."

"I'm looking forward to it."

"Ah, you say that now, but for the next few weeks, it's nothing but Christmas carols!"

I got on the bus and he waved and called up to me, "I think I'd listen to you recite the dictionary and I would still like it!"

I blushed and turned to Bernard and paid my fare even though he tried to wave me off and he raised his eyebrows at my desperate look to be underway. Before I could say anything back to Josh, or he could say anything else to me, Bernard shut the bus door behind me and lurched away from the curb.

"Thanks," I muttered and found a seat, digging through my bags for that Kit Kat I'd just bought him. The carriage was fuller this time around.

"Don't mention it, though he seemed like a nice fella."

"No, I mean, he *is*..."

"You got somebody else on your mind though?"

"Yeah," I said sheepishly. I took him his Kit Kat and he lit up, taking it from me and sliding it into his lunch pail by his seat.

"Somebody like ol' Bernard." He stuck his head up and puffed out his chest and I giggled.

"Sorry to burst your bubble, it's a local policeman, though."

"Ooo wee! One of our boys in blue?" he asked.

"Yeah," I acknowledged, returning to my seat.

"Good on you, girl!"

I giggled once again and said, "Yeah, well, we'll see."

"Where you at up in here, girl? Maybe I can get you closer," he said as we neared the stop.

"Oh, I'm two corners up," I declared, and he passed my stop and stopped at the corner closer to Poe's.

"Alright now, you be careful and I'll be seeing you."

"Thanks Bernard, you allergic to peanuts?" I asked.

"No, why?"

"Next time I see you, I'll bring you one of my signature cookies."

"You are too kind! Too kind," he declared as I stepped off the bus and with a wave, he shut the doors and trundled down the street that was filling with snow.

I sighed and made my way carefully down Poe's street, which didn't really have any sidewalks, and tried not to slip and die on the ice that was forming.

My arms and shoulders were screaming by the time I reached the steps on the side of his building. I was grateful to set things down outside his door so I could fish his key out of my pocket.

I turned the key in the lock with great big plans to bake and to cook, grateful that the oven would pull double duty and heat the apartment while I did it.

I had some pretty grandiose plans for dinner.

11

*P*oe...

The snow had started falling hard only midway through the shift. I rode home, but mother*fucker* was it dicey – and I wouldn't be riding into work the next day. Fuck that shit. I didn't want to damage the bike.

The good news was the crime rates usually dropped with the temperature – except for car theft, so it made for a pretty chill shift all in all. Still, I was freezing my balls off and all I really wanted, as crude as it sounded, was to be balls deep into Saylor Grace. I meant what I'd said, though. It really was up to her how far things went, if they even went anywhere.

I still didn't know what had possessed me to kiss her like that this morning as I'd left. To just kiss her, like she was my long-time girlfriend and I was just routinely giving her a kiss goodbye before my shift...

Maybe I was lonelier than I realized. Maybe, I was projecting. In any case, I'd felt guilty as hell about it until she'd told me to come back for more and holy shit was she responsive. I was getting hard again just thinking about it.

I keyed my way into the apartment having every intention of asking if she wanted to take a walk with me a few blocks to this Vietnamese joint for some hot soup, and I walked smack into a cacophony of delicious smells and some equally delicious heat that made my question die in my throat.

"What's all this?" I demanded.

"This is a lot of things," she said, closing my oven door and beaming at me.

"Where does the list start?" I asked, shutting the cold firmly on the outside and throwing the locks.

"Well, we're celebrating that I had over eighty bucks in loose coins in that Crown bag for one."

"Wow, nice!"

"Two, I wanted to say thank you for everything you've done." She reached out and I took her hand as she reeled me in closer to her, putting her arms around my waist, looking up at me with those stunning mismatched eyes of hers; smiling this charmed little smile.

"You're very welcome," I said softly. "You should know that by now."

"Mm-hm," she hummed and her smile turning slightly mischievous. She said, "And three, I really, really, *really* wanted to finish this morning's episode."

"Yeah?" I asked smiling too, my lips already descending towards hers.

"Yeah," she whispered, her warm breath brushing across my cold lips.

The kiss was an explosion of passion between us. She didn't hesitate, her lips parting, her tongue meeting mine, stroking against it boldly; her taste sweet from whatever she'd been drinking. Vaguely spicy, orangey, flavorful and bold.

"God, you taste divine," I growled against her mouth.

"Oh, you like that?" she murmured.

"Hmm, yeah, what is it?"

She reached off to the side, groping at one of the countertops and laughed, and I stepped back letting her go. God, it was reluctantly that I did it, but damn, I would have her in my arms soon enough. In my bed, holding her close, even if that was the only thing I got to do.

She slid a packet off the counter, a tea bag and put it in my hand. I read the label, the brand one I didn't readily recognize. It was a sweet orange spice flavor of tea and I gave a nod and an impressed look.

"Want me to hook you up?" she asked.

"Yeah, that'd be good," I said. "What else have you got going on in here?"

This woman had done *the works*. She had a chicken roasting in the oven, salad made with all kinds of extras like mushrooms, olives, cucumbers and bell peppers. She had *made* fresh popover rolls in my one muffin tin and even had a plate of these peanut butter cookies with the Hershey Kisses pressed into the top.

"Jesus, you've been busy!"

"Yeah and I have almost half that gift card left."

"Gift card? What gift card?" I asked.

"From the coin machine. If you get a gift card, you don't pay fees – take the cash and you have to give a percentage to the coin machine company."

"Huh, I didn't know that. Then again, I don't usually have a lot of pocket change. I use my card for almost everything."

"Makes sense. You know, by the time you grab a shower and change clothes, I'll have everything done and plated up."

"Sounds good, I could stand to get warm and into more comfortable clothes."

"Alright then." She stood on her tiptoes and puckered her lips and I laughed, giving her a quick chaste kiss.

"I'm really starting to enjoy those," she murmured.

I chuckled and went around the counter saying, "Plenty more where they came from."

By the time I got out, she'd made good on her promise. There were two plates made up and waiting and she was saying, "I guessed on the salad dressing and went with Ranch."

"I'm more of an Italian guy, but Ranch is good, too. I have to say, this is *really* a surprise."

"Good." Her smile lit up the space we occupied. "I'm glad. I wanted it to be."

"I was feeling pretty guilty about the lack of food in here. I think it's going to be a chill shift tomorrow. I maybe can hit up the –" She opened the freezer to show me another chicken in there as I put dressing on my salad.

"Soup tomorrow from whatever is left of this bird. We should be okay for the next couple of days."

"Nice," I said and nodded impressed.

"I have oatmeal for tomorrow morning. Milk. Plenty of flour, eggs, yeast, peanut butter… I can make a loaf of bread tomorrow. We'll still have popovers to go with the soup. No worries."

"You don't have to do all this," I said, tracing some of her longer, beachy waves behind her ear. She smiled up at me.

"I like to pull my own weight," she said.

"You've done admirably with all of this, let me just say."

"Shall we retire to the dining room?" she asked, and I chuckled and nodded.

"Let's, and ladies first."

We watched the tail end of the *Late Late Show* and I swear to God, I feasted. Her cooking was out of this world and probably a lot healthier than the noodle place when I stopped to think about it. We ate our fill and both of us cleaned up.

"I took a gamble that you weren't allergic to peanuts," she said and held up one of her bite-sized cookies. I let her feed it to me and it was really good… and I mean *really good.*

"Mm, wow," I said around a mouthful.

"Yeah?"

"Mm-hmm." I chewed and swallowed. "Those moutherfucker's are dangerous."

She laughed and sounded delighted.

"They're my signature cookie. My granddad and I made them every Christmas."

"You talk about him a lot," I mused and she nodded.

"He was my whole world," she said. "I miss him every day."

"I'm sorry," I murmured, setting the last dish in the dry rack and turning. She'd ripped apart the bird and I went to grab the pan she'd done it in and pour the drippings down the drain.

"Wait!" she cried. "Don't do that. I can use them for the soup tomorrow. Pour them in here." She thrust one of my Tupperware containers at me.

"Okay, you're the boss," I said amused.

"You put it in the fridge, scrape off the fat and are left with all the good stuff," she said. "Add water and it makes an okay stock."

"I am not going to lie," I told her. "I am your typical dude. I grill meat and can cook a steak, but my knowledge of cooking is fairly stunted."

"Kind of blows my mind," she said as she worked to put things away. "You have a really well-stocked kitchen."

"That was my mom and my sister," I told her. "I guess they figured if they hooked me up with enough decent cookware it would somehow magically teach me how to cook."

Saylor Grace giggled and put the container in the fridge.

I pulled her into my arms, and she bit her bottom lip, blushing.

"I don't know what exactly this is," I told her, "but I like it."

"I like it too," she murmured.

"I'd kind of like to know how far I'm allowed to go before I make any kind of misstep with you."

"I don't think you could mess this up… I'm more afraid that *I'm* going to do something to overstep."

"I guess we just have to be careful with each other. Keep the lines of communication open."

"I guess so," she whispered, her voice dropping into this husky, sexy tone that drove me a little wild. I tightened my hold on her and she sighed in contentment.

"I'm going to unwrap you like a present," I breathed against her ear.

"Yeah?" she asked. "Then what?"

"I'm going to love you long and slow. Take my time with you."

"Ooo, I like the sound of that," she said, voice a low and sultry purr. "Let's do that."

She tipped her face up and I met her halfway, pressing my lips to hers in an almost needy, certainly insistent kiss. Her lips parted in invitation, her arms went around my neck and I groaned as she buried her fingers in the back of my hair.

She whimpered, this soft, desperate sound against my mouth that sent fire through my blood. I held her tight against my body and she swooned into me. I swear to God, I don't think I had ever felt like so much of a man, so powerful, so virile, than I did in that moment when she yielded to me.

There was something so incredibly erotic about it, and we hadn't even gotten to the part where we were supposed to take our clothes off.

It was the strangest sensation, kissing Saylor Grace in my kitchen like that. It felt so natural, so pure; so *right*. She fit into my arms so perfectly, where she molded her body against mine – *goddamn* did it feel good. There was no comparison to any woman I'd ever had occasion to get with before. Our chemistry was off the charts, and I suddenly couldn't wait to get her naked and under me.

I kept to my word, though. Saylor Grace wasn't some quick fuck for me. She was a woman that I had every intention of savoring as long into the night as possible.

I led her out of the kitchen and around to the foot of my bed. I plucked at the buttons of her light and fluttery, completely inadequate for the temperature outside, flowery bohemian blouse. She had it tucked in the front, the tail out and hiding her shapely ass from me.

I pulled her tight against me by that gorgeous ass of hers as I devoured her from the mouth down, kneading her soft flesh through the thick denim of her jeans. She kissed me back just as fiercely, her hands delving beneath the hem of my tee. I moved my hands, grabbing the back of the neckline of my shirt and hauling it off over my head so I could pull her back against me.

Her skin against mine where her blouse gaped open was the softest thing I'd ever felt against my own. The woman's skin was satin, her scent intoxicating, and the way she moved against me, her reach eager, her kiss passionate fire, her touch sending lightning through my veins, making me come alive – she was just so perfect it was hard to maintain control.

"God, you feel good, Saylor Grace," I whispered against her ear, gripping her hair carefully, to control, not to hurt, as I played my lips along the side of her neck.

"Jeremy," she gasped, and I loved the sound of my name on her lips.

Her fingers tugged lightly at the drawstring of my flannel pajama bottoms as I pushed her blouse off her shoulders reverently, breaking our kiss so I could lay eyes on her, the flesh that was revealed pure and smooth, peaches and cream and begging for me to taste her.

Her blouse fluttered to the floor and I worked the tongue of her brown leather belt from its brass buckle, the leather sighing with its surrender as I opened it up to get to her button and zipper fly.

She pushed my pajama bottoms to the floor but left my boxers on, and I realized she was matching me. Piece by piece of clothing but she was getting ahead of herself. I pushed her jeans down, off over her hips and pressed her close again, my hands wandering to the clasp of her bra at her back, unhooking it a little too expertly in my haste to get it off so I could finally be nothing but skin on skin from the waist up.

Jesus, feeling all of her warm, silken flesh, the press of her small but perfect tits against my chest – I could die now. I could die and I would have only one regret, not knowing what it felt like to be inside her.

She whimpered beautifully against my mouth as I smoothed my hands up and down her back. She stepped on the cuffs of her jeans, marching in place to get her legs free. We were both barefoot, which helped – it just meant fewer clothes in our way.

I was straining at the front of my boxers, my hands wandering, caressing over her body and trailing to rest on her hips before I ventured bravely forth to plunge my hand down the front of her cotton panties.

"Oh, God, *Jeremy*," she whined against my mouth, her tone begging as my fingertips pressed against her pussy. I tapped my foot against the inside of her ankle, gently kicking her feet wider and she complied, her strong sure fingers wrapping around the head of my cock through my boxers.

"Oh, God, *Saylor*," I echoed her and our mouths clashed.

Jesus Christ she was so wet. My fingers slicked through her arousal and I teased the nib of flesh at the top of her sex. She squirmed on her feet and I dropped to my knees, taking her panties down and pressing my mouth to the front of her slit, delving my tongue between her folds, over her curls, tasting her, teasing that little kernel of nerve endings with my tongue, rolling my eyes to gaze up her body to those spectacular mismatched eyes of hers.

That view was everything, those gorgeous blue and green eyes staring down at me in wonder and lust between the valley of her breasts. Her chest rose and fell with shallow and uneven breaths, her fingers twining in my hair and her hands unconsciously pressing my mouth tighter to her body. Her legs trembled finely as she threw her head back and gasped as I found just the right spot with my tongue.

She shook her head and gasped out, "My legs, they're weak, I can't stand anymore."

I tore my mouth from her sex and turned her with my hands on her hips. She obeyed me, turning where I directed her and with a wicked grin, I pressed on her stomach and threw her down on the bed. She yipped and laughed but I wasn't done. I wrapped my arms around her thighs and dragged her back to the edge of the bottom of the bed, shouldering her knees apart and going right back down on her.

She moaned and gathered the comforter in her little fists at her hips which bucked unbidden, rising to meet my lips and tongue.

I put an arm across her hips and pressed her down to keep her at my mouth as I used my other hand to slip a finger or two inside of her.

She was hot to the touch, like silk against my tongue and hand. My dick throbbed painfully with a need to be inside her, but I denied myself. I was honestly worried I wouldn't be able to last very long once I was there, so I wanted to make her come a time or two first so as not to disappoint.

Mmm, she didn't disappoint *me*. Now that was for *sure*. She was so responsive, crying out yet trying to remain quiet, her body shuddering against the bed as she grew closer and closer to a final devastating orgasm. When she finally let go and took the plunge, it was beautiful. She cried out and arched, her hands flying from the blankets to her mouth to stop herself from screaming, her body which had been tauter than a bowstring had snapped closed, hurtling forward and I just needed to get the hell out of the way.

I jerked my head and shoulders back as her legs snapped shut and her knees rose to her stomach as she shook from involuntary muscle spasms brought on by her wracking waves of pleasure.

My fingers were still buried in her wet heat, and I relished the contractions around them, as her body tried to pull me deeper and I *had* to experience this sensation around my cock.

I waited until she calmed down, until she unfurled like a beautiful, delicate; night-blooming plant. Like the Casablanca lilies that grew in my mom's garden.

I slipped my fingers from inside her on a whimper of protest from her and stood, slipping my boxers off, staring down at her beautiful prone figure.

She looked up at me, eyes glassy with her burgeoning afterglow and I smiled.

"My turn," I murmured, and she smiled and reached her arms up, beckoning me to lie with her.

It was an invitation I wasn't about to refuse.

12

*S*aylor...

"My turn," he murmured with this devilishly debonair grin that I just adored. I reached my arms up, languidly, still unable to fully control my body much beyond the simple movement thanks to the incredibly devastating orgasm he had just graciously put me through.

He bit his bottom lip, excitement firing up his beautiful green eyes as he gazed upon my nude prone body on his bed. He had me at his mercy and he knew it, the slightly predatory look in his eyes incredibly arousing. There was no menace behind the expression, instead, there was something akin to joy, an almost gratitude, and though it was incredibly subtle, it was *there* and *palpable* and made all the difference.

He slipped his boxers off his hips and let them sweep down his legs to the floor. When he straightened, his cock was so hard, standing at full attention, the crown of it brushing just below his bellybutton. He was long, the head of him full, and the shaft not terribly over thick.

I was glad for that. I didn't have the biggest pussy, and the few partners I had been with willingly, had varied in size. The biggest of them had hurt and it had been disappointing to say the least – too big you couldn't get too rough and sometimes I liked sex to be a little on the enthusiastic side.

Poe was perfect and I was *really* looking forward to having him inside me.

He kneeled over me on the bed, kissing me softly, ramping me back up slowly and I was struck by how careful he was of me. His arm around me, hand at my lower back, lifting me gently to urge me further up onto the bed so he could get between my thighs.

I followed his motions with no resistance so that we could settle in the circle of one another's arms and kiss a while. He paused just a moment to search my face and asked,

"You want me to wear a condom?"

"Yeah," I whispered and he smiled.

"Didn't know your preference," he said.

"I got a free IUD from Planned Parenthood, but I still use protection just in case."

"Not a problem for me," he murmured, kissing the tip of my nose. "I was more asking about a latex allergy."

"Oh! No, I don't have one of those..." My curiosity got the better of me and I asked, "Were you with someone who had one?"

"For a minute, a long, long, time ago," he murmured and reached into the drawer beside the bed on 'his side' to bring out a square foil packet.

"What was she like?" I asked, for some reason wanting to torture myself a little. I mean, did he still have feelings for her? Did I look like her? Anxiety swirled in my chest and he gave me a one-sided smile.

"I don't want to talk about her," he said. "I want to talk about you."

I wrapped my fingers around his cock and massaged him gently to keep him erect, afraid our conversation would sideline things if it continued much longer.

"What about me?" I asked, stroking him. He closed his eyes and moaned, softly grunting as he tore open the condom packet eagerly. He fumbled a moment with the slick rubber, getting it lined up over the head of his dick, and I let him go, writhing a bit eagerly at his side, wanting him so badly.

"You're unlike anyone I've ever met before," he said, voice shaking with his nerves. His concentration on that borderline edge of loss.

"Oh?"

He got the condom on and got between my legs, kissing me, stroking over my skin with his strong hands, his fingers sure, his palms slightly rough. It was a tantalizing sensation that stoked the flame of my desire for him even higher.

"You're amazing," he murmured against my lips.

I smiled, warmed to a steady glow by both his touch and his words. I lay back and pulled him down over the top of me.

He slid his body against mine, thrusting blindly for purchase. It didn't take but one or two to find my opening. His cock slipped into my pussy and it was like we somehow completed one another, both of us losing ourselves in the moment.

I arched up to meet him, he bowed his head, hissing between gritted teeth, his lips pressing against my skin at the cap of my shoulder.

We danced. Bodies mingling, breathing harsh and clashing, moans following a delightful cadence, rising in pitch the closer I came to yet another orgasm.

He felt incredible moving in and out of me, and I relished holding him in my center. He folded over me, pressing my body into the mattress, and I swear to God, I'd never been closer to a man. I'd never felt so completed by another person, I'd never been so insanely attracted to any other man and *"Oh, God! Oh, God! Oh, God! Yes!"*

I pressed my body against his as I was wracked by another storm surge of pleasure, the waves cresting well above my head and crashing into me mercilessly, cruelly, and leaving nothing but the most wonderful and beautiful devastation in their wake. It was as if Poe's touch erased every other touch that had come before and as the waves of orgasm carried me to shore, they put me right back in his arms, which curved around my back and shoulders, holding me off the bed as he panted against the side of my neck.

It took me a few seconds to realize he wasn't moving anymore either. A few seconds more to even realize that he'd come too, with me...

I'd never done that before. Come in unison with someone. It had always been me, then him, or him and me not at all... never together like this.

We both lay quivering in each other's embrace, panting, incapable of words and that was alright. It wasn't like I really had the words to describe what it was I was feeling right now anyway.

"God, you feel so good," he breathed against my ear, capturing the lobe gently between his teeth.

I gasped and laughed at the shower of pleasing sparks that cascaded from the erogenous zone down the side of my neck to curl through my breast and down through my fingertips on that arm.

"So do you," I murmured, turning my mouth into his. We kissed languidly, and descended from our mutual height slowly, lazily, riding the thermals of our pleasure in a lazy spiral into the river of afterglow.

He searched my face from inches away, smoothing my hair back absently with his hand with such a look of wonder painted on his own features that I had to ask,

"What? What is it?"

"You," he said steadily as if that alone should answer my question and not just increase my confusion.

"What about me?" I answered almost automatically.

Color creeped up his neck and flooded his face and I laughed.

"What?" I cried playfully. "You can't leave me hanging *now*."

"I know! I know, that…" he trailed off and smoothed fingertips across my cheek as if he were trying to commit this moment to memory before he lost it forever.

"What is it?" I pushed and my tone had grown serious, losing all of its teasing edge, my laughter fled at how serious he'd grown.

"I don't want to freak you out," he murmured.

I cocked my head. "It takes quite a bit to do that," I told him truthfully.

He smiled and it held an almost shyness.

"Can you just trust me that it's good and not make me actually say it?" he asked.

I giggled and shook my head, biting my bottom lip saying, "No. Just tell me already!" Truthfully, my anxiety was trying to sound the alarm. Preparing me for something awful. Something that was going to wreck me, devastate my heart and I was starting to worry that maybe this had been a really bad idea.

"It's cheesy," he warned, and I fought not to smack him and demand he just tell me already.

I lost half that battle and gripping his upper arms where he held himself above me cried, "Will you just spit it out?"

"Fine," he said. He took a deep breath and I could see all over his face the fear and what he said wasn't at all what I had expected to come out of his mouth when he blurted, "I never believed love at first sight was a thing until I laid eyes on you."

I froze and blinked up at him, bewildered.

"What?" I sounded far away, even to myself.

"Shit," he muttered. "See, I told you I should have just kept it to myself. Now I've gone and scared you and I never meant to do that – not in a million yea –"

"Stop," I ordered him and refused to let go when he went to climb off of me. I wanted him here. Desperately.

"Just, stop," I echoed and to his credit, he did, staring at me apprehensively.

"I just don't know what to say, that's all," I murmured. His stiff posture eased and he came over me again, smoothing the fingers of his right hand through the hair at my temple in a soft caress.

"You don't have to say anything," he said.

"Well, maybe I want to," I said frowning. "Maybe I want to tell you that you *didn't* freak me out. That I don't know quite how I feel yet enough to express it in words but that I feel something deeply for you too. It's like this leviathan, deep, rising slowly, and I don't know what it is but it's not *bad*. It's just a mix of a lot of things..." I trailed off and heaved a heavy sigh. "I'm not always good at expressing myself," I complained. "Not just talking it out like this... but you make me want to try which is a lot more than I can say about *anyone* else."

He smiled at me then and said, "Saylor Grace, it may not feel like it, but you did a wonderful job just right there."

I smiled back and raised my head and neck off the bed and put my lips against his, kissing him slowly.

I fully confess my caginess was borne of habits learned on the street. There were a lot of situations I'd found myself in that you just *couldn't* show how much things affected you. To the degree that you never quite felt safe ever letting on how you really felt. Even when you felt the safest you had known in a very long time, *if ever*.

Poe laid his ear over my heart and listened, eyes closed, while I ran my fingers through his soft hair, stroking the soft strands while we simply silently soaked each other in, and I loved him for it. Loved that he seemed to get it, that he didn't hold it against me, and that he was satisfied to simply exist in one another's proximity with no more words for now.

Although, at some point, I felt I would need to come up with the right ones, I didn't have to for now, and I knew deep down that next time I would have them. Of course, I was *really* hoping there would be a next time.

I never took things like that for granted. It was one of the quickest ways to get your heart broken.

I'd learned that on the street, too.

13

*P*oe…

Having her nude body curled against mine as she slept made me feel like all was finally right in my world. Like everything had finally clicked into place and the puzzle was complete.

I'd never been so fucking content in my life, and I wanted to hold on to this feeling forever. I wanted to hold her, love her, and protect her, *forever* and the cognitive dissonance that these thoughts and feelings were causing was completely out of sorts with the rest of the feel good I had going on which was why I was still awake.

On the one hand, the feelings I had for her were so intense, so real, and they were coming from a place of only my very best intentions. That didn't stop me from knowing, or second guessing myself to death based on all my training and how things were societally.

I had this driving need to keep her right here, in my arms, and for all the right reasons but I still couldn't shake the overwhelming feeling that anybody from the outside would look at the situation and point out the *wrongness* of it.

The apprehension that caused was real and for some reason, right this moment, stifling and I felt the pressure, even though nothing had happened yet to warrant it. Just my mind, going off on its own fucking program.

Something it'd done since I realized just how fucking badly I'd fucked up as a kid when it came to that pedophile pastor.

"Poe?" Saylor's musical voice was thick with sleep as she pushed herself up to look at me groggily.

"Yeah, what's up, babe?" I asked her and her lips twitched with a smile.

"I could ask you the same thing," she murmured, and I loved how the glow of her nightlight caressed the side of her face.

"What do you mean?" I asked.

"You're the one lying awake muttering to yourself," she said.

"I am?" I asked.

"You were," she said.

"Sorry, beautiful." I kissed her mouth, darting forward, a quick press of lips, laying my head back down but the feel of her mouth on mine felt like it could and would linger for days.

"Look, I would *never* do *anything* to risk your job," she whispered and I reached up and caressed the side of her face.

"I know you wouldn't, it's not you I'm worried about – well, it *is* but not in that way," I said.

"Talk to me," she begged, her face crumbling into an expression of deep worry.

I hesitated and finally sighed out.

"It's Karma I'm worried about," I confessed, finally, and already it was as if a marginal amount of weight, of the burden I carried, lessened.

"Karma? But *why?*" she asked, pushing herself up into a sitting position. "Seriously, I can't imagine you doing *anything* that would warrant Karma to come knocking that hard on your life."

"That's just it," I said, knowing this would definitely be a make-or-break moment but needing it off my chest in the *worst* way possible.

"What is?" she asked and swallowed hard, the first stirrings of apprehension creeping into those glorious mismatched eyes of hers.

"It's what I *didn't* do," I said, swallowing equally as hard.

"Talk to me," she whispered and laid a hand on my chest, over my heart.

I told her the story. Of how I wasn't one of the kids that'd been molested but of how I liked Pastor Mike, and how looking back now, yeah, I was groomed, and I'd come damn close but as a kid – how I'd lied for him. How I had covered for him and called the boys he *had* touched liars. How I was afraid everyone would look at *me* like I'd been molested too and how I hadn't wanted that. How, no son of my dad's was that kind of a weakling. How I'd never told the truth and how Pastor Mike had gotten a slap on the wrist in part because of my testimony and how that made it my fault when Bryan McAdams, one of Pastor Mike's favorite boys, had committed suicide.

"You were *just a kid*," Saylor said, and the pain that went through her eyes went right through my heart.

"A cop's son," I amended. "A cop's son, who didn't do the right thing when the right thing was so obvious and right in front of me! The one thing that might have spared another kid his *life* if I had only spoken up and told the truth, but because I was afraid of what people might think of *me,* I didn't."

Saylor sat back on her heels in the middle of my bed and asked, "So why did you become a cop then? Because it was expected of you or because you wanted to fix it? Make up for it somehow... did you become a cop for atonement?"

I thought about it, but the truth was right there. I nodded, mutely, but she was right. I had become a cop to make it up to Bryan – even though I knew it was too late for that. That, I'd betrayed my friend and he'd died because of it – all because I was a lying sack of shit.

"That's something a good person does when they make a mistake," she whispered and I bit my bottom lip and nodded, afraid that if I said anything more, I was going to lose my shit.

I had never told anyone, not even one of the guys, what I'd done – or hadn't done, as the case may be.

"Why did you tell me this?" she asked and I swallowed hard.

"Because I don't deserve nice things," I said and she smiled down at me sadly.

"Yes, you do, Jeremy Poe. You deserve all of the very best things…" She settled down and laid her ear over the center of my chest. Holding to me tightly.

It was a cathartic conversation, for me, but I couldn't help but worry that I'd ruined things with Saylor before they had even had a chance to begin. Which I also couldn't help but feel like if that were the case, I'd earned it… She held to me as I quietly wept into the dark and didn't have the fucking words to tell her how scared I was to lose her but also just how much I had needed that type of shit off my chest.

It was confusing. Overwhelming. A dark night of the soul… and there would be nothing I could do until each of us had time to process things in our own way. There would be nothing I could do until the chips fell as they may.

When I woke, it was to sizzling and the smells of cooking. I frowned and dragged myself into a sitting position to the sight of Saylor

standing in my kitchen in my tee from the night before, smiling over at me as she asked, "How do you like your eggs?"

"You're still here," I muttered, scowling, wondering if my mental and emotional overload of the night before had really happened, or if it was just a dream.

Saylor cocked her head and asked, "Because of what you told me?"

Not a dream, but it definitely was going to bear some further conversation.

"Scrambled," I said, and she smiled and stirred whatever she had going on in the pan.

"No changing the subject," she said and smiled serenely at me. "What brought that up for you last night?"

I swallowed and sat there thinking about it. Finally, I told the truth which was, "I'm afraid that –" I stopped, even saying it out loud was dicey. Like what if what I was thinking was the truth and I had taken advantage of her? What if they only reason she'd fucked me last night was because she felt like she *had to*…

"I'm afraid that I've misread things and that what I did to you last night –"

"With me," she said curtly. "You didn't do anything to me that I didn't want you to," she said.

She fixed me with a look and as though she read my mind stated clearly, "What we did last night wasn't rape." It was her turn to swallow hard then she added, "I've been there, from a cop no less, but you aren't him. You're everything and then some of what he's not and could never be."

She dropped her eyes and I got up, out of bed and went around into the kitchen – not even caring that I was still butt-assed naked. There wasn't any way I was going to get hard after what had just come out of her mouth.

"I want to touch you," I said evenly and she brought her eyes up to mine. "I want to pull you into my arms and hold you tight and promise you that nothing like that is *ever* going to happen to you again. Not while I'm still breathing." There was a long pause as we stared at each other in my kitchen and I finally broke it with, "Can I do that? Can I touch you right now?"

Her expression softened, tears glimmering in her eyes as she took the pan off of the working eye of the stove and set it on a non-working burner before she practically dove into my open arms.

She held me tight, sniffing, and said, "Thank you, for asking."

"I don't want to be *that guy*," I told her. "I'm actually pretty fucking terrified of being *that guy*."

"You could never be that guy, Poe. Not with the way that you are."

"You want to talk about it?" I asked.

She sniffed and said, "Maybe another time. Right now, I just want you to hold me, then I want to feed your face and then I want you to kiss me goodbye before you leave for work like I'm a regular June Cleaver or some shit."

I laughed and held her closer, tighter, and rocked her back and forth, twisting from side to side gently.

"The amount of feelings I have for you are insane, and I don't know where they come from, but it's like I feel like I've known you forever. It's all so damn intense and real and I'm afraid I'm going to fuck things up but at the same time, I don't want you to think I'm something that I'm not and I know that's just as likely to fuck shit up. It's hella fucking confusing, you know?"

"I think, as apparently the voice of reason between the two of us," she teased and we both laughed, "that we both need to slow down just a little."

"What like no more of this?" I asked, gently tipping her face up to mine. I kissed her softly just in case it was going to be my last for the time being.

"Mm, no, definitely more of that," she said. "I mean that we need to not worry about what anyone else thinks about us when we are both still so worried about what the other thinks."

"You're worried about what I think of you?" I asked.

"Well, yeah."

I chuckled and smoothed some of her blonde beach waves behind the shell of her delicate ear.

"I think the world of you, Saylor Grace. Beautiful, strong, resourceful... You're the total package for me."

She rested her chin on my chest and looked up at me and it was both adorable and starting to make my cock stir.

"I pretty much adore you, too, Jeremy Poe."

"Yeah?"

"Yep." She lifted her chin and I brought a hand to my chest, the mood considerably lightened.

"Well, not that I'm fishing for compliments or anything but..." I trailed off to her peal of laughter and she turned back to the stove.

"You're hot, you're definitely generous, and you don't treat me any differently than anyone else."

"Oh, baby – I treat you *way* different," I promised her, leaning back against the opposite counter as she resumed cooking.

"Well, *okay*, I have to give you that one. I don't need you assuming something crazy like I think you're some kind of a man whore."

I shook my head.

"That was Golden before Lys came along."

She laughed and said, "Looking back, I think I could kind of believe that about him."

I chuckled and tried to ignore the obvious semi that was working its way into a full-on hard-on.

We bantered, the mood significantly lighter and my fears of fucking all this up warring with the internal self-sabotage I was pretty infamous for when it came to relationships with women, dissipated.

"I feel like we are taking this all extremely backwards," she said some time later as we munched on her breakfast scramble of leftover chicken and veggies.

"How so?" I asked.

"Well, we meet – I move in, then we become lovers, now I feel like we're becoming good friends – see, backwards."

I laughed slightly and nodded. "I think that's fair," I said.

"You aren't the only one worried about screwing things up, you know. And I'm not just worried about losing the roof you've provided over my head." She got quiet for a moment and said, "I think it would kill a part of me if I hurt you."

I didn't say it, but I wanted to… I just knew it would be overwhelming if I did. Still, I thought clearly to myself, *the only thing you could do that would hurt me right now, would be to walk out of my life.*

"Say something," she said, laughing nervously as I stared into my eggs. I looked up at her and smiled.

"Not going anywhere," I vowed and she smiled back.

I couldn't tell if it was really annoying we were so skittish of each other, or if it was adorable. Myself? I was caught somewhere between annoyed at myself and adoring her. Of course, I couldn't help but adore her. She deserved to be adored.

Fuck, I was smitten, and I needed to get my shit together on it. Fast. Before I wrecked everything.

I kissed her goodbye and there was nothing June Cleaver about it unless June sidelined as a pinup chick.

As soon as I was out the door and had the garage open, I called up Blaze and asked if he was up for a beer at the *10-13* as soon as I was off shift.

14

*S*aylor...

"Oh, *fantastic!*" he declared, relief in his voice when he stuck his head inside the apartment door and found me journal open at my side, guitar in my lap.

"What's up?" I asked curiously.

"I was hoping to find you here. I was going out for a beer with my buddy Blaze and I wanted to let you know I'd be late getting home."

"Ah, so the whole, don't worry about dinner, domesticated-bliss thing?" I asked curiously and the smile he rewarded me with brought an answering one to my lips.

"Yeah, and I would have called or texted, but we're doing this whole thing backwards and I don't have your social media or anything so to be on the safe side..." He stepped inside and shut the door on the swirling cold, holding out a bag.

I took it, curious.

"No strings attached," he said holding up his hands. "I got you a pay as you go phone. The screen's not cracked, and you should be able to load all your apps. Sorry you have to enter all your contacts by hand, but I didn't have you with me – I already programmed my number in there for you."

I set my guitar aside and went to him, wrapping him in a hug and looking up at him.

"You bought me a new phone so I wouldn't worry about you being late for dinner?" I asked.

"Well, yeah… I'm not trying to be a dick. I don't want you thinking I'm ghosting on you. I feel bad about my issues and the shit that went down last night and I was hoping to talk it out with my best friend over a beer tonight. I don't want to fuck any of this up, Saylor Grace."

"You still want to go with me tomorrow? You won't be too tired?"

"We can get coffee, I'll get like six shots. I'll be fine," he said.

I smiled a bit wryly.

"We can skip it if you'd like," I said and tried to keep my bitter disappointment at the thought hidden.

"Not on your life, babe," he murmured and kissed me.

"Okay," I whispered against his departing lips.

He reluctantly slipped from my grasp and said, "Don't wait up."

"I won't," I said. "But please, feel free to get handsy and molest me in my sleep."

He chuckled and said, "Consent is so fucking sexy when you put it that way."

"Glad you like it," I teased gently, and he ducked back out into the snow.

A voice called from down below and Poe called back, "Yeah! I'm comin', I'm comin'!"

I chuckled at the exchange, the smile lighting his face and his eyes as he shut the door lighting me up from the inside as well. I sighed and retook my seat on the bed to figure out the new phone and swap everything over and to set it up.

He didn't have to, but it was a gift I was grateful for. Right down to the bottom of my heart.

I HUMMED in pleasure as another kiss fell on my bare hip. I writhed a bit against the sheets and smiled when I realized it wasn't a dream, and that Poe was home and treating me to my heart's desire… which is to say he was kissing me awake. Light butterfly kisses on every bit of exposed skin, starting from my ankle on up.

"Hey," he whispered when he realized I was awake and I shifted, rolling onto my back, reaching for him.

He came to me, kneeling on the bed, bending over me, his skin hot and fragrant from the shower, his hair still damp where I delved my fingers through it, pulling his mouth to mine.

"Mm, you're so warm," he murmured against my mouth.

"So are you," I whispered. "I didn't even hear you come in."

"You were *out*, I hope I didn't scare you."

"Mm-mm, no," I murmured, my hips rising and falling unbidden, my arousal on autopilot. God, I wanted him.

"God, you're driving me nuts with that," he growled, his hand traveling down my flank and resting on my hip as I dry humped him like a teenage girl, pussy sliding against his cock which was hard and as hot as a brand.

"Good," I muttered. "I want you."

"Feeling is mutual, babe," he said between gritted teeth and I smiled at the effect I had on him.

"Get a condom," I ordered brazenly, and I didn't have to tell him twice. I didn't have to whine, and I didn't have to beg.

He simply reached up past me and plucked the condom he had at the ready off the nightstand and I smiled even wider.

"I love a man who's prepared," I joked.

"That's me," he said, tearing open the package with his teeth. "A regular boy scout."

"Next you'll whisper sweet nothings in my ear like 'Die Hard is a Christmas movie,'" I stated and I was only half joking on that one.

"Holy shit, it's like you were specifically *made* for me." He came back to me, cock sheathed in latex and I laughed, which turned into a hysterical fit of giggles when he attacked the side of my neck with his mouth, lips and teeth sorting out where I was most ticklish at and exploiting it.

He slid into my pussy while I was still laughing, and my laughter went from high and light to something deep and sultry relating to a moan. I breathed in, the combination of clean man, warmth, and our mutual arousal enough to completely flip my switch leaving me sinking into the softness of his bed and putting me at his mercy.

"Oh, God, yes, Poe! Like that. Just like that," I urged when he stroked in and out of me slowly but with such power behind his movements.

"You like that?" he growled in my ear and just beneath the mint of his toothpaste was hops and virility. I loved it. That he was letting whatever inhibitions that'd arisen last night after we'd coupled the first time, go.

That he was showing me just how much he wanted me. How much he wanted to claim me, with his tone – while *still* making sure I was getting my wants and needs met.

"Oh, yeah! Yes, yes, yes! Deeper!"

He obliged me, holding me tightly in his strong arms, driving into me with this deep desire, driven by his own need, and it was so base and beautiful. The way he claimed my body, the way he caged me in his arms, *safe, protected.* I could feel the love as he made love to me and I soaked it up like a damn sponge and did my very best to give as good as I got.

I gripped his face between my hands, kissed him savagely, and did everything to match his inward stroke with a downward one from me.

The feeling of him bottoming out against my cervix was a mix of pleasure and pain. The sensation a profound one, igniting sparks that were quickly roaring into an inferno, things tightening, throbbing, and aching for that sweet release.

This was not going to be a marathon. This was definitely going to be a sprint, although I believed wholeheartedly, we were *both* keen on arriving at an explosion rather than running from it.

"Oh God, yes, baby. Grip that cock, oh God!" he panted in my ear and I squeezed down tighter around him, the way he moved against my walls driving me nuts, but just this side of enough to make me come.

It's like he knew, rising up onto his knees, gazing down at me as I put my hands up against the wall and braced them there to keep the top of my head from banging into the wall.

He smiled, laughed slightly, but didn't stop or slow down. In fact, he picked up his pace, watching me pant beneath him, stretched, tits thrust into the air as he boldly drew the pad of his thumb across his tongue and delved it into the cleft at the top of my sex.

I screamed, crying out as the pad of his thumb stroked across that bundle of sensitive nerves.

He pinched one of my nipples with his other thumb against the side of his index finger and tugged on it lightly, his eyes on me, calculating, despite his own struggle not to come first, his jaw tight as he breathed in and out through his nose. I panted and tightened up just that little bit more and when I came? I exploded into a thousand points of light, disintegrating into pure bliss, his cock driving deep, losing his rhythm as he came with me, both of us tumbling through the dark, leaving our souls behind as we plunged, leaving them to catch up to us later.

He collapsed over me, groaning, panting, and I wrapped both my arms and legs around him, panting as well and whispering out between breaths, "God, I love you…"

"You have," he closed his mouth, swallowing, still gasping, "no idea, how much it means," he sat up to look at me, "to hear you say that."

I smiled.

It was true, and deep down inside, I knew he felt the same about me, too.

We just needed to get out of our own ways.

"You good?" he asked once our breathing had stilled to some semblance of normal.

"Better than good," I whispered and he kissed me.

Way better than good. I don't even think 'fantastic' came close.

15

P oe...

"You totally don't have to do this today, you know," she said softly, looking up at me as I locked up the apartment.

I laughed and asked, "Do I look that tired?"

She stretched out her bottom lip and sucked in air between her teeth and I laughed.

"Let's just get where we're going and coffee up," I said, throwing an arm around her shoulders.

"Sounds good, my treat." I laughed again and nodded.

"You got yourself a deal."

"Ah, ah, ah!" she admonished, giggling when I stopped outside the garage and I nodded.

"Oh, yeah, you're right. This is 'a day in the life of my Saylor Grace', no cutting corners."

She smiled pleased and tipped her face up for a kiss and I gave it to her. I would be lying if I said I wasn't worried about her. She'd layered up, but all of her clothes were so inadequate for an east coast winter.

She didn't complain, though I could tell she was cold. She just hunched her shoulders, leaned into me laughing and smiling, as we crunched over the ice and snow encrusted sidewalk to the main drag where the sidewalks got salted and the streets both salted and sanded.

She stopped at the bus stop, chattering about Bernard, her usual bus driver, and some guy named Josh at the coffee shop she'd found and now frequented.

"I think he's interested, but I'm not – obviously."

"He'd be crazy not to be interested, but I'm calling dibs for as long as you wanna let me," I said pressing a kiss against her temple, catching her silken hair on half of my lips and the rougher material of her slouching beanie with the other half.

She giggled and said, "I'm not sure that's how dibs works, like – you saw it first, you called dibs; that means it's yours."

I chuckled and said, "I know how dibs works, babe, but you're a person, not an object, so that makes things different."

"Okay, true, it does," she agreed, just as the bus pulled up.

"Yo, hey there, Saylor!"

"Hi, Bernard!" she called cheerfully and led me up into the warmer coach by my gloved hand. I followed her up, shrugging out of my cut but keeping my jacket on for the ride. She paid our fare and I frowned at her. Bernard eyed me.

"So, who's this?" Bernard asked and I couldn't say his look was entirely friendly.

"Officer Jeremy Poe, ICPD." I stuck out my hand and the older man's eyebrows went up.

"Well, now! Nice to meet you, Officer Poe. You one of them relatives to the writer?" he asked.

"Uh, yeah, actually, I am."

"What now?" Saylor asked, settling into a seat.

"You know!" Bernard crowed. "Poe! Quoth the Raven, *nevermore!*"

"No, shit?" Saylor asked, surprised.

"Uh, yeah. I'm one of his cousin's, Neilson's descendants," I said.

"How did I not know that?" Saylor asked.

Bernard and I shared a laugh. "I guess this is the first time it's come up in conversation," I said. "Doesn't come up as often as you would think."

"I guess not, I mean, was he local?" she asked.

We chatted about Edgar Allen, and how he didn't have any kids, but his cousin, my direct ancestor, Neilson Poe had had enough for the both of them, apparently. Saylor hadn't known that the Poe clan was native out here to Baltimore – having gotten it mixed up with Boston.

"So, uh, you the one Saylor's stayin' with?" Bernard asked.

"Yes, sir. I am," I affirmed.

"Do an old man a favor," he said. "If you got it, get this girl a proper coat, would yah?"

"I have a better coat," Saylor said, making a face. "It's just in my car in impound."

"I'll see what I can do," I promised Bernard, glad my girl had him looking out for her.

"You do that," he pulled up to the curb. "Here's your stop, now."

"Thanks as always, Bernard. Merry Christmas!" Saylor quipped, getting up.

"Oooh! A Merry Christmas to you, too, darlin'. You come back through and sing me a Christmas carol on your next ride."

"Hopefully, I'll catch you later today," she said, hopping off the bus. I followed her and swung into my cut saying, "Nice to meet you, Bernard."

"Likewise, five-oh. Likewise," he called, shutting the door with a pneumatic hiss, the coach lumbering back into traffic.

I smiled at Saylor and said, "Ladies lead the way."

"Oh, I like that!" she declared and led me up the sidewalk and down about three-quarters through the next block.

We ducked down a few steps and into this French bakery, a young hipster-looking dude behind the counter looking up and smiling. He was all eyes on Saylor and his smile dimmed and became more rigid when he caught sight of me coming in behind her.

"Hey, Saylor – looks like you've got company."

"Hi, Josh and this is Jeremy Poe! The friend I've been staying with." Saylor grasped my index and middle finger of my right hand and swung them between us. It was plucky and adorable, and it made Josh almost visibly deflate.

"You want your usual?" he asked her and she smiled and said, "Yeah." She turned to me and raised her eyebrows.

"A promise is a promise," she declared. "Josh makes some of the best coffee in the city, so what cha want?"

"Uh, I'll take a quad shot peppermint mocha," I said.

"Tis the season," Josh said, and it held an edge of winter outside but was quickly thawing.

Saylor's usual was a mocha and a chocolate croissant. She wouldn't hear of me just getting the coffee, so I ordered a plate of beignets drizzled with honey fully intending to foist some off on Saylor – which wasn't difficult.

"Oh, my God. I am so going to have to get these next time," she said, licking powdered sugar off of her bottom lip.

"Have you never had a beignet?" I asked.

"No!" she cried. "Seattle was a great place for food, don't get me wrong, and they had this great French bakery at Pike's Place – but this wasn't on their menu."

"It's good stuff, they're missing out," I said.

"Yeah, they are!" she agreed.

"So where do you typically go next?" I asked when we were almost all the way through our breakfast and the shop started to really fill up with the morning rush.

"Anywhere along here, typically. It's a good touristy spot and stays pretty busy. There's a Christmas tree farm that has a stand set up just inside the park. Might be able to get some change singing Christmas carols there, so I'll give it a go for an hour or two."

"Sounds good."

"You going to wait here?" she asked and I laughed.

"Hell no, I'm coming with you – watch you do your thing."

She laughed and said, "It's going to get *really* cold!"

"So? I'd bargain I'm dressed better for it than you are," I said, and she wrinkled her nose in a mix of defiance and capitulation that was cute as hell.

"Touché," she sighed.

"I'll keep you in coffee and cocoa," I said.

"Actually, hot water with lemon and honey will do my voice way better."

"Oh, yeah?" I asked, standing and getting my coat back on. "Where'd you learn that?"

"Granddad," she answered. "He taught me everything I ever needed to know about busking."

"That's awesome," I declared as we made our way out the door and up the street to the corner so we could cross.

The tree farmer was happy to have Saylor play and didn't mind me hanging around to watch and listen. She sang like an angel, voice light and clear, carried on the wind to passersby. Not a lot, but a few came down to listen, dropping change and dollar bills into her open guitar case. A couple going on to buy a fresh wreath or evergreen swag for their apartment or house.

She went for about an hour, caught my eye and gave me a raised set of eyebrows and a nod, and with a salute, I jogged back to the French bakery to get a cup of hot water doctored with lemon and honey.

Josh was at the counter when I came in and I asked for the hot water and some lemon – they had honey at the little counter with the sugar and sweeteners, the half-and-half, and milk.

"This for Saylor?" he asked and I nodded.

"Yeah, she's a great girl. Could see it the second she stepped inside here."

"I know exactly what you're talking about, man. I saw it too. First moment I laid eyes on her."

He chuckled and said, "You just got to her first, I guess."

"Nah, man," I shook my head. "Saylor is a free spirit. She goes where she wants to go and loves who she wants to love. I just happen to be the luckiest son of a bitch alive that right now? I apparently get to be that person."

He looked at me thoughtfully and handed over the cup of hot water he'd drawn from the tap on the espresso machine and a lid to go with it.

"You know, you're alright," he said finally. "No charge for hot water, lemon," he said sliding a slice he'd retrieved from the back to float on the top of the cup, "is on the house."

"Thanks, man." I winked at him and he laughed and waved me off. I went over and added honey and stirred it with one of the wooden stir-sticks, popped the lid back on, and with a wave got it back out to Saylor. She was starting to shiver, just barely finished her song and reached out for the cup gratefully, wrapping her frozen fingers around it and shuddering.

"Ohh, thank you!"

"Okay," I said laughing, "it's been swell, but you're frozen and as such – the swelling's gone down. Time to get you warmed up and to move on, and I think I got just the place."

She laughed and sipped from her cup.

"Okay, I'll bite, where we headed?"

"It's a surprise. Now what do I need to do here?"

"Um, gather up the money, obviously," she said chuckling.

"On it." I gathered it up and stuffed it in my jacket pocket for safe-keeping.

"Guitar goes back in the case," she said, and I helped her unhook the strap and laid it in there for her, closing it up, hooking the hasps and I stood, gripping it by the handle.

"Usually I put the money in my Crown bag, but it's in my backpack and I'm freezing so we'll sort that out and check our haul later."

"Sounds good, and it's *your* haul."

"Street kid code as per my granddad, you assist me, you get half the haul."

I shook my head. "Not taking your money, baby. I got a main hustle and money aplenty all my own."

She laughed lightly. "And because I know you're not on the struggle bus, I'll let you win this round."

"Good deal," I said and with a goodbye to the tree seller, we set off for the bus stop.

Bernard swung by about twenty minutes later on his circuit and I stuck my head in and asked, "What line do we gotta take to get over to the old Indigo Arcade building?"

"Oh, yeah, yeah, yeah! That'd be a good spot for Ms. Thang out there, that away. You need to take the ol' green line. The number six bus. You can't get it from here, but trek on in about two three blocks and you should be able to get it over on Muller outside that fancy bar y'all cops like to hang out at."

"Thank you, kindly! I sure appreciate it."

"Ain't no thing! Y'all have a nice day now. Hope you make lots o' money, girl!"

"I hope so too!" Saylor cried, shivering and I backed out of the coach's door.

"Come on, I know just how to warm you up while we wait to get where we're going."

"Sounds good," she said breathing out and I took her hand and started walking.

We got in by a couple blocks and I oriented myself on the one-way street. I wasn't used to coming at it on foot, and it took a second to remember which direction the *10-13* was in. I started us that way and

Saylor didn't speak, just tried to keep up. We made it, and I knew the place was closed so I didn't bother – instead, I went for the door up to Skids' place and hit the buzzer.

"This better be fuckin' good, I was gettin' laid." His grizzled voice came over the speaker and I could hear Coco's hysterical fit of giggles in the background.

"Hey, yeah, it's Poe. Put some pants on Chief, I got Saylor with me and she's fuckin' *freezing*. We're waiting on the next bus."

"Bus?" Skids sounded confused and I heard a "What in the hell?" just before the buzzer took over and I yanked open the door, ushering Saylor in ahead of me.

"Up the stairs," I ordered lightly, and she nodded and took them two at a time, determined to keep moving and keep warm.

Saylor paused at the top of the stairs and jumped when Skids' door opened and leaned out.

"Just what in the fuck are you two doing out in this?" he demanded. "And this fuckin' early! Get in here!"

Saylor laughed nervously and went in before me.

"It's a day in the life of Saylor Grace," I said, leaning her guitar in its case against the wall by the door. Coco was in the kitchen at the electric kettle heating up water, eying Saylor in her mostly denim outfit and looking worried.

"Sit down," Skids demanded, and he was looking Saylor over too.

"Girl, where are your *clothes?*" he demanded.

"Ahh, I'm wearing everything I've got," she said shivering.

"Well it ain't enough!" Skids declared.

"I know," I said unhappily. "Her car is in impound and they wouldn't let her take her stuff. I had to pull some shady shit just to get her guitar and the things she's got on."

"How long ago was that?" Skids demanded.

"Only a few days, Chief."

He nodded and said, "Lemme make a call."

"Look, it isn't much, but can I at least lend you a pair of fleece-lined leggings for under your jeans until you can get some of your own?" Coco asked.

"Oh, I don't know, you've only just met me!" Saylor cried.

"And?" Coco demanded rolling her eyes. "You're with Poe. It's not like I'm not going to see you to get 'em back, and even if I don't, I have like a million pairs. I'm a dancer. I have like no body fat, remember?"

Saylor laughed and finally gave in and nodded.

"Okay, now you're talking." Coco followed her man back to their bedroom. When she opened the door, he looked up, phone pressed to his ear as he spoke to someone on the line earnestly.

I started to relax. Grateful that my squad had seemingly accepted that Saylor and I were a thing. I was so thankful for that. For the fact that the chips had fallen where they had to bring us here. The fates were finally smiling onto my girl, and I was grateful for it. I mean, it was about fucking time for her, wasn't it?

Coco returned with a pair of sleek black leggings over her shoulder and it wasn't lost on me that she was wearing a pair of her own in navy with one of Skids' button-down shirts on over it. She looked casual and comfortable, and Skids was just behind her in a pair of flannel pajama bottoms and no shirt, just like he'd answered the door.

His scar right down the middle of his chest from where they'd had to do open heart surgery after his heart attack was mostly faded from an angry red to a muted pink and that was another thing I was grateful for… that he was still with us.

"You guys are coming up on your one-year anniversary, aren't you?" I asked.

"Actually, just missed it," Skids said, scratching an itch on his left shoulder.

"The bathroom is the first door on the left, go put these on. I'll have some hot tea waiting out here," Coco said, handing the leggings over to Saylor.

"Thank you," Saylor said, setting down her near-empty cup of hot honey-lemon water down on the kitchen table. She took the offered garment from Coco and went down the hall.

"We can get her stuff from impound, you got a place to store it?" Skids asked.

"Yeah, there's a chain-link fenced area in the garage under my place I can keep stuff. I don't have a lot in there, so it should work."

"You, uh, thinking about maybe moving up your timeline some on getting a real place?" Skids asked.

"It's been on my mind," I answered truthfully. It had been one of the things chewing me up silently since our first night as a couple. It was the truth that sex changed everything, and I'd already been turning the idea over in my head even before we'd done it.

There were some problems involved, though. Like location was everything. A commute for me wasn't anything, but for Saylor? She needed to be in the city to do what she loved and moving to the suburb might be a deal breaker. I knew I really wanted a house, though. Something with a yard. So, I just didn't know how anything would play out and to be honest? Everything was still so brand new.

I think Skids could read it on my face because he gave a lopsided grin and said, "Don't rush into anything. Rome wasn't built in a day."

I gave a nod and Coco smiled over at the counter where she was pouring hot water into mugs. She said to Skids, "And you thought *we* moved fast."

Skids chuckled and shook his head but didn't say anything.

"Tea or cocoa?" she asked me.

"Cocoa," I answered. "Please."

"You better not," Skids raised an eyebrow and winked, and I laughed slightly and shook my head.

"She's all yours, Chief," I said.

"Speaking of which," he declared as the bathroom door opened back up and I smiled and nodded.

Saylor came back out and said, "I have *got* to find me some of these. I bet they cost an arm and a leg, though."

"Nope, got them at Walmart. They're like fifteen bucks for a two-pack."

"Two pair for fifteen dollars?" Saylor echoed. "You just saved my life."

"Do I see a trip to the 'burbs' in our future?" I asked.

Saylor twisted her lips back and forth. "I could order them online, but I don't have a credit card or bank card or anything."

"Have you ever had a bank account?" Coco asked. "I mean, living the life you do is pretty wild, but I've never really thought about what it *means* you know? Like how *do* you do certain things?"

"Well, I've been kind of bouncing around as a street kid since I was fifteen, so no – I actually don't have a bank account and never have. I mean, it's not like I've really needed one. I've always been cash-only."

"Do you even have your birth certificate? Social security card?" Skids asked, frowning.

"Sure do. I keep it all in my journal and on me at all times. Not the *safest* thing to do, I know, but when you don't have a permanent place, it's even less safe to keep your permanent documents somewhere that you're not."

"Tea or cocoa?" Coco asked and Saylor smiled.

"Tea, please."

"Here, have a seat, the both of you." Skids pulled out a chair for himself and Saylor and I followed suit across from each other.

"Can I see how much we pulled at the Christmas tree stand?" she asked me, and I immediately emptied my pockets for her. She shrugged out of her backpack and got into it for her Crown bag and her journal.

We chatted about her systems to keep things in check while living on the street and it was a fascinating and heartbreaking look into the life of someone poor and down on their luck.

She was an amazingly good sport about it. Didn't have to share but shared freely anyway as she counted up her money and marked things down in her journal.

"Why keep track so hard?" Coco asked.

"So I can pay my taxes." Saylor smiled and we all laughed before Skids looked at her and said, "Oh, shit, you're serious."

"My granddad didn't raise a freeloader. It's hard, but anything over a certain threshold and I owe tax on it. I'm pretty behind on my taxes, but it's the only debt I have, so I guess there's that."

"Wow, you really don't sugarcoat nothin' do you?" Skids asked.

"Why?" she shrugged. "I am who I am, not entirely perfect because who is? Live and let live is how I was raised. I mean, I know how lucky I am compared to most. Believe me. But I don't feel the need to be embarrassed about being poor or about taking care of myself. I'm pretty secure in who I am and how I live. I don't drink to excess, I don't do drugs, I'm responsible with my body and have never been pregnant – but that isn't going to stop people from judging me, and that says more about them than it does about me." She smiled then and said, "Six bucks and eighty-seven cents. Not exactly raking it in, but not bad for an hour's work either."

"You sure do keep it positive," Skids remarked.

"I like that about you," Coco chimed in and Saylor smiled.

She'd said she wasn't perfect, but I wanted to disagree so hard, because right then, I knew she was absolutely perfect for me.

"So, about the rest of her shit in her car," Skids said, turning to me.

We spent the rest of our time warming up, making arrangements to get her things with the help of Youngblood and his truck to get them over to my place. Saylor sat in stunned silence for several moments and finally settled in to the steady pace of the Indigo Knights taking care of one of their own.

See. Perfect.

Perfect for me.

16

*S*aylor...

One day bled into the next as the page leafs on the calendar flew off counting up to Christmas. In that time, my belongings had made it out of impound and my car had been signed away to the city for scrap.

I'd been able to go through the boxes, and almost everything was safe and unharmed, held in the storage area below the tiny studio apartment we inhabited. I would be lying if I said things weren't starting to feel pretty tight up here, though.

My winter clothes alone were starting to make things feel claustrophobic as I was coming back to the tiny studio more and more tired, which just made things worse for me mentally. I constantly worried that at any moment Poe would decide I was taking up too much space and I'd be out. It wasn't entirely an irrational fear. It'd happened to me once before back in the Pacific Northwest.

On a positive, I was killing it at the Arcade, and outside of Ally and Dawnie's funky little boutique in the city's Old Town district. It was only a few blocks away from where the *10-13* resided and I had to say – Indigo City was a lot kinder than I'd expected.

I'd pulled in enough cash to pay ahead on my phone, which I had stocked up on prepaid cards for, and I had seamlessly made myself responsible for dinners and cooking. Poe had let me, and I was looking forward to the holiday with him and his family now that I knew I could afford some small gifts. He'd come home two nights ago and had told me he'd spoken to his mother and that I was expected at the Christmas dinner table as his new girlfriend.

I was nervous. Even more nervous that I didn't even know what his family *liked*. Which led us to this moment, curled up in bed, the blankets piled on as we snuggled as much to be close as for warmth.

The power was out, the lines brought down by heavy ice and snow.

"Okay, okay, but what about your mom?" I asked. We'd just gone over what his dad was into and both of us were at a loss on that one.

"This has got to be the most painfully awkward conversation I've ever been in," he said and I frowned, jerking my head back to look at him.

"What? Why?"

The night was dark, and the only light we had was from the three-wick scented candle burning on one of the nightstands and the flashing orange light of the utility company's truck outside as they tried to repair the line.

Everything out there was beautiful – encased in a layer of crystalline ice. Beautiful, but dangerous.

"We're talking about my *parents*," he said, rolling his eyes.

"And?" I asked curiously.

"Post-sex, in the nude. I would pretty much rather be talking about *anything* else."

I laughed and snuggled closer.

"I am in serious need of help here!" I cried.

"We both are," he said dryly and chuckled, sighing out in satisfaction.

"Mm, I just really want to make a good impression," I told him. We'd already agreed that we would tell his family the truth about us. He couldn't bear to lie to them, and even though I had a nagging bad feeling about it, I had agreed. I mean, I didn't want to say anything out loud – but I knew how even kind people could be judgmental about street kids like me. Even though I wasn't a kid anymore, I certainly didn't feel like the adultiest adult. You know what I mean?

"Hey." He pressed a hand to the side of my head and pressed my temple to his lips. I closed my eyes, weak against that kind of attention. A forehead kiss got me every time. No matter what, a forehead kiss and an 'I'm sorry' could get a guy out of trouble with me every time. I was such a sucker for it. Temple and forehead kisses for no reason, like Poe was prone to handing out like candy, just had me swooning for his fine ass that much harder.

I was catching myself all too often dreaming about what a 'forever' with him would look like and it honestly scared me how much I wanted it. I mean, I wanted it so bad I could taste it.

"What do you want for Christmas?" he asked me casually and I smiled.

"I don't need anything," I murmured. "Everything I think I have ever wanted I have right here and right now; with you."

He held me tighter and the sigh that emanated from him was one of the purest sounds of contentment I think I'd ever heard.

"I want to buy a house," he said out of the blue sometime later. "With you."

"What?" I sat up, pushing off of his chest so I could look him in the eye.

"I mean it," he said. "I've been thinking about it. Something close enough to catch transit into the downtown core. So you can keep doing what you do."

I swallowed hard, hardly believing I was hearing what I was hearing.

"I've always been solid on buying a place of my own," he said. "I have a sizeable down payment and let's face it, this place isn't big enough. It's alright for now, but I really want to think about a future… with you."

"Are you asking me to marry you?" I asked, startled.

He smiled slow and sweet. "Not yet. I'll have a ring or get down on one knee when I get around to that. Why? Does it shock you that I've been thinking about this at all?"

"Yeah," I said honestly, resting my hand on the center of his chest gently. "It's been a really long time since I last thought past my next meal let alone getting through the next day – I've never really thought about life beyond any of that, you know? About *years* from now… I guess the future has always been this distant *thing*, not really real…" *until now*, I wanted to say but at the same time I was so afraid to say it. I laid back down, my head on his shoulder and he chuckled.

"Until now," he said kindly, a very echo of what I'd been thinking.

"I-I-guess," I stammered, throat growing thick with tears that threatened to spill.

"You don't sound so sure," he murmured and rubbed the back of my neck, pinching and kneading the muscles at the base of my skull.

"Maybe I'm just a little bit in shock."

"That's okay," he whispered. "Take your time and think about it. No matter what, though, I'd like you to help me pick a place."

"For us?" I asked, still hardly willing to believe it.

"For us," he agreed. "A house, for us to live in, to make into a *home*."

"I've never shopped for anything as big as a *house* before."

He chuckled again as he could tell I was warming up to the idea.

"First thing's first," he said. "We gotta decide our budget and find a real estate agent."

"You're really serious," I said, and my shock was giving way to joy.

"I'm really serious, babe."

Holy shit...

"Can we just get through meeting your family first?" I asked.

"You sound afraid," he murmured, pressing his lips to my hair, breathing me in and sighing out.

"I mean, I *am*. What if they don't like me?" I asked.

"I don't need them to," he said simply. "I mean, they're my family so obviously I want them to like you, but I really don't need them to because honestly, as much as I love them, my dad is a flawed individual and my mom? She goes right along with whatever Dad says and tries to smooth things over to keep him happy."

"And your sister?"

He chuckled. "The disgraced one for the most part. She's divorced, two kids, two boys, actually. Five and two. To be honest, it might be nice to take some of the heat off of her for once."

"The heat?" I asked, looking up.

"Yeah, my dad actually *liked* my brother-in-law. Honestly, Trish and I kind of feel like he would have swapped the both of us for the guy given half a chance."

"Gross," I muttered.

"Like I said, my family's not perfect by any means and I don't need them to like you, not when I love you like I do, just the way you are."

His words stilled the breath in my lungs, and I pushed up off of him so I could gaze down into his eyes.

"You trying to get laid again?" I asked to break the sudden tension that was probably wholly of my imagination. Or, really, just internal. I really sucked at dealing with my feelings. Especially the more intense ones; and Poe? He brought out *a lot* of intense feelings.

He laughed and raised his eyebrows. "Maybe. Did it work?"

I sat up onto my knees and flung a leg over his hips, straddling him. He didn't miss a beat, smoothing his hands over my skin, letting them travel up my body to cradle my small tits. I gyrated, rubbing my pussy lips along his hardening length.

"Mmm," he hummed out appreciatively.

"Now, let's start with your sister," I murmured and he groaned.

"Seriously?" he demanded.

"Seriously!" I cried and he sat up, capturing me, his arms around me as he turned us, me shrieking, him laughing, to press me into his bed.

He silenced my giggles with his mouth on mine, grinding against me, teasing me with his cock which despite bringing up his sister had remained hard.

"Can we table this discussion until tomorrow morning?" he asked gruffly, gently biting along the side of my neck in the way that made me gasp and want to give him the very stars from the sky if only he would continue.

"Deal," I whispered, breathily.

He made this darkling little growl of victory and kissed my skin which heated to branding-iron hot beneath his touch.

I was no shrinking violet when it came to sex with Poe. No way. I adored him too much for that. So I twined my arms around his shoulders, buried my fingers in his sable soft brown hair, and arched, pressing my flesh further against his lips, into his mouth, inviting him to devour me if he so chose.

It didn't take him long to work me up. Hell, we'd barely come down from our last love-making session.

Each touch, each kiss, each nibble from his teeth and blush of warm air from his breath did things to wake nerve endings I hadn't even realized I'd had until I'd met him.

"Hmm, baby, I'm gonna make you feel so good," he promised in a whisper against my ribs as he worked his way lower.

"Put a condom on," I whispered and it was half begging and half a command.

"Now?" he asked, a teasing edge to his voice. "But I'm just getting started."

"Nuh-uh, fuck that," I declared. "I want you inside me now."

He laughed and sat up, reaching over to the bedside table. I scooted back, kneeling up and took the condom from him when he turned back around.

"Lie down," I ordered. "It's my turn to do all the work."

"Yes, ma'am," he murmured, and his arousal was clear.

He laid down, hands behind his head, and I wasted no time in straddling him once more, his cock between us, long and thick, veins standing out with how turgid he was.

I tore open the condom wrapper at its little notch to make opening it easier and took the slick, rubbery disc between my fingers. I slid it onto him, slow and sensual, watching his eyes and the desire flare in them as his mouth dropped open and he gave this little 'ah' like it was almost too much having my hands on him.

"Hmm, yeah, baby, c'mere," he whispered when I kneeled up to take him inside me, walking forward half a pace on my knees to line him up with my entrance, pressing him against my pussy which was slick with fresh arousal.

I made eye contact with him as I slid down his length and the things that were silently communicated between us were beautiful.

Making love to Poe was like poetry or music. Beautiful music, the notes soft, the melody gentle. The cadence and rhythm set were ones that we could dance to all night and past dawn, the golden glow of sunlight a mere glimmer on the distant horizon in comparison to the rays of light beginning low in my body, curling through my limbs like a fine mist off the bay.

"Tell me you feel something, *anything* for me," he grunted and I stilled for a moment. His words catching me off guard as much as the desperation in his voice.

"I love you," I whispered, and the words slipped out much easier than I anticipated they would.

"Yeah?" he whispered back, and I could feel the vulnerability he held in this moment. He was opening up to me like we hadn't been open to each other just yet and rather than frightening, the way I expected it to be, there was something… comforting about it.

I smiled down at him and captured my bottom lip between my teeth, rolling my hips, moving him inside me. It felt so good, I couldn't help but throw my head back and gasp for a moment.

"It scares me," I confessed. "How strongly I feel things when I'm with you. I may not always be good at displaying how I feel, but that's only when I feel something so deeply, it's overwhelming." I bowed my head and whimpered but didn't stop riding him. I didn't slow down. I didn't stop… and it was killing me sweetly, slowly, the fact I was on that razor-thin edge of orgasm.

"Oh, God," he moaned and I could tell he was close too.

"I love everything about you," I whispered. "Your kindness, your generosity, your protection, how you touch me, how you kiss me, how you hold me when I need it without me even having to ask. You complete me and that scares me so much." I bit my lips together, afraid I was babbling.

We dissolved into panting breaths and dew-slicked skins, his hands gripping my hips, thumbs smoothing over my skin as he urged me to change angles *just so* and oh my God! It was like he had unlocked a door and all the good things I kept hidden and locked away behind it came spilling out, rushing through me, lifting me high on a tide of bliss and just plain feel good.

I gazed down at Jeremy Poe and I could tell he was along for the ride, both of us glowing, both of us luminous, eyes bright as we gazed at each other through muted candlelight.

Coming was like an out-of-body experience. Like we both diffused into the flickering fire of the candle's flames, diffused into beings of light ourselves and I didn't ever want to go back to the dark.

17

*P*oe...

"What about this one?" she asked and tilted her phone in my direction as we shivered on the sidewalk outside our apartment.

"What's the square footage?" I asked.

"Twelve hundred," she answered.

"What is that? Two-bedroom, one bath?"

I shifted in my boots, a box of Christmas gifts for my family in my arms, Saylor's backpack loaded on her back. She was crazy. Had insisted on wrapping everything herself, despite my attempts at short-cutting things and having a gift-wrap person do some of them at the mall. She'd also insisted that they all had to match. Had bought this big roll of brown paper for a dollar at the dollar store and used this twine she'd found from somewhere else as a sort of rustic ribbon. Then she'd decorated every damn package with real tree bits and pine cones. Some she'd glittered to look like they held snow.

She'd spent hours poring over online tutorial videos on creative wrapping and folds and everything had come out totally spectacular, but she really hadn't needed to go to such effort.

I loved her for it, though. It was just another kind thing she did. She did such amazing things with the small things and didn't take *anything* for granted and it was eye opening, charming, and so damn down-to-earth.

She was an angel, she had these glorious wings, yet somehow, she gave me roots.

"Two bedrooms, one-and-a-half bath," she said after scrolling through the listing.

"Neighborhood?" I asked.

"Uhhhh, Burrington Heights?"

I gave a low whistle. "That's going to set us back a pretty penny," I said.

"Listing says it's within your budget," she said confused as I looked up the street wondering where the fuck our rideshare guy was. Resisting the urge to check the app, I was starting to wonder if the dude had canceled the ride on us.

"Ohhhh, it's a fixer upper in need of electrical and plumbing. Never mind."

"Eh, I got guys for that depending on *how much* electrical and plumbing it needs," I declared.

"It's got a nice open floor plan and windows for light. I think that would be good for you," she said, scrutinizing the screen of her phone and I chuckled.

"You think so, huh? That neighborhood is pretty well gentrified from what it was before, I think. I'm going to guess that those lots of windows still have bars on 'em, though."

"They do, but the outside of the place still looks nice and it has a detached garage in back." She flashed the picture of the front of the house at me.

Sure enough, bars on the windows, the driveway an overgrown narrow dirt track, leading past the house to a one-car garage thing in the back that looked like the roof was sagging pretty hard. I couldn't deny the appeal of the place, so it was a hard 'maybe'. I opened my mouth to tell her as much when the ride I'd ordered turned the corner from the main drag onto our street.

"There's our ride, I think," she said before I could, looking up as the Lexus rounded the corner, tucking her phone in her jacket pocket. She'd had a decent winter coat in her car. An old Navy surplus wool peacoat. I'd been glad for it. It was way better than her denim jacket; that was for sure.

"Thank fuck, I was beginning to freeze my balls off," I declared.

"Fleece-lined leggings, I'm tellin' yah," she said and I laughed.

"I got my long johns, there's no way you're going to convert me to wearing girly-ass leggings," I said.

"Uh huh, we'll see about that," she said. "Lose a testicle out here and you'll be begging me for them."

I threw back my head and laughed as the car pulled up to the curb. She opened up the back door, pulling her arms through her backpack straps so she wouldn't crush it, and slid into the car first.

"I'm serious!" she declared, reaching for the box I held, and I handed it to her before shrugging out of my cut and getting in behind her.

"Sorry about the delay, folks. Traffic is moving at the speed of snail out there," the driver declared.

"Aw, it's alright man. I'd rather get where we're going safely than quickly."

"Man, you sound like a cop," he said laughing.

"Guilty," Saylor sang out.

We bantered lightly with the driver, a newsstand owner that drove on the side to make ends meet. He was around as old as my dad, which was to say somewhere in his sixties, and was a careful driver despite all his chatter.

Saylor was bright eyed and beautiful, the snow swirling past outside her window as we made our way carefully out of the city and toward the Bay Bridge, headed to my parents.

I'd been *shocked* when she'd suggested that it was alright to leave her guitar and journal behind. Shocked, and warmed that she trusted me enough to take care of her. That she felt secure enough to come back here and that they would be waiting, right where she'd left them. She'd told me about how she never went anywhere without certain items and the reasoning behind the decision and I could respect that about her.

The fact she'd been willing to make this Christmas Eve trip with me, and that she was willing to leave those items behind for an overnight… that was huge, and I knew how huge it was and it made me feel so… I don't know, loved? Admired? Trusted? All three?

It was a heady and intoxicating mix, and I was drunk as fuck on Saylor Grace Dresden.

We wound through gridlock, the holiday traffic murder, and I could just feel the cost of this ride racking up. Still, it was either this or the bike and I wasn't about to risk Saylor and her carefully procured Christmas gifts on the icy streets. That, and I *really* wasn't about to risk the bike.

I was no fair-weather rider, but I did have my limits – mostly put in place by the bounds of my own sanity.

"I'm still really nervous," Saylor declared as the driver pulled up to the curb in front of my parents' nice suburban retirement home.

"It's okay to be nervous," I said. "Just be yourself. You do that, and everything is going to be great."

"I really hope so," she said.

"Ah, you'll do fine, kid!" the driver said, coming to a complete stop.

"Thanks, man," I said and opened up the door, sliding out carefully onto the icy sidewalk. Dad had salted it, but with how bad the weather had been? It was still dicey as fuck.

Saylor held out the box of gifts and I balanced it on one arm, reaching my other hand down to help her climb to her feet. She hefted her stuffed backpack onto her shoulder and breath pluming the air said, "Ah, we're expected."

I looked up to the house at my Mom standing in the front door waving excitedly and crying, "You made it!"

"Of course we did!" I called, shutting the door to our ride with a final wave.

The car crunched over the ice and snow as it carefully lumbered away from the curb, leaving me and Saylor to traverse the rest of the distance to my parents' front steps.

"You must be Saylor!" my mom cried. "I am so happy to meet you! Please, God, come inside! You must be freezing!"

"Oh, I'm alright!" Saylor declared. "I've got fleeced-lined leggings on under my jeans."

I laughed and shook my head as she went past my mom and I kissed my mom's cheek on the way by.

"Hey, Ma."

"We're so glad you're here!" she declared, hugging me fiercely.

"Gifts under the tree?" I asked unable to hug her back with my arms loaded by the box as they were.

"Oh! Yeah, go on into the living room, your dad's in there – say 'hi.'"

"Kay." I jerked a head at Saylor to follow me and she smiled, letting her bulging pack down and holding it in front of her to follow me into the family room off to the right.

"Hey, Dad!" I called and he grunted and put his hands to his knees, getting up and turning.

"Well, hey there, boy! Was wondering when you were gonna finally get here." He hugged me and pounded me on the back enough to rattle my ribs like a wind chime.

"Yeah, the weather was rough, traffic was rougher," I said and turned to wave Saylor up. "Dad, I want you to meet Saylor Grace, my girlfriend."

"Oh, wow! Nice to meet you, Saylor." He stuck out a hand and she took a step forward with a shy smile and shook it.

I could see she was petrified, and I knew my dad could have that effect on some people. Former Marine, and an ex-cop, my pops had hardass written all over him even when he was trying to be nice, which I could tell, he was.

"Ho, look at what you got here!" he cried as we started unloading Saylor's carefully wrapped gifts under the Christmas tree. I smiled and waited patiently for her to empty all the smaller ones out of her pack.

My mom always put on an impressive tree each year. Christmas was always her favorite holiday, and when she and Dad downsized into this fancier two-bedroom house after his retirement, one of the best things about it, to her, was the impressive front windows.

The living room had vaulted ceilings, the windows at the front of the house cathedral-like and beautiful. Her Christmas tree towering and green, swathed in white lights, taking up center stage. Saylor's lips were quirked in a gently pleased smile, the lights reflected in her beautifully mismatched eyes like star scatter. It made her breathtaking in the dimmer light of the living room.

"It's almost too perfect," she remarked. "Like a Christmas tree in a shopping mall display. I didn't think people had trees like this in real life."

"Yeah," my dad said. "My Laura's always been special like that."

I chuckled. I knew what he meant, that my mom was genuinely *special* to him. Not *special* as in the modern connotation. He was so not declaring that my mom rode the short bus, but that was my dad. Simple, down-to-earth and didn't give a flying fuck about modern language conventions or slang terms.

Saylor's eyes widened slightly, and I chuckled. I'd have to explain it to her when I got the chance. If, I got the chance. My sister Trish poked her head around the corner and smiled. It was tired and I figured my nephews had been wild.

"Hey! There you are! Where're Sam and Will?" I asked.

"Their dad has them this year," she said pained and I shook my head.

"Shit, I'm sorry."

"It's okay, you didn't know."

She came over and hugged me and I hugged her back saying, "I got their presents here and I'd like you to meet Saylor."

Saylor peeked around me and stepped out from between me, my father, and the tree.

"Hello!"

"Hi, it's very nice to meet you," Trish said, smiling. She disengaged from my side and sighed.

"Mom's heating up dinner for you two, come on back to the kitchen," Trish said.

"Oh, perfect! I'm sorry we're so late," I said and I looked over my shoulder at Dad.

"You coming, Pops?" I asked him.

"Hell, no. I already ate. You two go on ahead. I'll be right here in my chair with my beer and my sports' highlights until y'all come back and usurp my TV for your damn Christmas movies."

I laughed and nodded, putting my arm around Saylor and said, "Okay, then. C'mon, babe. You're probably as hungry as I am."

"Famished," Saylor agreed, and we followed my sister back into the kitchen.

My mom and Trish sat with us at the table while we ate, drinking coffee and having their dessert, a slice of mom's cranberry-almond apple pie.

"So, Jer-bear, how did you and Saylor here meet?" my mother asked, and I traded a look with Saylor who positively looked like the jig was up. I should have taken the look to heart. After all, Saylor had been in this position before – but I literally thought my family was good people. Accepting, Christian in the truest sense of the word. Especially my mom.

I was about to find out that couldn't be further from the damn truth.

"On a call, actually," I said and my mom didn't seem phased at first. The more the story came out, the more worried she looked. Her good nature and kind demeanor didn't diminish in the slightest, but that was my mother, unfailingly polite. My sister raised her eyebrows and gave me a look that could only be interpreted as *'I'm so glad I'm not you right now,'* but I brushed it off.

"I think we should follow through with our Christmas Eve tradition," my sister declared when Saylor and I had finished up eating.

"Leave your plates," my mother declared. "I'll clean up in a bit."

Now *that* was unlike mother. I smelled an ambush, I just hoped like hell that they didn't do it in front of Saylor.

We went into the living room and my mom rooted around under the tree handing out boxes.

"Okay, Trish here's yours. The boys' are here too, but we'll just have to get them over to them later." My mom gave a gusty sigh and I knew she was disappointed the boys weren't here but that wasn't Trish's fault. I shot my sister an apologetic look and she rolled her eyes behind mom's back when Dad wasn't looking.

I tried not to crack up and Saylor blushed with good cheer and tried not to snicker herself.

"Okay, here's yours Jer-bear and here's yours Saylor." My mom handed over boxes and Saylor laughed lightly.

"You didn't have to get me anything," she said and my mom waved her off, handing my dad his box and dragging her own out from under the tree.

"Nonsense," my mother declared. "It's a Christmas Eve tradition in this house."

"We all open one gift on Christmas Eve," I explained. "Then we watch Christmas movies way too late into the night and sleep in on Christmas morning –"

"As much as the boys usually let us," my mom interjected and I took a deep and even breath, wishing she would let it go already as my sister sat on the other end of the big sectional setting herself as far away from our parents as she could get while still remaining present. I didn't miss how my sister closed her eyes and seemed to count to ten and I had to guess Mom had been at it for a while about her grandbabies not being present.

Dad was on the other end, feet up with the built-in recliner, a beer in its cozy in the drop-down arm rest's cup holder. He grumbled under his breath. "Time to drop it, Laura," my dad admonished, and my mother looked genuinely affronted by his tone.

"What?" Mom demanded, before waving her hands over the present in her lap and saying, "You know what? Never mind. Everybody's got their box, it's time to open!"

The awkwardness hung thick as the sound of tearing paper filled the living room. I wasn't quite looking at what I had on my lap. I knew what it was, same as it was every year. It was a new set of pajamas picked out by either my mom or my sister, my favorite movie snacks, and a holiday movie – whatever I'd picked that year.

I was more interested in what would come out of Saylor's box. I'd called ahead and had given my mom the low-down. Had spent several days cultivating what it was that she liked. Her favorite color, her favorite movie snacks, her favorite candy and what she thought was the ultimate Christmas movie.

Her answer had both surprised me and hadn't at the same time. I guess her grandfather had as much love for 80s and 90s action movies as my own dad. Her favorite holiday movie pick had been a tie between *The Nightmare Before Christmas* and *Die Hard*. We'd had a hell of a spirited discussion on if *The Nightmare Before Christmas* was actually a Christmas movie or if it was more of a Halloween movie and after a lot of tickling, laughter, and some deep penetrative, hot sex, she'd finally conceded in my favor that it was a Halloween film.

"Oh, my God, seriously?" Saylor demanded, laughing as she plucked the DVD off the top. She giggled as she held it up for all of us to see and my mom laughed lightly with her, my dad chuckling. "And pajamas, *and* Red Vines?" She picked up the pajama top, a deep, dark blue, the matching pants beneath them spangled with shiny silver stars.

"Merry Christmas, babe," I said evenly and just soaked up her *joy.*

"Thank you all, *so much!*" she said enthusiastically.

"What'd you get?" my sister asked and I looked down into my box.

"Nice!" I held up *Die Hard 2* and my dad said, "Decided to make a theme of it this year," as he held up *The Long Kiss Good Night.*

My mom rolled her eyes and held up her movie choice. "Fine, but tomorrow it's mine and Trish's choices," she said as she held up *Scrooged.* My sister smiled a little sadly and held up *The Polar Express,* which I knew was her choice because it was her favorite for the boys to watch.

"Nice, Trish," I said gently and asked, "What kind of pajama's did you get?"

I held up mine – a red plaid flannel set with a gray thermal top, the neckline, cuffs and hem lined with the said red plaid pattern that dominated the pants.

Trish smiled down into her box, pleased and held up hers, a purple set with snowflakes.

"Niiiiice!" Saylor said smiling and Trish nodded.

"Right, Saylor, the bathroom is just down the hall past the kitchen, first door on the right. Why don't you go first and try yours on?"

"Thanks," she said rising. "I will."

I smiled and gave her hand a gentle squeeze as she went past me to go change. It was suddenly tense and as cold in the living room as it was outside.

I fucking knew it.

As soon as she was out of earshot my dad heaved a big sigh and said, "On a call? You really went there, did you, Son?"

Crap.

18

*S*aylor...

I set the pajamas on the edge of the sink and ran my finger-tips over the warm, soft material. The tags were still on them. They were only fifteen dollars from Walmart, but they were also probably the nicest pajama set I'd owned in the last ten years. Of course, when you were a couch-surfing street kid you pretty much slept in whatever. Pajama sets weren't really a thing you got to own. At least, not complete sets.

I bent at the waist and swiftly untied and toed off my boots, one after the other. I quickly changed, bundled my clothes neatly and smoothly stepped back out into the hallway to a strained silence.

"I mean, just because she hasn't got an adult record doesn't mean she isn't a criminal, Jeremy. It just means she probably hasn't been caught yet. I didn't raise you to do something this stupid!"

I froze at Poe's father's harsh tone.

"So you won't even give her a chance?" Poe asked defiantly.

"Jer-bear," his mother started gently.

"No, Ma. Him I expect this kind of thing out of, but you?"

I didn't want to hear anymore. Instead, I slipped back into the bathroom, my heart breaking, and got dressed.

When I slipped back out it was to hear Poe's father say, "And what is taking her so damn long back there? How do you know she ain't robbing us blind?" he demanded, and I stepped back into the living room.

"I'm not," I said and hated how my voice cracked. I cleared my throat. "I was getting dressed again. I'm really sorry that you don't approve of me and I really don't want to ruin your Christmas. Um," I reached into my pocket and pulled out my cash, "this is all I've got – it should be more than enough to get back to the city… could someone call a car for me?"

"Babe…" Poe trailed off but he didn't say 'no', he just shook his head and looked so disappointed that my heart broke that much more.

"No, you know what, you're good. I'm coming with you," he said.

"Jeremy!" his mother exclaimed.

"What? No!" His dad was equally vehement.

"I can drive you," his sister said meekly.

"Trisha Anne Poe!" his mother barked.

"Tell us why we should stay?" Poe demanded. "Seriously. Saylor is with me, and she's had a rough life and background. Tell me how any of what you've said about her in the last five minutes is even remotely okay or the Christian thing *on Christmas!*" Poe was angry now and made a noise of disgust.

"You know what, Dad? You didn't raise me that way. I'd like to say you guys raised me better." He set his package of movies and pajamas aside and stood. "You certainly raised me to call bullshit when bullshit was present, and this right here is bullshit!"

His mom covered her mouth and his dad looked *pissed*.

"I don't want to ruin you all's Christmas," I said gently. "So I'm happy to go –"

"No," his mom said, plaintively unhappy.

"It's late," Poe's dad agreed. "It's icy out, and my son…" He looked like he was swallowing something exceedingly bitter when he said, "My son isn't exactly wrong."

I scuffed the toe of my boot against the lip of the hardwood half-step leading down into the sunken living room. Twisting it back and forth in an effort to alleviate my high-strung anxiety.

"I know I don't have the best background, but I promise – I'm not a bad person, I just come from a long series of unfortunate events. My granddad raised me right, I wouldn't do anything to cross him, especially now that he's gone."

I sniffed. I couldn't help it and Poe's mom visibly crumbled in apology and his sister in empathy.

Poe came over to me and pulled me into his chest, shielding me from his family's eyes and murmured into my hair, "I'm so sorry, babe. This wasn't how I expected our first Christmas to go."

"It's okay," I whimpered, and the lie was bitter ash on my tongue. It wasn't okay. It was as far from okay as it could get. "I just really wanted everyone to like me, but I get it. *Homeless* and *street kid* are hard to get around."

"Jesus Christ, rub it in why don't you?" his dad grumbled and I stiffened.

"Dad!" Trish barked sharply.

"Look…" His mom got up. "We're really sorry –"

"You're just worried about your son. Yeah, no, I get it, believe me I do,"

I said, taking a step back and dashing at the corner of my eye with the heel of my hand.

"So you staying or you going?" his dad grumbled, and I knew he felt like an asshole just from his tone. He wasn't a bad guy – he was just super rough around the edges. My granddad had been much the same way. The same type of guy cut from the same cloth. No nonsense, no filter, with the best of intentions and the absolute worst way of going about them.

I looked up to Poe for the answer and he sighed. He smiled wanly and traced some of my errant hair behind one of my ears, letting his fingertip run along the outer edge of my ear that sent a pleasant wash of tingles down the side of my neck and across my breast and back. I blushed faintly.

"What do you say, babe? Give this pack of assholes another chance?" he whispered. His dad snorted with humor, his mother wisely didn't say a word and just took it and I looked past him to his sister who was grinning ear to ear like she'd been gifted Christmas just by virtue of her brother calling their folks out on their bullshit. It was kind of like Christmas magic for me, too. I don't think anyone since my granddad had ever stood up for me like Poe did just now.

I nodded softly. "Okay," I murmured.

"Okay," he whispered back.

I resisted the urge to look past him at his father and ask if he would like me to turn out the rest of my pockets to assure him I hadn't and wouldn't steal anything, but I didn't exactly want to stoke the fire back up.

Poe turned back to me and my bundle of pajamas in my arms and said, "Okay, we're staying, but I'm going to take a minute with Saylor in the other room. Trish, toss me my PJs."

His sister got up swiftly and brought them over to him and he took them. "Thanks."

"Welcome."

"Be back in a minute," he said, and we left them all sitting there as he took me by the arm and led me back into the bathroom, shutting the door behind us both.

I immediately burst into tears, doing everything I could to keep them silent.

"Shit, babe, come on, come here," he whispered quietly and pulled me into his arms.

He held me tight while I cried my burned and broken feelings out into the front of his shirt, and not once did he try to stop me. He simply held me until the storm had passed.

"I'm so embarrassed," I confessed.

"Why?" he asked and lifted a shoulder in a shrug. "You have no reason to feel that way. They do. Without a doubt they do, but you? Mm not so much, baby. You are *definitely* not the asshole here."

I gave a little broken laugh and sighed. He turned on the tap and pulled a washcloth from one of the drawers, wetting it. He squeezed it out and handed it over. It was cool and inviting against the hot skin around my eyes from crying and I pressed the cloth to my eyes and scrubbed my face with it.

"There you go," he said, pulling his dark gray thermal Henley over his head, taking the white crewneck tee he had on underneath it with it.

He never disappointed. I almost swallowed my tongue looking at him and he chuckled lightly, reaching for the hem of my sweater and tugging on it.

"No dice, babe. I'm letting my sister take the guest room. We can stay out on the couch."

"I'm okay with that," I murmured.

"Figured you would be, beautiful."

"Your family loves you," I whispered.

"Doesn't keep them from being jerks," he said.

"No, true, but I'm used to it, so don't take it out on them too hard, okay?" I didn't want Christmas to be wrecked. I really didn't. I mean… I didn't feel like I was honestly worth having it wrecked over. I was just me and even though I was starting to figure out I was special to Poe, I didn't want to be the kind of special that broke up a family on Christmas.

We didn't say anything for a long minute. I mean, what was there to say? Finally, Poe smoothed his hands over my hair and tilted my head up to look at him, hands to either side of my face. He pressed his lips firmly against my forehead and sighed out.

"Let's get changed. We'll go out and pretend like nothing happened – which I know is hard because it did and I'm not happy, and I'm not over it. But in the interest of making it through tonight and tomorrow, we'll watch some movies, cuddle up and sleep, and as soon as we finish opening presents tomorrow, we'll find an excuse and jet."

"Okay," I whispered.

"I love you, Saylor Grace."

"I love you, too, Jeremy Poe."

"K, come on, let's get dressed."

"Okay."

We changed after that, and with our bundles of clothes, went back out to the living room. His dad was changed into his set of flannel pajamas, and his mother too, into a long-sleeved flannel nightgown, white with faint blue snowflakes. His sister hadn't reappeared yet.

"Oh, don't you both look adorable," his mother declared, and his dad nodded without looking.

Poe squeezed my hand and stepped down into the living room first, and I followed to the end of the couch where my bag sat. I stuffed my things into my backpack and kept it close, my boots at the ready in case I needed them.

"I put in *Die Hard* first," his dad said, and I smiled and tried to take the peace offering for what it was.

This Christmas, while not as bad as some I'd had, seriously couldn't get over with soon enough for my tastes.

I just wanted to be back in Poe's bed, in his too-tiny apartment, away from all the unpleasantness.

19

*P*oe...

"Mom, can you grab me a blanket out of the hall closet before you go?" I asked. We were half way through *Die Hard 2* and she was calling it a night. She looked at me and at Saylor sleeping lightly on my chest and nodded.

"Thanks," I said.

"She out?" my dad asked.

"I think so," I said. "Can't say I blame her."

"No, me either, I guess," my dad sighed.

We'd watched *Die Hard*, and at the end of the first movie, Trish had turned in. We were just into the second film when Mom had gotten up declaring she needed an early night. She came back over, shuffling in her slippers with a blanket from the hall closet in her hands.

"Thanks, Mom," I murmured as she laid one of those thin, but warm, furry blankets over the both of us. It was warm enough in the house, the woodstove going in the corner between the living room and open

178

kitchen. Still, I knew Saylor, she'd told me she had a hard time sleeping if one; there wasn't even a little light, and two, if she didn't have anything to cover up with. Even on the hottest days, she'd said she at least needed a sheet.

I knew that about her, just like she knew peculiar little details about me. Because I told her. I told her *everything*. Even the things I would never tell my sister or my mother. Things I even kept from some of the guys.

I trusted her and believed in her to keep my secrets safe and it was one of the best feelings, knowing I had someone to rely on like that.

"Goodnight, baby," my mother said with a big yawn. "See you in the morning."

"Night, Mom," I said simply. I was still pretty upset with both her and my dad, but I was trying not to let it creep and fuck up Christmas any more than they already had. Enough damage was done. Still, I couldn't wait to take Saylor home.

"Boy," my dad said, drawing out the word. "I don't think I ever remember a time you were so pissed at your mother and me."

"I can't honestly remember a time you guys so thoroughly fucked up. I mean, I know you're human, but that's what's killing me... I thought you were *human*, you know?"

Again, my dad gave a gusty sigh, this time edged with annoyance.

"Watch yourself, Jeremy," he grumbled.

"I am," I said, steely.

"Hmm, I think it's high time I got my ass to bed, too." My dad heaved himself to his feet.

"Night," I said clipped.

"You want this light out?" he demanded and I thought about it.

"She's afraid of the dark, were you planning on leaving the tree on?" I asked.

"I wasn't, but you're in here and it's well-watered so go ahead and leave it on." He snapped out the light over the kitchen stove, the one he'd asked about.

"You got the remotes close enough?"

"Yeah, Dad. Thanks."

"You're welcome, and son?"

I looked over curiously. "Your mother and me? We're only human. The nice thing about humans is they *can* learn from their mistakes."

"Yeah," I said, "they can." I was waiting for his usual caveat, and I wasn't disappointed.

"Most of 'em don't want to," he said and usually he left it at that. "But the good ones do," he added.

"Yeah, Dad and I know you and Ma are good people, Trish too. Maybe convince Ma to cut her only daughter some slack when it comes to the boys this Christmas? She misses them, too, and she doesn't tell you the half of what that sorry son of a bitch gets up to. She calls *me*."

"Eh?" My dad straightened, his brow wrinkling.

"She thinks you like her ex better than you like the two of us combined." His brow smoothed out in surprise, his eyebrows shooting up into his hairline. At least that was one thing we had going for us, the men of the Poe line. We may get the occasional receding hairline, but male pattern baldness wasn't our thing.

"You're sure full of hard truths tonight, aren't you?" he demanded, and while he didn't sound happy about it, I thought I could hear the edge of something else. Something like pride?

"Guess Saylor is rubbing off on me," I said, looking down at the crown of golden blonde hair on the top of her head. Her breathing deep and even, her hand warm on my chest. "She's so honest it hurts, but she's never brutal or unkind about it."

"Salt-of-the-earth is what they call folks like that," my dad said.

"Yeah. She's one of those. Take my word for it until you can see it for yourself. She's been shy, pretty much terrified to meet you guys. She just wanted you all to like her so damn much. Didn't want to lie, even though I did –"

"And look where the truth got her." My dad nodded and didn't look happy with himself.

"Yeah."

"You got a right to be pissed," he said.

"Treat her better tomorrow or we walk," I told him.

"You've made your point," he declared acidly, and I backed off.

"Night, Dad."

"Night, Son."

And that was that.

Any more and it would have been a screaming match and I didn't want to wake Saylor up.

She sighed out and cuddled closer whispering, "Thank you."

"For what?" I asked as Bruce Willis shot it out with terrorists in the backstage baggage area of the Washington D.C. airport.

"Standing up for me like that, especially to your family."

"I told you I would –"

"Yeah, but a lot of men *say* a lot of things but then when it comes time to pony up, they fold like cheap paper in front of their mom or dad and I get it, I really do – it's hard to stand up to your family and the people who raised you, but no one has ever done that for me before."

I kissed her forehead. "My parents, especially my dad, can be rough around the edges but they *are* good people at heart."

She nodded her head against my chest, and I kissed the top of it again, her hair silky against my lips and her breath warm where she sighed out in contentment and it penetrated the weave of my shirt.

"You've had it rough enough. Let me carry things for a while and give you a much-needed break."

"Not for too long, though, okay?" she said. "I don't want to get too soft."

I chuckled. "I don't see that happening. You're too much of a feminine badass."

She snorted and held to me tightly before asking meekly, "You want me to get off of you?"

"Not on your life," I answered, soothing my hands over the blanket covering her.

"K, good, because I'm reeeeeally comfy."

"Can you see the TV?" I asked.

"Yeah, mm-hmm."

"Okay, good."

I don't know about my precious and beautiful woman, but my Christmas Eve got a whole lot better after that. Her in my arms, an action movie on the screen, warm, safe, bathed in the light of the tree.

Only thing that could possibly make it better would be if we were naked, in our own house, the both of us freshly fucked.

All in good time, I guess.

～

CHRISTMAS MORNING, I couldn't tell if Saylor was genuinely asleep or not, just like I hadn't been able to tell the night before. At any rate, my mom woke *me* up with a touch to my shoulder, holding a steaming mug of coffee out to me.

"Do you know if Saylor likes coffee?" she asked me in a dramatic whisper and Saylor contracted slightly with a bit of laughter.

"Coffee would be lovely, Mrs. Poe."

"Oh, please," my mother waved her off, "call me Laura."

"Yes, ma'am." Saylor carefully pushed herself up off of me taking her warmth and the blanket with her.

The room was still fairly warm, but not warm enough. I held my mug out to the side over the protective area rug as my mom moved off and I waited for the slight flurry of activity to settle down. Once I was sure I wasn't going to spill, I sat up slowly.

"Morning," my dad grunted, shuffling into the room in his deerskin slippers.

"Morning," I groaned, a little stiff from the couch but mostly from not moving all night. It was like that with Saylor. I slept so deep, so hard, when I was with her, I swear I *didn't move* all night long.

She smiled at me sleepily and asked, "You okay?"

"I'm good," I declared, taking a careful sip of hot coffee.

"Saylor, honey, what do you like in your coffee? Would you like to come fix it to taste for yourself?"

"Coming," Saylor said, and it was probably only to me that she sounded so guarded.

She rose gracefully and stepped around the storage ottoman that tripled as a coffee table to step up into the kitchen.

"Is there anything I can do to help with breakfast?" she asked and I smiled. Despite what they thought of her, the conclusions they'd readily jumped to about my bohemian babe, she was still trying to help out.

"Oh, no! I've got it, and Trish will be up to help, soon."

"Okay, I just thought I'd offer. I actually like to cook."

"Who taught you how?" my dad asked. I mentally face palmed, but she answered before I could say anything. That one was just my dad being my dad. A question popped into his head and he asked, whether it was appropriate or not given whatever circumstances.

"My granddad, actually. When I was six or seven."

My dad gave a low whistle.

"Awfully young," my mother remarked slightly disapproving.

"He wanted to make sure I could take care of myself before he went," she said. "He was in good health, so we thought, but he always worried about it. About what I would do when he was gone."

"How come?" Trish asked from the kitchen entryway with a yawn and a stretch.

"Uh, when I was two or three, my dad murdered my mom and then killed himself. My grandmother had cancer and died not too long after, so it was just me and my granddad. When he went, he knew it would just be me and when he *did* go in his sleep, from a heart attack, I was only fifteen. It was the foster care system after that and *that* was a joke. I've pretty much been on my own and a street kid ever since."

"You've been homeless for *ten years?*" my mother asked, agape.

"Yeah, well, I mean I've had places but rent out in the Pacific Northwest is *expensive* and I've always managed to get by." She shrugged and raised the coffee mug between her hands to her lips to blow across the surface. She'd been moving around the kitchen, doctoring herself up a cup as she'd been talking.

"That's intense," Trish commented, getting herself a cup of coffee.

"I mean, I guess." Saylor laughed a little nervously. "I got my GED and I didn't want to drown in student debt, so I sort of skipped the whole college thing. I'm just happy to make my music," she said.

"Oh, so you're a musician," my mom said.

"I told you that, Ma," I said gently.

"That's me," Saylor said with a sad sort of smile. "On the corner singing for my supper."

"That's no way to live," my dad said, and his tone wasn't dispassionate or disapproving, it was more like a little sad.

"Really?" I said. "Because I'm pretty sure she does it every day."

Saylor smiled at me and mouthed 'It's okay' but it wasn't – still, my dad got the picture and my mom changed the subject.

I didn't even want to open presents, I just wanted to get the fuck out of here – take Saylor out of here – but my sister's pleading look told me I needed to stay, if only so I wouldn't abandon her in the middle of the brewing family shitstorm.

I honestly couldn't do that to her.

We managed to get through breakfast by sticking to safe topics and staying out of Saylor's past. Of course, that meant focusing on mine some and because nobody can fuck with you like family? That meant dredging up some really awful and embarrassing childhood memories. Memories I could have lived with never letting see the light of day ever again.

It was worth it to see Saylor laugh lightly and there were a couple it was nice to watch her cringe in solidarity. I actually couldn't wait to be alone with her again to have a real discussion about a few of them. She somehow made me feel better, she soothed me about some of the darkest parts of me – the things that really bothered me even though for anyone else they might seem like no big deal.

"Right, I think that we've all been held in suspense long enough," my dad said, and my mom smiled.

"Presents anyone?" she asked, and some genuine smiles broke out among us.

I had no idea what Saylor had been up to, but I did know she'd managed to source something for everyone and with her own earnings. Some, she'd confided, she'd traded services for. Singing outside the shops and luring in some business, running the odd errand for shop owners during their busiest times.

"Who's going to be Santa this year and hand out gifts?" Mom asked.

"I can," Saylor said immediately. "I'd like to do *something* to help."

"Have at it, girl." My dad smiled at her and she nodded.

I didn't honestly care that much about what was under the tree if it didn't have that simple, beautifully folded brown paper wrapping.

I know it sounded petty as hell and it was shitty on my part, but I sort of suffered through my parent's typical gifts of socks and tee shirts, a nice watch and a really nice shave kit. Don't get me wrong, I *liked* these things, and I even needed them, but I really wanted to know what Saylor had done.

She'd gifted my sister a piece of street art that was absolutely amazing. A canvas that'd been spray painted, the silhouette of a mother and two young children beneath a large tree, playing on a swing. The scene was set at dusk and done all in purples and lavenders, my sister's favorite colors.

It made Trish tear up and gave my mom serious pause. Even my dad had complimented it rather than giving one of his trademark monosyllabic grunts of approval.

For my dad, she'd gone hard and had bought him an expert whittling knife for his little figures he liked to carve. My dad liked miniatures but didn't really like the store-bought lead figures, so he preferred to make his own. He had a whole representation of old Indigo City and the 1912 riots out there as his latest project. When he was finished with them, he usually found a museum to donate them to and they almost always took what he had to offer, gladly.

"Thank you, Saylor," my dad said in a tone that bordered on chagrined. "It'll get a lot of use, I promise you that."

Saylor smiled simply and nodded and dare I say cracked my pop's icy facade with that gift. I'd had no idea what she was going to get him. I had suggested the hobby paints he used but she'd definitely gone above and beyond.

For my mother, she'd gotten hand-crocheted kitchen pot holders and a handmade pottery mixing bowl from Ally and Dawnie's funky little boutique. It may not seem like much, but my mom *loved* to bake and she was positively giddy with the gift.

That just left me, and the tiny little box between my hands that rattled with what had to be a snaking chain pooled in the bottom.

I opened it to a white gold chain, a pendant like a compass rose sitting on the coils. I looked up at Saylor.

"It was my granddad's," she said softly, twisting her lips back and forth, her nervousness palpable.

I didn't know what to say. I knew how much it meant to her, and I honestly didn't know what to say. It said everything she wasn't able to – that this was *definitely* a forever kind of thing going on between us, and I made the decision right then and there that yeah – it *was*.

I pulled her into my arms and hugged her tightly, kissing her temple and swearing I would never let her go. That no matter what, I would always keep tabs on her, even if she told me to fuck off, to know that she was safe.

I really loved this woman so damn much in such a short amount of time that the idea of soulmates didn't seem so farfetched anymore.

"God, I love you," I muttered, and I didn't care what my family thought.

They'd better get used to it because Saylor wasn't going anywhere.

20

$\mathcal{S}$aylor...

He bought me a lute. All because I said it would be nice to learn how to play one. It would be different, and I was always afraid of losing or having my granddad's guitar damaged beyond repair and I couldn't believe he'd gone to such an expense.

The piece he had bought for me was *expensive*, the body hand-painted with beautiful flowering vines and timeless, the blonde wood all aglow under its fresh, sparkly coat of sealant. I loved it. He'd even sprung for the hard-sided case, lined in a rich red velvet that was eye catching.

His mother had gifted me a warm natural fiber wool sweater that hung to mid-thigh and wore wonderfully like a dress. Paired with leggings, a thin brown belt I owned cinching it at the waist, it would make a wonderful dress and I adored it. Even though I couldn't quite be sure that was what his mom had intended... even if she had purchased it or what have you before she learned about how her son and I had met.

His dad had gotten me a gift card to a popular music shop in Indigo

City that still had vinyl records and CD's not understanding that when Poe had said music shop, he'd meant where you could buy instruments and things for them such as guitar strings which I had been in need of, but that was okay.

His sister had gotten me a pretty pewter hair clip with acorns and leaves. Something my hippy bohemian-chic ass had *loved*.

Going above and beyond her wonderful Christmas gift, Trish provided us a swift exit from their parents' house by giving me and Poe a ride back to the city, dropping us off in front of his apartment building.

"Thanks, Trish," he said, going back to her open driver's side window, hugging her through it. "Call me if you need anything," he said.

"It was really nice to meet you, Saylor!" she called back to me, waving and I smiled.

"You too!" I called, and I meant it. I liked his sister. She was quiet but sweet.

I had most of the gifts to both him and me in my backpack. My hand in a death grip on the case's handle that held my new lute as Poe trudged through the piled snow at the curb to reach the icy sidewalk where I stood.

Trish pulled away, her Volvo angry at the foul driving conditions and slip sliding a bit on the icy street.

"Slow and steady, Trish," Poe muttered looking after her.

"I would really hate driving in this," I remarked. "Maybe it's a good thing my car is already totaled? Saved me the trouble of doing it myself."

Poe laughed and took my lute case from me, tossing an arm around my shoulders.

"Let's get inside and warm up," he said. "I know just the thing."

"Please tell me it involves getting naked and horizontal in bed," I said.

"You read my mind," he affirmed.

Well, actually, I only half read his mind. As soon as we were inside, he turned and handed my new instrument back to me and went into the kitchen, switching on the electric kettle to heat some water. It was cold in here! So he asked me to turn up the heat.

"Want me to find homes for some of this?" I asked, turning up the dial on the thermostat.

"Yeah, could you? I'll make us some hot tea and we can get cozy."

"I should get some laundry going, between you and me we have a load."

"Sure."

It was domesticated bliss. I mean, it felt really good just the two of us in the too-small space getting things accomplished.

"You know since I had this year off, next year I'll be working Christmas unless I can find a guy who worked it this year to trade off with," he said from the kitchen.

We made small talk about how scheduling for holidays worked at his job while he made up some hot tea for the both of us. I got the washer running just as he came around with two steaming mugs.

"Find something on TV we don't care about so when we finish our tea and start making out, we don't care about missing it?" he asked.

"God, it's like we're made for each other," I said and winked over the rim of my mug.

Now that the apartment had warmed some, we hung our coats, took off our shoes, and whisked our socks into the filling washing machine before settling onto the bed and taking up our mugs from our respective nightstands.

"I would kill for a couch," he said.

"Oh, and a living room, with a corner and some instrument stands?" I said wistfully.

Poe smiled at me, this charmed smile, and said, "I think that's the first time you've ever been brave enough to dream with me instead of for me."

"What do you mean?" I asked.

"I mean every time we talk about a bigger place or a house, you say things like 'this would be good for you' or 'I can picture you in X' it's never included *you* or your things and I really want it to."

I felt my shoulders drop and my expression soften as I stared into his deep green eyes. Not that the color was deep, which it was, but more the emotion in them as he looked at me was unfathomable.

The fact that he turned that type of gaze on me melted me like chocolate, and I felt as though everything was slanted in his direction. I ran to him, rich with the warmth he instilled in me, as I set my mug aside and slid over the covers to straddle his lap.

He quickly set his mug aside and leaning back against the wall at the head of the bed, put his hands on my waist, gazing up at me with equal parts love and lust. I turned a decidedly different type of molten under that gaze, capturing his face between my hands, running my fingers through his hair and gripping handfuls of it to tilt his mouth up to mine.

I kissed him, pouring every ounce of joy, every drop of the devotion I had for him into it. My tongue sweeping past his lips, rubbing tantalizingly against his as he groaned into my mouth, kissing me back with intense fervor.

His hands smoothed over my hips around to my lower back, down to cup my ass. His strong fingers gripping it, urging me to dry hump him like a horny teenager which wasn't a big ask. I rubbed myself over his growing hardness through our clothes and I know the both of us became more aroused for it.

It was a slow burn, teasing; a torturously sedate build. His hands delved below the waistband of my jeans as far as his fingers could reach before getting trapped, and I hummed into his mouth in a desire for more. I smoothed my hands down his body so I could unbutton and unzip my jeans to give him better access.

We went tit for tat, exchanging an article of clothing for another chance at putting lips against skin, to revel in each other's warmth as the cold pressed in on the small apartment from the outside. We laughed and giggled our way through getting out of our pants. Neither of us wanting to let go of the other as we struggled to peel the clinging cotton denim off our legs – shoving it all into a heap off the side of the bed, dying sweetly at every new kiss, lick, or touch against previously hidden skin.

"God, baby you feel so good," he whispered harshly against my ribs as I leaned way back, straddling him once more, but almost over-whelmed by his hands and his lips on my body. I wanted him inside me *so* badly, but I was enjoying the sweet torture, the exquisite agony of wanting him, of having his stiff cock in contact with my pussy, of sliding myself up and down the hot velvet length of him in foreplay – but not penetrating me. Not yet.

Good God, I wanted it, though. I wanted to feel him move inside of me. I wanted to love him and be loved by him until we lost all sense of time and space and the room fell away, and it was just down to the feel of his body in mine, against mine, the touches, the panting breaths, the feral cries of pleasure and the sparks and stars behind my eyelids.

"I know it's wrong to want it, but I want you just like this," he declared. "No barriers, just skin on skin and I don't know how to feel about the fact that I want it so bad." He grunted and thrust against me by way of emphasis. Sliding against my wetness, the feel of him nude against me sending delightful shivers up my spine as he confessed,

"I've never wanted it with anyone before. I've never wanted something so much in my life."

He was asking my permission while at the same time too afraid to ask outright, but he needn't have worried – I wanted the same thing. I had an IUD, and I knew how effective it was, but I had always been so afraid of getting pregnant. Of bringing another life into this world when there were days I could barely take care of myself, I almost always insisted on another layer of protection for peace of mind.

Sliding him inside of me without that extra layer sent a thrill through me. As though we were suddenly indulging in the forbidden, and the thrill was two-fold for me. The fact that this was *my* choice, *my* decision, that I was the one to hold the power however slight and that he had conceded that power to me when he could have so easily forced the decision. God, it was so sexy, so erotic, and as I felt him go deeper, inch by inch, I think I was the wettest I had ever been in my life.

"Fuck, Saylor," he gasped and swiped his thumbs in an encouraging caress against my hips as he drove upwards to meet my downward stroke, sending a little shock of pleasure through me, causing me to throw my head back to *surrender* just as readily to him as he surrendered himself to me.

It was beautiful. It was everything. It was the most complete sharing of myself to him, and I felt, in equal measure, of himself to me that I had ever had the grace and good fortune to encounter.

I felt so fortunate, so loved, and I loved him back with a slow, languorous roll of my hips, living for the slide of his dick against my inner walls that I clenched around him, gripping him, making it good for us both as best that I could... and *God* he gave good dick. Thrusting up just enough as I came down to nudge just that little bit further. Opening me up, sending pleasure and euphoria swirling through my entire being, my body like a night-blooming flower, unfurling under his touch which was as gentle as the touch of the light of the moon.

Silvery and sweet, gentle and magic. I lived for his touch and the caress of his gaze as he watched me move above him, his hands constantly touching, sweeping over my skin, smoothing out the goosebumps that raised on my flesh, warming me where I started to chill.

I leaned over him and pressed my mouth to his and he didn't hesitate, his hips rising and falling off the bed to keep the spark of joy alive, fanning it to a flame that rose higher and higher, generating enough heat so that when I spread my wings, I could ride the thermal even higher than that.

God, I was getting close. So close. So close that all I needed to do was reach fingertips up to touch the sun.

"That's it, baby," he murmured in encouragement as my physical fingertips pressed against my clit.

I arched up, leaning back, his body driven into mine as far as it could go, the contact of my fingertips against that sensitive bundle of nerves driving me full on into the warm golden glow of the sun, my feathers burning, my resolve evaporating as I burst into shredded ribbons, the streamers falling beautifully apart, fluttering back down to earth, spiraling down until I coalesced back into my body and the safety of his arms.

21

P oe...

She cuddled against me in a blissful silence. As in she was so blissful, she couldn't speak, and I was close to feeling the same except I had the opposite thing going on the chatter. Like, I suddenly couldn't *wait* to talk more about where to move to. All because I couldn't *wait* to start my life with her. I couldn't wait to the point I wished we could head to the real estate office right now and get an agent looking for us because we weren't entirely doing awesome on our own.

I felt that now she was really on board and willing to dream with me, that it was time to really get off my ass and to make those dreams a reality.

She cuddled closer and sighed happily, and I chuckled and kissed her forehead and asked, "So, now that it's settled and you want to move with me, I gotta know, what's the most important feature of a new house for you? Big kitchen? Master bedroom? Open floor plan? Because this isn't going to be *my house*, baby. It's going to be *our* house, and these are important things to know."

"I know it's probably really dumb," she whispered, "but I *really* like that one I found before we went to your parents."

"The Burrington Heights one?" I asked.

"Yeah."

"How come?"

"I think part of it is what you told me," she confessed. "That it comes from what used to be a rough neighborhood. I actually *like* that it needs work. I mean, I know it's a pain in the ass to do that kind of remodeling and I know it can be expensive, but that kind of thing is what can really make it *ours*. Doing as much of the work as we can ourselves would save on labor and – I don't know... can we just go look at it?"

I was silent for a second to let my brain catch up and sort through the pros and cons of everything she'd just said when she added the most adorable and whimsical little girl, *"Pleeeeaase?"* that just absolutely did me in.

I laughed and said, "I could never say no when you ask like that."

She laughed slightly too and said, "Good to know."

"So, let's go take a look at it," I murmured, and she looked up at me.

"Really?"

"Yeah, really."

"You mean it."

I laughed again. "Of course, I mean it!"

"God, I love that it's so *easy* to love you," she said, and I thought it was a weird thing to say before I stopped to *really* think about it and I guessed, in a way, she was right. Some people made it a real pain in the ass to love them and I just wasn't that guy. I didn't need to make things difficult for the sake of being difficult. Saylor didn't have anything to prove to me. Just like I didn't have anything to really prove to her. We were just comfortable with each other. We'd clicked. Two peas in a pod.

She was really easy to love herself.

~

NEW YEAR'S Eve was spent at the *10-13* with the rest of the guys and their women. We all pretty much agreed we wished Thanksgiving and Christmas were an option for all of us, but blood relations like mine still demanded attention – except the older I got, the more I questioned why. If the ones you were born to made you so damn unhappy through no fault of your own, why push it?

It was a question I sometimes thought I had the answer to, but then I would go second guessing myself. The short answer was, for some of us, it wasn't worth pushing ourselves into the situation at all. For me, I loved my mom and dad. I loved my sister, too, and while it wasn't worth it some years for me, I couldn't and wouldn't give up hope that my mom and dad who weren't bad people, would work on their more obnoxious flaws.

I knew I wasn't perfect, but *goddamn* I was tired of my mom and dad saying judgy shit to Trish only to have her call me crying. She was doing her fucking best and her ex was seriously a goddamn psychopath with some of the shit he was pulling to make her life miserable. The latest was to enlist our own fucking parents against Trish to get his own fucking way when it came to the custody arrangement with the boys.

It was ugly, and I was over it. I was glad that the one holiday during the winter season I got with my club and my woman was *mine*. No parents. No judging. No fuckery except the fun kind.

It'd been a much-needed night for the lot of us to cut loose.

As soon as the holiday was over, and things were back to normal – the first day off I had that everyone else was back from their holidays – I took Saylor with me to the realtor's office so we could do more than just talk about it and could get crackin' on a plan for the rest of our lives together.

The rotten luck she'd had in life had seemed to lift with the changing of the year and the house she'd so wistfully had fallen in love with in the Burrington Heights district of the city was not only still available, it was right up our alley in price – including the home-improvement loans it would take to really make it ours.

We got to take a look, and even I was in love with it when I laid eyes on it in person, and the more animated Saylor got with her suggestions – all extremely modest and doable – the more excited I got. Still, I wasn't going to take what the realtor had to say about it at face value. I called up Backdraft and we made a second appointment to walk through and have a look at things.

I'd waited with bated breath while my club brother walked through with us. Blaze had tagged along at my request because he'd likely be doing a lot of this shit with us. As my best friend, I think he'd have been pissed if we didn't let him help out – plus I had to admit, he had a lot more home-improvement know-how than I did, just not quite as much as Backdraft who was a true jack-of-all-trades, and practically a master of all of them. And no, none of us knew how he did it.

They'd both agreed there wasn't anything out of pocket about the place, and I'd be insane not to put an offer in. Saylor had practically jumped up and down for joy.

We'd sealed the deal and lucky us, with it being fucking January the owners had taken it solid. We'd gotten it slightly below asking price and apparently, they were just thrilled to have it gone so soon.

"Looks like your luck is turning, baby," I'd told Saylor when I'd gotten home that night and she'd tackled me onto the bed, and it was the hottest sex to date.

We'd closed on the house last week and it was a done deal.

Now it was Thursday night, the club was holding church and part of the discussion was moving day for me and my girl who was out on the sidewalk singing her fucking heart out to anybody passing by on the street.

I don't think I'd ever felt so alive. I felt like the world was our damn oyster and there was nothing but laughter and smiles going on around the table.

"You look the happiest I think I've ever seen you, man. Looks good on you," Oz declared.

"I know for a fact he ain't ever been this happy, and it *does* look good on him." Blaze winked in my direction.

I shook my head and agreed, "I *am* happy."

"So, what's the big plan, then?" Skids asked.

"Well, I'm paid up until the end of the month. If we're lucky, we'll be able to get into the new house as-is before dropping another month's rent and go from there."

"How much stuff we talking?" Youngblood asked.

"Honestly, none. Just what's in the apartment and what's in my storage cage down below it. There was a bunch of shit left behind in the garage at the new house. It would be nice to get that cleared out, so I have a place to secure the bike before making the move. Think I can borrow you and your truck next time I'm off to deal with that?" I asked Blaze.

"Sure!"

"Might need to have a look at the garage's roof, it's sagging in a couple places. Might need to redo it – I don't know how much that would take though."

"I can run by and have a look at it once you get it cleared out, any idea when you'll get the keys?"

"The place was unoccupied, I actually pick up the keys tomorrow."

"Nice!" Youngblood took a drink out of the bottle he'd been nursing.

"You're really doing it." Golden gave me a crooked smile and with a wink said, "I'm proud of you, kid."

I chuckled. "Thanks. Saylor found some kind of weird paint with glitter in it and is begging to do one wall in it. I'm not sure what to do with that."

"Pick a room and paint the damn wall in glitter," Reflash said dryly and the guys laughed with me.

We sat around shooting the shit and making plans in between, and it was good to know they had my back. No one was trying to talk me out of shit, and no one damn sure had anything negative to say about Saylor and I knew her, I knew she would never give them a reason to.

All was right in my world.

"Right, so we'll call this good and get out there and enjoy some time with the girls before we gotta call this a night, what do you say, boys? Adjourned?"

"Adjourned!" we all enthusiastically agreed.

I got up along with a lot of the other guys to go out to see our women. Blaze got up with me and followed me out to thread through the tables in the bar area out on to the street to collect Saylor and her new lute.

There was nobody out on the sidewalk when we emerged, so she simply cut playing and smiled at us saying, "Hey, you guys. Done already?"

"What do you mean 'already?'" Blaze asked. "I thought that shit was never gonna end."

Saylor laughed lightly and pulled her lute off over her head, coming around to the front of her case and laying it reverently inside.

"No luck out here tonight, huh?" I asked, noting how empty the case was.

"Nope, not tonight. That's just the way the cookie crumbles." She gave a gusty sigh that plumed the frozen air.

"I hear you guys get to pick up the keys tomorrow," Blaze said.

"Mm-hmm, I'm excited."

"I'm off, why don't we ding out the garage then?" he asked.

"Yeah?" I asked.

"Yeah. Let's get it done."

"Alright!" Saylor enthusiastically agreed.

"You ready to head home?" I asked.

"Ready when you are," she stated and picked up her case, rising gracefully to her feet and stretching her back.

"Aw, man, I was hoping for at least one round of pool or darts or something, but yeah. Best get her out of the cold. I'll be by in my truck say around nine o'clock?" Blaze asked.

"Nine it is," I agreed.

"Cool, cool."

"You know, we can stay for one more drink if you want," Saylor said and I smiled.

"Nah, I want to get you home and warmed through," I said as she shivered on the sidewalk.

"Okay." She smiled, easy going either way.

"Dress warm for tomorrow," Blaze said. "We'll get your keys and get shit handled."

"Get it done," I agreed and clasped hands with my best friend. We knocked shoulders and Blaze grinned.

"See you tomorrow, Saylor."

"See you tomorrow!" she quipped back cheerfully.

I took her back to our apartment, selfishly, greedy for just her company and to have her body writhing under me.

When we got through the door, she apparently had the same idea and I don't think I had ever been happier in my life.

22

*S*aylor...

Blaze came over early, like nine o'clock as promised, and gave us both a ride in his pickup to the realtor's office for our appointment to pick up our keys. That done, it was an immediate ride with barely suppressed excitement to our new house.

The three of us worked all day and took three loads of trash out of the garage to take to the nearest dump. It was a lot, but it was worth it. It was a little daunting with how much the roof sagged over our heads as we worked, and once the debris was cleared, and the few treasures we'd found were carefully set aside, we all stood staring at the deepening night sky through the hole in the roof.

Blaze and Poe were taking pictures with their phones.

"What do you think? A whole new roof?" Poe asked.

"Yeah, but it looks like all the support beams are okay. We're talking just plywood, tar paper, shingles… the house's roof looks good, so I think it's just going to be out here."

"How long you think it'll take?"

"What, like is this a weeklong or a weekend project?"

"Exactly."

"Backdraft will have to weigh in with a final answer but I'm cautiously optimistic and will say 'weekend' for now. Roofs aren't my usual thing. I'm more interior finishing work."

Both of their phones went off at once and they traded a look and looked at their screens.

"What?" I asked. When they both frowned heavily, I reiterated the question. "What is it?"

"Trouble," Poe said.

"Glad you brought your guitar. We have to head to the *10-13* like right now." Blaze and Poe started moving.

"What's wrong?" I asked again.

"Officer involved shooting," Poe said and I gasped.

"Oh my God! Who? Are they alright?"

"Driller, and I think he's okay. No word on the specifics yet, that's why we need to go in."

I helped them lock up, rushing around and securing the house doors and windows while Blaze secured the tailgate on his truck against the last load of trash which I guess was going with us.

"Come on, baby, up you go." Poe helped me into the back seat of the truck where my granddad's guitar waited. I didn't know why, I just had wanted it with me today instead of my lute. Even though I didn't intend on playing anywhere, I was glad I had it with me now. Sounded like we were going to be at the *10-13* for a while.

"You guys okay?" I ventured, as we carefully but as quickly as possible navigated icy side streets.

Blaze did his best to keep his truck from meandering sideways through a turn and said through a clenched jaw and gritted teeth, "Ask me again after the emergency church meeting."

"You got it," I uttered quietly, and Poe reached back to squeeze my hand. I squeezed back and smiled at him, but the worry wouldn't leave his eyes and for that I could not blame him. I was worried, too. I liked Driller, Narcos, and Everleigh.

We got lucky and found parking right up the block from the *10-13*, and even though it was dicey parallel parking on an icy street over the berm of dirty snow left by plow trucks, Blaze had the know-how and the four-wheel drive to make it happen.

"Country boy in the city has some uses, huh?" Poe asked.

"Damn straight," Blaze agreed.

We got out of the truck, Poe taking my granddad's guitar and passing it off to Blaze to help me down even though he didn't need to. I loved that about him, though. That he was always a gentleman.

"Thanks," I murmured, and Blaze held out my guitar to me and said 'Welcome' with a wink. I rolled my eyes and tucked myself into Poe's side as we walked the dreaded walk to the waiting doors of the *10-13* to find out what had become of our friend.

23

*P*oe...

"Thanks, man," I said as Reflash held open the door to the *10-13* for the three of us to step through.

"Is Driller okay?" Saylor asked of him before even a greeting could cross her lips and I loved her for that.

"Physically? Yeah. Yeah, he'll be alright. His vest took it and he's bruised but it ain't a bullet he's gotta worry about with this one."

"Okay, babe. Looks like you're the only ol' lady here. Get yourself a hot drink and I'll see you when I can." I kissed her forehead and she nodded.

"I love you," she said impulsively, and it made me smile. Usually, she saves the 'I love yous' for when it was just her and me, alone together. It meant a lot, her calling it out like that in front of Reflash and Blaze.

"I love you, too. Be back as soon as I can." Her hand lingered in mine and she smiled at me, letting her fingers slip and dropping her arm to her side as I trailed after Reflash, Blaze bringing up the rear. Looked like we were the last to arrive.

When we got into the fishbowl, Skids was looking dour. Not surprisingly, we were missing Driller and Narcos.

"Somebody catch us up, all we know is what we got in the text to be here," I said.

"It's not good. Media is turning it into a shitstorm. White cop shoots unarmed black teen."

"Unarmed? I thought Driller caught one in the vest?" Blaze and I took our seats, but he took the words right out of my mouth.

"He did," Youngblood said. "Guy that shot him took off; he managed to get up and pursue."

"How the hell did he pull *that* off?" I demanded.

"He's one tough son of a bitch," Golden grunted.

Catching one to the vest was a lot like taking a charge from a rhino. It wasn't easy to get your wind back let alone pursue. His adrenaline must have been running buck wild.

"They're talking charges," Yale declared. "I've already recused myself."

"Charges!? What? Why?" Oz looked pissed.

"The kid he shot wasn't the suspect. I shouldn't even be talking to you about this –"

"Wait, he literally *did* shoot an unarmed kid?" Backdraft's mouth dropped open.

"Looks like it, but that doesn't mean he didn't *think* it was the kid. It's complicated," Skids declared, sighing out.

"The optics are a shitshow," Reflash declared.

"Hence, why I called you all in here." Skids didn't look happy.

"We're standing by him," Golden snapped.

"Now, I didn't say that we weren't." Skids raised his hands to ward off whatever G. was going to say next.

"Sure as fuck sounded like you were." Oz scowled at him.

"This is a lot different from what happened to you over the summer," Reflash declared.

"I know that," Oz said harshly.

"Look," Youngblood said coolly. "I think this meeting was called to see how we could best support Driller through this."

"Exactly," Skids said, his tone both chastising and inviting no argument.

"So what do we need to do?" I asked. Like everyone else, I was eager to pitch in.

"First off, fuck the media," Oz declared and there were grunts of agreement around the table.

"Agreed," Skids said. "We all know if it bleeds it leads. We don't need to feed into the sensationalized bullshit surrounding this."

"No comment is the rule of the day," Yale said, and his dark eyes were cold, flicking from one face to the next.

"He going to need a defense fund?" I asked and the table went quiet and grim.

"Probably." Yale nodded.

"Should we start lookin' for a lawyer?" Golden asked and Angel, who was sitting across from his brother, looked grim.

"Can Chrissy take it?" Youngblood asked.

"No, too big of a conflict of interest. She can't take on something like this if she wants to stay employed in the prosecutor's office."

"How sure are we that this is even going to go to trial?" Oz demanded. "I mean, it just happened so –"

"With the current narrative nationwide, the prosecutor's office of Indigo City is *not* trying to seem either corrupt or weak. The fact of the matter is, the boy Driller shot was unarmed and was *not* the boy that shot Driller."

"Driller is not a racist ass motherfucker," Oz declared.

"No, he is not," Skids said with a sigh.

"He's really in a lot of trouble, isn't he?" Blaze asked, dismayed.

"We won't know for a bit, but yeah… I think worst-case scenario is in play here." Yale shook his head with a sigh.

"Hey!"

Something crashed out in the bar and we all turned our heads.

"God fucking damn it," Skids growled and got up. The rest of us getting up with him. "This ain't that kind of a place and tonight is *not* the night."

I was at the back of the line so I didn't see what was up, but gathered quickly it was a dude that'd had too much and it was time for him to fucking go.

I looked for Saylor and saw her out the front window, to the side of the front door, singing and playing her heart out.

The guy who'd started the ruckus had backed into Coco who was trying to mop up her tray of drinks and broken glass as the dude kept trying to drunkenly help and apologize.

"That's *enough*, my dude. You've got to go!" Golden barked at him and the guy stood up, looking at my brother blearily with his hands up.

"Awright! You ain't gotta be such a dick about it." He shuffled off in the direction of the front door mumbling and we all stood by watching to see what he would do or where he would go and I swear to God, it was the biggest fucking mistake of my life.

He pushed through the door outside and wobbled slightly on his feet. I started forward when he turned to Saylor and it was like the whole world slowed down to show me my folly in high-definition.

He turned to Saylor and said something, his breath pluming the air, but she didn't stop playing or singing, she simply smiled slightly around her vocals and the guy said something else. He lurched in her direction and I started forward. Golden was in front of me muttering, "God fucking damn it," when the guy cocked back and let fly.

He punched her. He punched her *hard* and I suddenly didn't care who I had to leap over to get to her.

She sprawled back against the glass and slid down it, and I screamed out, "*Angel!*"

We poured out of the bar en masse and Golden and Oz took the motherfucker on, full-on brawling with him and taking him to the ground. My eyes were on Saylor who was lying crumpled against the edge of the building, below the windows, out cold.

"Angel!" I screamed and he was striding for me and Saylor.

"Saylor, baby, come on wake up," I muttered as Angel stopped my hands from reaching for her.

"Hang on, he caught her in the temple, I need to make sure her c-spine isn't compromised."

"Fuck," I whispered.

"Somebody call a bus!" Angel shouted and I turned, Blaze nodding at me, his cell pressed to his ear.

Oz was riding the dude's back holding him in a choke hold while Golden rubbed his jaw.

"I can't fuckin' breathe!" the dude wheezed.

"I don't fuckin' care!" Oz shot back.

"You talkin' ain't 'cha? You can breathe just fine," Golden growled.

"Guys, we need that bus, we need a hospital right now," Angel shouted, and I was back to Saylor. "Help me get this off of her," he demanded, and I went for the strap on her guitar. Backdraft was helping Angel, while I handed her guitar off to Coco who slid her case out of the way and saw to it that it was put away safe.

"What's wrong?" I demanded.

"Head trauma, bad, might be brain swelling."

"Ambulance is on its way, two minutes!" Blaze called out.

I stared helpless as Saylor lay there prone, Angel stabilizing her head, Backdraft taking her vitals and she *just wouldn't wake up.*

"Please, God, let her wake up," I muttered.

"How is she?"

I looked up from where I sat beside her hospital bed, eyes red rimmed as much from lack of sleep as from crying.

"Same, man."

Skids came more fully into the room.

"She'll come out of it, man. Just give it some time."

"She went down *two nights ago*, Chief. I don't know… I just don't know."

I broke down again, I couldn't stop myself. I was beside myself with worry. My club's president came over and stood sentinel, squeezing my shoulder, giving me silent strength and I was grateful for it.

"What's the doctor say?" he asked.

"That her, uh, scans look good. That the swelling is coming down and to just be patient."

"Then that's all you can do, Son."

I nodded, but it was the last thing I wanted to hear. What I wanted to hear was Saylor's voice. What I wanted to see was her open those beautifully mismatched eyes even through the swelling and bruising on one side.

He'd hit her so hard, right in the temple. The emergency doctor had said she was lucky she hadn't broken anything. Her x-rays ruled out a busted orbital socket. Still, there was a lot of bruising, a lot of swelling, and that drunk ass motherfucker was up on a whole host of charges that, frustratingly, would either get plead down or dismissed altogether.

It was times like these it was clear as day just how fundamentally broken the system was.

Driller could go to prison for life for trying to protect these streets and this guy would probably walk with barely a fine for being a menace to them.

Driller killed a kid... even if he didn't mean to. Drunk guy hurt Saylor, and thank God, she's still here. The thoughts did nothing to comfort me. None at all.

"You want me to stay awhile?" Skids asked and I nodded, mutely.

"You got it," he murmured and pulled up a chair of his own next to mine to stand watch with me.

"Wake up, baby," I whispered, silent tears tracking down my cheeks. "Please, wake up."

If she could hear me, feel me smooth her hair lightly back from her forehead, she made no movement to acknowledge it. It killed me, worrying about her. Facing the monstrous thought that this could be it. That there was a possibility that she would never wake up. It was too hard to tell. All the doctors could and would say was that things looked good and she would come to on her own time and I hated that.

I hated that too much was left to chance, and I hated that this had even happened to her. That I had been *right there,* and I'd still failed to protect her.

I hated myself so damn much that she was even here.

24

*S*aylor...

I winced, mouth dry, a foul metallic taste in it and cracked my eyelids. It was dark in the room but there was a bright light coming from somewhere over and behind me. I raised a hand and felt the pull of tape on the back of it, the rub of plastic tubing and I grimaced.

That grimace lessened when that raised hand touched a head of silky soft and familiar hair. I glanced down at my side and was suddenly transfixed by the play of my fingers through the thatch of medium brown hair atop Poe's sleeping head, his face turned away from me.

I groaned quietly, not wanting to wake him up and tried to swallow. I was on oxygen, and I couldn't remember how I got here.

I mean, the last thing I remembered was standing in our garage – we'd been cleaning it out.

What'd happened? How did I end up here? Why did my head hurt?

Had the roof collapsed and beaned me on the head?

So many questions and it felt as though my head was stuffed with cotton and too thick to think through them all. I closed my eyes and just concentrated on the feel of Poe's hair under my hand.

That felt nice, that felt good, and I would take it. I don't think I had ever felt so rough in my life and I'd been through some tight scrapes.

One of my eyes felt thick and I couldn't open it all the way. I hated that. Hated that I didn't know how I got here or what was going on... but I wasn't willing to wake Poe up to find out. Not yet. So, I just contented myself as best I could with the feel of his hair under my hand. I concentrated on the sound of the machines I was hooked up to, which sounded super loud in my ears, right along with my own rushing heartbeat.

God, I feel like shit.

I closed my eyes and tried to rest.

"Hi."

I opened my eyes at the feminine whisper.

"There you are. Hi."

A bubbly little blonde nurse was on my other side where my hand wasn't mutilated by an IV in the back of it. She smiled and placed two fingers against the inside of my wrist.

"Hi," I barely croaked and she smiled bigger.

"I'm Kristina Canaday, and I'm your nurse. Do you know where you are?" she asked.

"Hospital, um. Indigo City?"

"That's right. Can you tell me your name?"

"Saylor Grace Dresden."

"Your date of birth?"

I gave it to her, and her smiles just kept growing with every right answer. The year, the president, the only slight frown came when she asked if I knew how I got here, and I told her I couldn't remember.

"That's normal," she whispered. "I'm going to get the doctor. Your man will be *very* happy to see you. He hasn't left your side since you came in."

"Thank you," I whispered. I'm not surprised. My love for Poe suffusing me with warmth. "Can I have some water?"

"I'll bring you some ice chips. How's your pain?"

"Not good, I have a headache."

"Okay, I'll tell your doctor. I'll be right back."

She breezed out of the room and I gripped Poe's hair gently, glad for the tactile sensation against my hand. Wishing he would wake up but still unwilling to wake him.

A moment later he sucked in a sharp breath and brought his head up slightly and with a final squeeze, I let go of his hair. He sat up carefully and looked over at me and the sight of my eyes open, my careful look, and he sat up fully.

"Saylor, baby, is that you? Are you awake?"

"Of course I'm awake," I uttered and it didn't exactly have the effect I'd expected.

This beautiful strong man of mine crumbled right before my eyes and *cried.*

"I was so worried," he declared, and I tried to smile and reached up my arms wanting him to close the gap and hug me. I needed it. I wanted it. I craved being in his arms like nobody's business.

He came to me and carefully hugged me and practically sobbed into the crook of my neck.

"Shhh, I'm okay," I whispered. "It's alright, I'm okay…"

"I thought I was going to lose you," he gasped into the side of my neck.

"I don't even know why I'm here," I murmured.

"You don't?" he asked, leaning up to look down at me, his warm green eyes traveling over me, head to toe.

"No, did the roof collapse?" I asked.

"The roof?" he asked, confusion traipsing across his face, leaving his expression muddied and confused.

"Yeah, the roof. The roof of the garage. Did it collapse? Did it bonk me on the head? I can't remember –"

"Retrograde amnesia, it's perfectly normal with injuries like yours. Hi, Saylor. I'm Dr. Minarde, how are you feeling?"

Poe turned, stepping aside to reveal a doctor that looked awfully young. He held a clip board with my chart, and Kristina, my nurse, waved from around behind his back.

"My head hurts," I murmured.

"Also to be expected with injuries like yours. Is it alright if I come in and we have a chat?"

"Of course," I murmured. "Can Poe stay?"

"Of course he can."

I had been asleep, or knocked out, or in a coma or whatever for three going on four days. My brain had swelled, although it hadn't bled, and the doctors were fairly confident that I would make a full recovery in time. They said I'd gotten lucky, for how serious a state I had been in, and that I needed to take things easy. Take them slow getting back into them.

I was shocked at first, then the panic, the worry, and the dread set in…

How was I going to pay for all of this?

"Don't worry about that right now," Poe soothed. "Yale is working on some things, and the rest of the club. You've got a family now and we're going to take care of you. *I'm* going to take care of you."

He kissed the temple that wasn't horribly bruised from the sucker punch I had absolutely no memory of and I asked the doctor, "Can I have something to eat? I'm starving."

The doctor broke into a wide grin and said, "That's encouraging. Nurse Canaday will order you something from the cafeteria if you'd like. Stop if you feel nauseous and let her know."

"I will, thank you. How long until I can go home?" I asked.

"I'd like to keep you a day or two for observation and get at least one more set of scans," the doctor said, and Poe was nodding beside me. I sighed inwardly and deflated a little. I just wanted to be out of here – I didn't like that I had already apparently been here for so long.

"Thank you, doctor," I murmured and with a nod, he departed.

"You want to have a look at the menu?" the nurse asked.

"Sure." I nodded and stopped partway through the motion. Too soon. I guess maybe staying here a little longer was a good idea. I looked over the menu and ordered some dinner and pretty soon I was settled back down, and it was just me and Poe again.

"Have you been to work?" I asked when Kristina had left, and he shook his head.

"I never take sick time, so I've got plenty. They know what's going on and a bunch of the guys in my precinct are happy for the overtime. I do need to get back to it in the next couple of days, though."

"Knock, knock!" a deep masculine voice called out from the front of the room. I was by the window, the curtain pulled between my bed and the next, which was empty.

"Yeah, we're good!" Poe called back softly.

Driller appeared around the curtain with a big bouquet of flowers wrapped in white butcher paper and I smiled. They reminded me of the big bouquets you could get at Pike's Place Market back in Seattle. How I loved the flower sellers there, the women in their quilted jackets with their mandarin collars, expertly weaving individual blooms, spinning and adding, fleshing out each bouquet into a riot of color and foliage.

The bouquet that Driller handed down to me was no exception and I carefully hugged it to me and breathed in, hoping to catch a sweet scent from some of the blossoms it contained.

"From Lys' flower shop and the greenhouses Everleigh works with her bees. Everybody's worried about you, kid."

I snorted and said, "I'm not a kid and –" I stopped, something coming back to me. "And what about you? I remember now, we left the garage because you got some texts that Driller was hurt or in trouble." I directed the last at Poe.

Driller grimaced. "Deep bruising, a cracked rib or two, nothing that won't heal. As for trouble? I'm in plenty of that… but just how much remains yet to be seen." My face crumbled into lines of sympathy while Driller's crumbled around the edges with his rapidly crumbling hope for his situation.

"What brings you here?" Poe asked, taking the big vase from Driller's other hand. A simple glass cylinder.

"Flower delivery and I figured since I'm on administrative leave, I could hang with Saylor Grace while you got your ass back to work – or did you forget you got a mortgage now?"

"Trust me, I ain't forget shit," Poe declared and I smiled to myself. He sounded like Oz just then.

"Alright, then."

"What time is it?" I asked softly.

"About time for him to head on in if he's going on tonight's tour," Driller answered.

Poe nodded. "They're expecting me," he said and didn't sound happy about it. He filled the vase at the sink and turned back holding out his hands for my flowers. I passed them to Driller who passed them to Poe.

"Thanks, man."

"No problem," Driller said. "You know how long until they spring you?" he asked me.

"A couple more days, maybe? They weren't super clear. They want me to do more scans."

"Cool, cool. What're we watching?" he asked and took Poe's seat and turned on my television.

"Whatever you can get on bad hospital TV," I answered.

He surfed channels while Poe arranged my flowers for me and said, "I hate leaving."

"I know, but you have to, I'm sorry I slept so long."

"Technically, you were in a coma," Driller supplied, and I made a face.

Poe arranged my flowers beautifully and set them in my window. I had a good view out of it, over the tops of some buildings and out over the bay, the winking lights of the Bay Bridge soothing to the soul as the water lapped at the supports far below them.

Poe both did and did not rush out of there to get to work and I found myself wishing I had woken up just a day earlier. Still, I understood. He'd already taken almost three days off and he'd just bought a house for us.

I worried now. I mean, we were supposed to start moving this week, we needed to be out of the apartment before the first, and now I was in here and nothing was getting packed and –

"Hey."

I turned my head slowly and looked at Driller who gently grasped my IV'ed hand and gave it a light squeeze.

"Stop worrying about it."

"About what?" I asked, trying to play innocent.

"I don't know what – but whatever it is, stop it, okay? Money, moving, the new house, whatever – just stop worrying about it. We've got you." He jiggled my hand back and forth lightly.

"It's going to be okay, isn't it?" I asked a little stunned when the realization hit me.

"What's going on with you, what's going on with me, it's all going to be fine. Maybe not right away, but in the end? Whatever is supposed to happen is going to happen. So we just both need to relax and heal up."

I nodded carefully and my nurse, Kristina, breezed in and gave a little startled 'Oh!' when she saw Driller who was looking a little broody which made him super, duper, hot to look at.

I still missed Poe with a fierce ache in the center of my chest, though.

"Poe had to head to work," I said softly. "This is Driller."

Driller gave Kristina a nod and sat back so she could put my tray of food on the rolling table cart thing over my lap.

I used the buttons on the bed railing to slowly sit up and sighed in discomfort of the catheter they had in me.

"We can get that out in a little while, after we assess your fall risk."

"Thank you," I said softly, understanding that if I cooperated, I would get out of here faster.

"You just give me the all clear when you're ready to send out the text that you're awake. The girls all want to come see you," Driller said as I took my first hesitant bite of chicken soup.

"You can tell everybody," I said. "I'd feel bad if you didn't."

"You sure now?"

"I'm sure."

He smiled and said, "Okay, hold on to your butt, mass text going out now."

I smiled and asked, "Seriously, how are *you* doing?"

His face became guarded and he answered, "I thought the kid was the one who shot me. Same height, same build, both wearing hoodies that were nearly identical in color... I feel like shit, Saylor. I feel guilty as hell – and I'm scared... but I'll take whatever is coming at me."

I reached out and took his hand and gave it a reassuring squeeze.

"You didn't do anything wrong," I whispered with conviction.

He swallowed hard and nodded, but said, "Yeah, but I feel like I did."

"Me too."

"All you did was stand on the corner singing your songs," he said.

"I can't remember, though... and I guess I've always lowkey felt like I was doing something wrong. I mean... I'm a homeless girl from a poor family. Mom murdered, dad committed suicide, grandma died of cancer, granddad died of a heart attack. Maybe this is a sign not to go thinking I should get above my station in life. I don't know."

Driller snorted indelicately and snickered saying, "Or maybe whatever demon is on your back is losing hold and this was its last-ditch effort to hold on. I don't think you're rising above your station, girl. I think you're rising to be who you were meant to be from the get-go despite life trying to hold you down."

He sighed and continued, "Poe is a good man that deserves good things, and honestly in all the time I've known him? You're the best thing that's ever happened to him. He loves you. You love him. This is just one more bump in the road called life and you're both going to get through just fine."

"Well, same to you, then."

"Nah." He shook his head. "Not the same thing at all."

I considered him and finally said, "Agree to disagree."

He snorted and gave a nod. "Eat your soup."

25

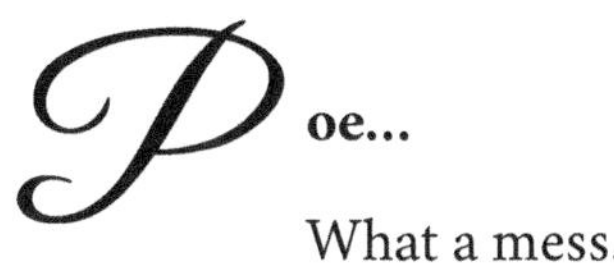oe…

What a mess.

We only had 'X' amount of days to get shit done and ready at the new house to move our shit from the apartment and those days were dwindling fast. Still, Saylor was in the hospital, but she was getting out today.

We should have been painting in the new place and packing up the old place but none of it had gotten done with the sudden emergency. Now I only had two days off, she was still on the injured roster, and the next set of days off I had was the move.

I went to the hospital when I got off work until she kicked me out to go get some real sleep. Then I came back in the morning for an hour or two before rushing back to work. I didn't give myself time for anything else… not even church, which was fine. The guys all gave me a pass and I technically didn't need to be at *every* meeting. It wasn't how we were set up.

I was definitely feeling the crunch and was cursing myself for going on autopilot through the crisis. Now, now we would be getting back on track, though. Saylor was coming home.

I pulled on my jacket and cut just as Blaze knocked on my door twice and tried it. I had it locked, out of habit since Saylor had come to live with me, and so I called out, "Just a sec!" I heard some feminine giggles out there with him and frowned as I unlatched the door.

"Whoa, what're you guys doing here?" Ally, Everleigh, Claire, and Coco were on my front step with a harried looking Blaze.

"Saylor sent us!" Coco quipped, jangling Saylor's keys.

"We're here to pack," Claire said with a wink. Everleigh nodded enthusiastically while Ally looked like she was trying to figure out what she could say that would get her into enough trouble and kinky fuckery with Yale.

I felt my eyebrows go up and shook my head.

"Where there's a will there's a way with that woman," I said and nodded, holding the door open wider for the girls to file past.

They'd even brought boxes. Claire and Everleigh each having a flattened stack under an arm. Ally with a bag of packing tape on her wrist.

"You drive them?" I asked Blaze.

"Nope, they got here all on their own."

I laughed and said, "Okay, let's go get my woman. You ladies try to stay out of trouble, now." Coco stopped in front of me and held out Saylor's granddad's guitar in its case. She'd held onto it, had taken it upstairs to her and Skids' place during the scuffle.

"You're a lifesaver!" I declared and took it from her.

"I know she would die if you didn't bring it, I'm not sure if it didn't get damaged. I don't know anything about guitars. Might want to have her look. If it did get hurt, I looked up some repair shops in the city."

"They exist?" Blaze asked impressed. I was right there with him. I mean, this *was* a disposable society.

Coco rolled her eyes and said, "They exist but the guys sounded way more interested in selling me a new one – they admitted to doing repairs, though."

"I could kiss you for going the extra mile."

"I know how heartbroken she would be," she said, and her face crumbled into lines of empathy.

"Thank you," I said, hefting the guitar.

"Let's blaze," I told my best friend.

"Har, har, har," he shot back, unamused.

"I thought it was funny," I said with a shrug.

We went out and shut the door on my too-crowded place full of feminine chatter and the sounds of cardboard boxes being assembled.

"Hey, yo!" I looked over the railing down on Youngblood and Driller, both their pickups pulled up to the curb. "You wanna get this door open?" Driller called up.

"While they're in there packing up, we can start loading up what's in your storage," Youngblood called.

"You guys fuckin' serious right now?" I demanded.

"If you're gonna bring your woman home, you might as well bring her *home*," Skids called up, jumping out the passenger side of Youngblood's ride.

"We got you, brother. Go get her. Take Lys's grocery getter, Blaze you can stay here with your truck. Just more likely to get it in one load." Golden and Angel were walking up the street, G. jangling a set of keys at me.

"I am *not* gonna argue," I declared, excitement taking hold.

"We'll meet you at the new place, get you set up in no time. You ain't got that much shit," Blaze said.

"You knew about this?" I asked. He held his hands open and tilted his head.

It was his idea.

"Bro, I owe you so big." I clapped my hand in his and pulled him into a hard hug.

"Move it or lose it. Go spring your woman before they wrack up more charges to your bill."

I laughed some and nodded. "Fucking hospitals, man."

"Fucking hospitals," he agreed.

I jogged down the steps, passed off my garage door key and the rest of my ring to Golden and took the offered key to Lys' car.

"We'll see you over there, man. Shouldn't be more than a couple hours at most. The rest of us are over there cleaning and getting primer on some walls."

"Dude, I owe you like so fuckin' big," I declared.

"You don't owe us shit. You're family. This is how we do," Skids said.

"Yeah, well, I won't forget it!" I called out, already on my way up the sidewalk to find Lys' car and to go get Saylor.

The parking garage under Trinity General was a hot mess, and by the time I made it to Saylor's room, she was dressed and sitting on the edge of the bed almost ready to go, just waiting on her discharge papers. Her eyes lit up at the sight of her granddad's guitar case in my hands but when she looked at me, she turned absolutely luminous. Radiant in a way that left me no doubt – she was the one for me.

Forever and ever, the woman for me.

I went to her and bent down, kissing her carefully but soundly.

"Hey, stranger," she whispered against my mouth.

"You're kind of incredible," I whispered back and she smiled so bright.

"Oh, yeah? How's that?" she asked.

"You know damn well what I mean."

"I take it the girls showed up to make up for lost time on the packing?"

"And the guys," I said. "They're moving our shit as we speak."

"Excellent!" she cried delighted.

I laughed.

"How much longer until I can spring you?"

"Just waiting on the paperwork."

"Cool. You wanna check this out while we wait? Make sure no harm was done?"

"Oh, shit. You think it might have broken?"

"If it did, there's nothing to worry about. Coco already scoped out the city's repair shops and we'll get it in right away."

She teared up as she set the case on the bed.

"You haven't even looked at it!" I cried, chuckling softly.

"Okay, unlike *you* it's been a minute since I've had anyone looking out for me like you do for me and like the rest of your club does."

"Hey." I touched the side of her face and she looked up at me. "They're your club too, now, baby. We've got you."

She smiled and took a deep slow breath and let it out just as measured and slow.

"Okay, moment of truth." She unlatched the case and threw back the lid, carefully running her fingertips over the instrument that lay inside.

"Well?" I asked.

She lifted it from its ragged velvet and turned it over in her hands. Examining the neck, the frets, the strings, and the tuning pegs. She nodded and let out a rushed breath of relief.

"It looks okay."

I felt my own face crack into a wide and relieved grin and gave a nod.

"You know you're not allowed to do anything when we get home," I said.

"What? How fair is that?" she demanded.

"Until I know you're fit for duty, you're on the injured list," I declared.

"Are you kidding me?" she scoffed. "We have so much to get done to make our house a home!"

"And you can start by saying 'yes.'" I said, and I don't know what made me say it except that it felt right, and I needed to.

"Yes to what?" she asked curiously, cocking her head gently to one side, her beautifully mismatched eyes roving my face, her lips curled into a gentle smile.

"Will you marry me?" I asked evenly.

Her smile intensified and she raised an eyebrow.

"I don't have a ring, yet. And if it's alright with you, I wouldn't mind re-doing this in front of the guys with the ring, and you know, a bunch of fanfare and all of that, but right now..." I got down on one knee and took her hands into mine.

"I really need you to do me the honor of making me whole. Say 'yes' and let me make you the happiest woman to ever live. Let me be your family now."

Tears brimmed along her lower lashes and she nodded. "Yes," she said on a little broken sob and I carefully, got off my knee and stood, gathering her to me and hugging her firmly but gently.

She clung to me back, her granddad's guitar laid haphazardly in its case, her small form sheltered by my larger one.

"I love you," I whispered into her hair and she sniffled.

"I love you, too," came muffled from my chest.

That was how her nurse found us, both clinging to each other. Both the happiest we could be given the circumstances of her hospital stay.

We would take things one day at a time from here on out, but together.

26

*S*aylor...

There was cheering when Poe escorted me through our front door. God. That was still so surreal… saying *our* door. My smile was brittle, and I felt like I was on the brink of another spate of happy tears. All of it just so overwhelming and *real* and so *new* and *God I wish my granddad could see me now…* I thought.

"Welcome home!" Ellie crowed, lowering her paint roller from the wall.

"Oh, so they got the professional artist slinging paint on the walls, huh?" I asked, laughing, going in for the hug.

"Well, primer, but yeah," she said.

"God is *everybody* in on this?" Poe asked.

"Yup," Narcos replied.

We'd seen Backdraft out back at the garage, up on a ladder with a nail gun, tacking tar paper to a fresh sheet of plywood on the roof.

"About time you got here," Yale said and Poe laughed.

"Need a handle to get up high, huh?" Poe asked and Yale glared at him.

"Fuck you."

"What can I do?" I asked and though my head throbbed a little, I otherwise felt okay and wanted to do something.

"Nothing," Poe declared, taking off his jacket and motorcycle vest which I'd handed him in the little driveway. He wouldn't wear it in a car. He always draped it across my lap.

"Oh, come on! I'd like to do *something*."

"Play us a song, then," Yale said.

I smiled and said, "Now that I can do."

I went and sat on the stairs with my granddad's guitar, it was the most out of the way place I could be while they painted primer up and down the living room walls and coated the ceiling with it.

I strummed a few experimental notes and satisfied I was in tune, began to play.

When we met you were my sweet
Said there's nothing that could hold you back from me.
Talked all day and we dreamed all night
But I never saw the truth until the morning light

You promised me your love.
And I walked miles and miles and miles and miles and miles...

To find that slamming door
Babe I should have seen it coming
I've been here before
I come close and you start gunning
Well Cupid he don't shoot no bow
He's got an Mk 48

Left me standing on your stairs
You called me "honey, baby, sugar" now you don't care
I spit on the ground, I cussed your name
And if there's a God I prayed to him that you would go up in flames

You tossed me off that cliff
After I drove miles and miles and miles and miles and miles...

To find that slamming door
Babe I should have seen it coming
I've been here before
I come close and you start gunning
Well Cupid he don't shoot no bow
He's got an Mk 48

Well I fell down hard I broke apart
But there's no better lesson 'bout a man like you
Than crawling in the streets looking for the pieces of my
Broken heart...

So you'd better hide behind that slamming door
And pray you never see me coming
I've been here before
So you'd better start to running
I'm not a girl in ribbons and bows
I've got an Mk 48

A rowdy round of applause and whistling went up and I laughed. It felt good to sing and to play again after days of not being able to.

It was cold in here, the doors and windows open to vent the primer fumes. I continued to play and intermittently sang, but my head still throbbed so I honestly didn't want to overdo it. So while I kept playing, I quit with the singing pretty soon after that first song.

The atmosphere was light and animated, as our little house came together. Once the primer job was done downstairs, they moved upstairs and when the boxes arrived, we parceled them into one room, the better bathroom got set up and the bed was set up in the middle of the living room until we could finish one of the bedrooms.

The whole thing ended in laughter, traded stories, talk of what kinds of furniture we would be looking at when and pizza on paper plates and soda out of plastic cups.

It was a whirlwind of activity, and once the last person had left, it was just me and Poe in our little house, his bike tucked safely in the little freshly roofed garage.

"Wow," I said with a little laughter.

"Yeah, going to have to find the boxes with the bedding," he said laughing.

"Shit, oh no!" I covered my mouth with my hands.

He laughed nodding and said, "I'll go look. You stay down here."

"I'd like to help," I said, and he looked me over from the bottom step where I sat on the edge of the bed.

"How's your head?" he asked gently.

"A little throbby but otherwise, okay."

"You take anything for it?" he asked.

"No," I laughed a little. "I didn't think to."

"They gave you that prescription Tylenol shit, where is it?" he asked, stepping down and coming back to me.

"Um, side pocket of my backpack."

"Let me get it for you, babe." I smiled and he got me a pill and some more soda for my cup. I took it and smiled up at him.

"Tired?" he asked softly.

I nodded slightly.

"Yeah."

"Me too, it was a big day."

"I'm still more than a little boggled that we're *moved*. I mean, just like that!"

"Just like that," he agreed, grinning down at me. He brought his mouth to mine in a gentle kiss and I smiled against his mouth, kissing him back.

"I've slept like shit without you," he whispered.

"They kept waking me up to give me a sleeping pill," I whined, pouting out my bottom lip. He laughed.

"Sounds like every hospital ever known anywhere."

"Right?" I asked and laughed slightly.

He sighed happily.

"I can't wait to marry you," he said.

"Me either."

"Do you ever think that this is crazy?" he asked and sat down next to me. "Like, do you ever doubt that I'm sincere in any way?"

I searched his face, his beautiful green eyes and shook my head slightly.

"No."

"Sometimes I do, but it all feels just so *right* and for, I think, the first time in my life ever *I don't care* what other people think. There is something just so beautiful, so freeing about knowing you." He traced some of my hair behind my ear. "Something about being with you is better than any rush I've ever gotten flying down the highway. I just don't know how to put it into words how much I love you. How much I love being with you."

"You're all I've ever wanted," I whispered, tearing up. "Somebody to love. Somebody to love *me*… a home… a real life. *Roots.*"

"I give you roots, you give me wings," he muttered and closed the distance between us again with a kiss that sealed both of our fates.

This was the stuff of fairy tales, of legends, true love in action, and as he kissed me, laying me back on the bare mattress, the glimmer of magic that was the love between us warmed us in the cold house and sent a shimmer of delight over our skins.

"Mm, stop, let's make the bed," I murmured.

"I need you so bad, right now, baby –"

"I know, I need you too, but when we're done, are we really going to want to move?" I giggled and he chuckled back.

"Fair. Point to you, my love."

"God, I hope they labeled those boxes clearly."

"Me, too!"

We got up and went upstairs and into the room full of boxes. It was a pain in the ass, finding the ones we were looking for, but we did and then found the pillows and comforter wrapped in heavy trash bags to keep them clean.

"Do we need to find clothes?" I asked.

"We might as well. We also better find towels."

"Oh, shower! Good point. I feel gross after so many days without one."

"Want to do that first?" he asked as we sorted through things looking for fresh towels.

"God, that's a tough decision."

"How about take a bath with me," he said.

"Oh, shit! We have a bathtub now!"

"Yes we do!"

"I am so down," I said and he seemed well pleased with the decision.

I found my box with my three-wick candles that I'd gotten on sale and kept for the eventuality that I would ever have a home of my own. These were the ridiculously expensive candles from that bath shop that only held a sale once a year. I got mine for like ten dollars apiece, but even ten dollars at the time was cringe-worthy pricey.

It meant something to me to open one and light it now. On our first night in our new home.

We made the bed first and I lit one of the candles downstairs in the middle of the empty floor where it was safe from catching anything else. The Primer was mostly dry, the fumes damped down by a lot, and Poe had said he was sure it would be alright.

I took a second one up to the bathroom with us and set it on the back of the toilet, the warm golden glow overpowered by the naked bulbs aglow above the sink for now while the tub started to fill and gently steam.

Poe got in before me, and I shut out the light, relief flooding in at the muted glow of candlelight versus the harsh electric.

"Come here," he murmured and held out a hand to me to help me down into the tub. I got in, between his legs, carefully leaning back into his warmth, the water rising quickly at our displacement.

I hummed out in happiness as his arms went around me and he laughingly shut off the tap with his foot before we could overflow.

The sudden silence was soothing as he held me close and kissed the back of my shoulder and along the side of my neck.

"I missed you so much," he murmured.

"Oh, yeah? What'd you miss the most?" I asked.

"Hmm, tough call. Coming home to you, holding you, telling you about my shift and falling asleep with you in my arms… I mean it. I slept like shit while you were gone. It just wasn't the same."

"I'm so sorry," I whispered softly. "I seriously wish I could remember. I mean, I don't remember a thing past closing up the garage."

"There is absolutely nothing you need to be sorry for, baby. If anybody needs to be sorry it should be me for not getting to you soon enough."

"You had no way to know from what everyone else said."

"Yeah, no, I know… it's just… fuck. I wish I could have gotten to you in time."

I cuddled back into him and sighed. "It was worth the headache," I joked and he laughed slightly.

"I was so scared I'd lost you," he said after a long silence and we both sobered rather quickly.

"I'm here," I whispered, and he held me so tight, his lips pressed against the side of my neck as he breathed me in.

"You smell like a hospital, your hair… sit up for me."

I obeyed, trusting him implicitly, hugging my knees as he dipped one of the plastic cups from downstairs into the water and brought it up to douse my hair.

He lovingly, reverently, washed me. Starting with my hair which he carefully shampooed and rinsed, careful of my eyes, making sure he got every bit of soap out of my strands. Gently detangling them, before moving on with a washcloth to scrub my body.

I moaned softly, tipping my head back against his shoulder as he dragged the warm, wet, soapy cloth along my skin slowly in a tantalizing and thoroughly erotic fashion that drove me deep into a submissive headspace.

I wanted so badly to cede control, to lay myself in his hands and trust him implicitly that he would take care of me and for the first time in my life, I actually *did.* I trusted him completely enough to just *let go* and it was a wonderful feeling.

He washed my body as carefully and completely as he washed my hair and I was done in by him. Relaxing totally against his body, closing my eyes and dipping into an almost meditative state as he slid a hand down between my breasts, nipples pebbled hard in the cooler air that kissed them from above the waterline. He dipped that hand between my legs, and I stiffened against him.

"Relax," he breathed against my ear. "You're safe, you're all good. I've got you, baby… Just relax."

I relaxed, marginally, incrementally, and listened as he soothed me. He knew. He knew everything about me. What bothered me; what didn't. What brought up the ghosts of old memories past, and what laid them to rest. He was determined to right the wrongs of my beginnings and to make me feel good if only I'd let him and God, yes, how I wanted him to.

I lay back against his hard chest and closed my eyes, his other arm crossing over me, holding me close as the hand below the waterline teased at my pussy, sliding firm but gentle fingertips against its lips, parting them, a finger delving inside me causing my hips to jerk, the heel of his hand working a delicious friction against my clit, working me up slowly into a shivering mass of want and need.

The water began to grow cooler against my heating skin, and it lent another delicious contrast in sensations as Poe worked tirelessly but methodically to bring me to orgasm against his body.

I moaned, helpless in his arms, breath quickening; silver sparks molten and alive traveling through nerve endings I hadn't known existed.

The water made a musical sound against the edge of the tub as I jerked in his grasp, slowly coming down from the clouds to land gently back in his arms where he both soothed me and praised me essentially for an orgasm well done.

I don't know what the appeal was, but I glowed from not just his touch but his praise, but damned if the water hadn't started to grow cold and double damn if I didn't want *more.* This little orgasm was more like a preview of coming attractions and I wanted him so badly back downstairs and in our bed, I almost couldn't stand it.

I wanted him over me, inside of me, stroking deep, pressing me back into the bed. I wanted to feel loved and safe, caged in the unimaginable strength of his arms. He felt invincible to me when we were like that, and I so loved the illusion deeply, with everything that I was and everything that we could be when we spiraled high and higher, drunk off each other and our love.

"Come on, baby. Careful now, but up you go."

He helped me stand when I was ready, my legs still trembling finely as I stepped carefully out of the tub onto the spare towel he laid on the floor before we got in. When he was sure, he let go of my hand and got up after me, stepping out and taking the towel from my hands as I unfurled it to wrap it around me and to rub me briskly through the cloth, drying me.

"You take such good care of me," I whispered, feeling absolutely spoiled by this man and he grinned, bringing his mouth to mine to kiss me.

"That's the whole point," he said. "You're long overdue."

I smiled and brought up his towel and tried to do the same for him, but he would have none of it.

He dried himself quickly and wrapped the towel around his lean hips, tucking the corner to secure it, his erection tenting it comically in the front.

I did likewise, tucking the towel I held around me, securing the corner in my armpit before taking his hand, blowing out the candle up here, and letting him lead me downstairs.

"We have a lot to figure out about this place," he said quietly.

"The bedrooms up here are fine, they just need paint."

"Yeah," he agreed. "What colors, though? And which wall are you going to slather in your crafting herpes?"

I snorted and laughed and shaking my head said, "I just want an accent wall and I don't even know which color glitter yet."

"Guess we're taking a ride to the edge of the city and the hardware store tomorrow."

"Do you think we can get the paint we want delivered?"

"I think so," he said as he pulled back the blankets on our bed.

I shivered and he pulled the corner of my towel, letting it drop to the hardwood flooring that was somewhat desperately in the need of a refinish but at the same time, I liked its old and worn appearance. I felt it lent it character. Another thing we would have to discuss. Refinishing would require equipment we didn't have and *a lot* of sawdust.

"Your mind is going a mile a minute now, isn't it?" he asked, dropping his own towel and sliding into bed next to me.

Dropping the blankets down over us severed the chill of the ambient air and we quickly warmed beneath the covers.

"It is," I agreed, and he stroked a hand over my body, a gentle caress, a loving touch and I hummed in appreciation, snuggling closer.

"It's all going to be here tomorrow when we wake up," he murmured.

"Yeah," I whispered and we naturally just sort of fell into each other, kissing softly, lips touching, tongues mingling, the temperature rising to a pleasant warmth as he rolled us, him on top, me on my back, between the sheets.

I moaned softly into his mouth and he groaned back, and I loved the sound.

"Tomorrow," he whispered against my skin, pulling the blankets over his head, kissing along the side of my neck, my shoulder, over my collarbone.

"Mm-mm! Now, right now," I whispered and giggled.

"Got better things to be doing right now," he growled against my skin.

"Like what?" I asked breathy, gasping as he kissed a nipple.

"Like you," he answered before taking it into the wet heat of his mouth, his teeth careful but sharp as he grasped it between them, tugging it lightly, sending waves of arousing sensation through me.

"Okay, you win. Not going to argue," I whispered quickly, suddenly unable to catch my breath.

"That's what I thought," he said with a dark little chuckle and *oh damn*, I was nearly undone.

*P*oe...

Her skin was soft as silk beneath my lips, her breathing in a wonderfully deep cadence as I teased her into a deep state of arousal. I kissed my way down her body, teasing her with my lips, letting my warm breath fan along her ribs, my fingertips trailing after. Her little pants and moans that followed each new sensation driving me nuts in all the right ways.

"Jeremy, please," she whimpered and how could I ever deny a plea like that?

"Please what?" I teased lightly.

"Come up here and kiss me," she begged.

I kissed my way slowly back up her body and she shuddered beneath me, spreading her legs, locking her ankles behind my back the higher I climbed up her body.

I laughed as she pulled me into her, my cock slipping against her pussy which was so wet with her arousal and I smiled, rocking against her, but not penetrating her. Not yet.

"Jeremy Poe!" she chastised, and I chuckled deeply as I licked and kissed the side of her neck. Teasing that spot that made her gasp, that sent her hips rocking against mine. The delicious friction of her velvet pussy lips against my shaft edging me on.

I moaned and kissed her deeply. She kissed me back, and I took over thrusting, sliding myself against her, our bodies finding a sync that sent us both into this slide of pleasure that stopped time, or at least severely slowed it to a mere crawl.

I worked my hips, my body against hers, just sort of naturally seeking purchase. My cock finding her opening naturally before I sank slowly inside. God, her walls were warm, tight, slick, and felt so good where they pressed around me, gripping me, pulling me deeper into her.

"Shit, baby, slow down. I'm not ready," I hissed between gritted teeth and her deep and sultry moan did nothing to help keep me in check. I might not have a choice. It's not like a man could truly stop himself from coming. Sometimes a dude's body just went on its own fucking program.

The way she held me, the way she buried her hands in my hair, the way she locked her ankles behind my back, the way she *moved*, writhing beneath me in this sensual dance of lust and desire. It was hard as fuck holding off.

Her pussy pressed around me, drawing me deeper, her walls soft and yet with this iron grip. God, she felt so good. Feminine and soft with this edge of dangerous steel, a core of iron, a true partner in everything.

She was tough yet yielding, and I loved the unique dichotomy.

"Oh, fuck! Baby!"

I struggled to hold back, to make her come first, but I couldn't. Not this time. I squeezed my eyes shut, my whole body getting involved, my balls tingling then tightening up, white sparks flooding my vision as colors exploded behind my eyelids and I lost the fight, spilling hot and ready, deep inside of my woman as she cried out and arched beneath me, her body pressing tight to mine.

Flashbulbs went off behind my eyelids, as I cried out and collapsed on top of her, barely holding myself up enough to not crush her into the mattress. Not like she cared, with her hands on my back, pulling me down on top of her, cuddling into me like she was. If she were a cat, she would purr, her pussy certainly doing so, throbbing with little aftershocks, her orgasm nearly perfectly timed with my own.

God that was nice.

A perfect circle, her and me, me into her.

"God, I love you," she whimpered and held me close and I don't think I had ever felt so close to perfect in my life.

"The bedroom?" I tried and she smiled and laughed lightly.

"You'd be okay with a sparkly wall in the bedroom?" she asked me.

"Why not? Maybe behind the bed, silver glitter like star spangle or something. Could be nice."

She hummed and pressed tighter to my side, snuggling her head against my shoulder, her fingertips walking over my abs beneath the blanket.

"That sounds really nice, actually."

"Better than the bathroom," I said.

We were cuddled close, the candle burning in the middle of what would be the dining room giving just enough light to cast shadows and to beat back the dark for my woman.

"You'd really be okay with a great big glittering wall in our bedroom?" she asked softly and I smiled.

"Would it make you happy?" I asked.

"Yes." She laughed lightly, more of a light giggle, like a babbling brook.

"Then yeah, because I would do anything and then some to make you happy."

"Yeah?" she asked looking up at me.

"Mm-hm. You glow when you're happy," I murmured. "Like the light of the moon."

She laughed outright then, and I laughed too.

"What?" I demanded.

"You, being all romantic."

"You rather I not?"

"I didn't say that. I guess I'm just not used to it is all, it's still so new."

"Ahh, you best get used to it," I murmured and kissed her forehead. Her eyes drifted shut, her eyelashes tickling my chest in a butterfly kiss which is how I knew.

"I never dreamed in a million years that this could be my life," she confessed.

"You know what? Me either."

"I'm so happy."

"Me too."

"I'm almost scared to be this happy, you know?"

"Why d'you say that?" I asked.

"Feels like anytime something good happens to me, something bad is sure to follow."

"Oh, baby... that's just life. Good, bad, indifferent," I murmured, stroking her absently.

She was silent for so long, but I knew she wasn't asleep yet. I smiled softly in the dark and declared, "Doesn't matter. Good, bad, indifferent… I'm here, in it, with you until the bitter end."

She pushed herself up and looked down at me, the soft play of candlelight making her luminous.

"I believe you," she whispered and smiled at me.

"You better, because I'll never lie to you. Not about the big things, and this is one of the biggest."

"What would you lie about?" she asked frowning, her smile ruining it.

I grinned. "I might lie to get you someplace to surprise you."

"That's a *surprise* though!" she cried. "Not the same thing at all."

"I don't know, but how about this… the next time one comes up, I promise to tell you."

"Oh, you promise to tell me you lied to me!" she laughed then, and I swear I smiled so big the grin would like to split my face.

"Should sleep, babe. We got a big day tomorrow."

"Hmm… I suppose we do. Wait, what are we doing?"

"Hopefully, getting our bedroom done upstairs. All it needs is paint, now."

"Yeah," she whispered dreamily. "Paint, furniture, and us."

"Mm-hm."

Sounded just about right.

We slept hard, but we didn't get to sleep late. We woke to Blaze pounding on the door raising a fuss, ready to help us take on the day.

"I thought you had work today," I said and he shrugged.

"Called off, took a mental health day or whatever. Figured you'd need to hit the hardware store and you needed the truck."

"Seriously?" I laughed and shook my head.

"Well fuck you, too, buddy! See if I come help out of the goodness of my heart again."

"Yeah, well you're in for it now. Saylor wants her glitter wall in the bedroom, so you know what that means…"

"Oh, shit – is it too late to bounce?" he asked.

"Yup!" she called down from upstairs as I sat in bed, a blanket wrapped around my waist which is how I answered the door seeing as our clothes were all upstairs.

"Shit," Blaze swore softly. "Guess we better get to it."

"Yup."

I left him with my girl downstairs and went and rooted through some shit to find some clothes I didn't give a fuck about, seeing as we would be painting today.

At the hardware store, I stopped Blaze on the paint aisle, Saylor chatting amicably with the hardware store clerk that was mixing a misty blue-gray color for the rest of the bedroom to make her silver accent wall really pop.

"Dude, I need your help at some point."

"With what?" he asked, perusing the rollers and brushes, snatching an edging tool off the shelf and flipping it into the cart.

"Picking a ring. I asked Saylor to marry me in the hospital yesterday and she said 'yes' but I told her I wanted to find a proper ring and ask in front of the guys. I don't want everybody feeling like I cut them out –"

"You're fucking serious!" he whisper-shouted harshly and I thought I was fucked. That I'd upset him or something for a second there – but not Blaze.

He jerked his elbow back and let out an excited "Yes!" then lunged at me to hug me all fierce. We both looked over to Saylor and the clerk looking at us funny, Saylor's eyes sparkling with glee as she laughed lightly and went back to talking to the clerk like everything was normal, ordinary, and for us I guess it was.

"Hell yeah, I'll go ring shopping with you, bro. Just name the date and time and tell me where we're going."

"I'd also really love it if you wouldn't spill to the rest of the club and if you would be my best man."

"Bro! You got it, man. Whatever you want, whatever you need, I'm here for you. You know that."

I felt a weight come off my shoulders that I hadn't realized was resting on it.

"Cool. Let's get this shit and get out of here. I'm hoping to get at least this one room done by tonight."

"Let's do it," Blaze agreed, and we wheeled our shopping cart full of the goods back out to the main paint center to load up on the cans of paint for the bedroom.

I didn't even bat an eye at the bill, which was way big, to accommodate the fucking glitter paint which was definitely the lion's share of it. I did accept Saylor's contribution of her meager earnings to help cover it. Not because I wanted or needed her to, but because she seemed to need to and I got it. I really did. She wanted this to be as much of a partnership as possible. Not just me paying for everything and her just existing.

I *did* insist she take it easy, even though she insisted she was fine. And even though she said she didn't need one, I talked her into taking one of her beefed-up Tylenol prescription pills before any pain could start.

I loved her, and I wanted what was best for her and for her to be comfortable.

We went back to the house, relocated some drop cloths to the bedroom we decided would be the master – although *both* bedrooms seemed to be of an equal size up here, and we got to work.

"So how does this shit work?" Blaze asked, looking at one of the smaller cans of the silver glitter paint she'd picked.

"Paint goes up first on all four walls, ceiling gets painted white, then when the paint's dry, you do as many coats as you can get out of this glitter paint onto the wall picked as an accent wall, let it dry, and that's that."

"Okay then, what'd you want to do first?" I asked.

"Walls are already taped off from the primer, so let's hit the ceiling first."

"You're the boss," Blaze declared and we got to work.

With the three of us at it, the ceiling went fast. I got up on the step stool somebody had scrounged from somewhere and edged the ceiling with a brush while Saylor and Blaze went at it with the rollers on their extended handles.

We pulled tape off the walls, turned on the heat in the room and shut the door and did the ceiling in the next bedroom giving the paint a chance to do some drying before we pulled tape, taped off the ceiling and baseboards, and went at the walls.

It was an honest day's work, and by the time we had the walls in the master bedroom done with the regular paint, it was time to basically call it a day for now. They had to dry before we could get into the glitter paint she wanted on the accent wall.

"Dude, I'm starving," Blaze declared, rinsing brushes in the kitchen sink downstairs while Saylor disposed of paint tray liners in a big black trash bag.

"Kitchen isn't exactly conducive to cooking right now," Saylor declared. "Did anybody even grab any food from the old apartment?"

"We don't have a fridge yet, so that's okay. I still need to clean over there before handing in the keys and the like."

"They got boxes marked kitchen in here," Blaze said opening one up.

"Looks like all the dry goods and non-perishables from the kitchen cabinets," Saylor mused, looking back over her shoulder. "Nothing I can do anything with without a stove or even a microwave." She made a face.

"Where is the microwave, anyway?" Blaze asked. "I know you had one."

"It's around here somewhere," Saylor said with a shrug, giving the rest of the too-empty kitchen a scan.

"It's no problem," I said with a shake of my head and a shrug. "Let's just hit the *10-13*. Reflash'll be more than happy to make sure we're fed."

"When exactly were you guys planning on ordering up things like furniture and appliances?" Blaze asked. "Did you even set anything aside for that shit?"

I rolled my eyes. "Dude, you sound like my mom or my dad, of course I did. We just have to figure out what we want to do – like what kind of appliances and shit and do up the kitchen before we have them delivered."

"Ooo, hold on, I grabbed some of those paint chip cards and some wallpaper samples for the kitchen."

"Later!" Blaze cried. "I'm going to die of starvation. Can't you see I'm wasting away over here?"

"He's right, babe. That sandwich on the way back from the hardware store wore off a while ago."

"Okay! Okay, I'll curb my enthusiasm for now," she caved and I smiled, throwing an arm over her shoulders.

"Let's eat," I declared and steered her to the front of the house, Blaze falling into step with us.

28

*S*aylor...

The *10-13* was way busy and it took me half a second to realize that a big part of that was the crowd of Indigo Knights and the rest of their women scattered throughout the fishbowl and out on the barroom floor.

"Hey, look who it is!" Skids called, raising a glass over by the pool tables in his dapper leather vest with all its patches. I smiled and waved and Reflash who was near him in his typical cook's attire asked us, "You three hungry?"

"Starving!" Blaze called back.

"Head on up to the fishbowl, the three of you, and grab a seat at the big table," Skids ordered, and I wrapped both of my arms around Poe's one, twining my fingers of one hand through his and let him lead the way.

"Get much done today?" Oz asked as we walked by, Ellie tucked against his side.

"All the upstairs ceilings and the walls of the master bedroom. Things needed to dry before we can hit the accent wall in the master, but all in all I'd say we did pretty good. All that primer going up yesterday really helped out," Poe answered.

"Awesome," Oz declared, lowering his beer glass from his lips and smacking them around the word.

"We can come help some more next weekend with whatever you haven't gotten done," Lys called and Golden laughed and raised an eyebrow. She rolled her eyes and smacked him lightly in the chest. "And by 'we' I mean me and the rest of the girls."

"More painting?" Ellie declared. "You know I'm always ready for that."

"I know," Oz said in his sarcastic way and pulled her closer, smacking a kiss on her temple. I smiled and felt relaxed among the banter.

"I'm holding you all to it!" I said and we whisked by to head up to the fishbowl.

Narcos, Everleigh, and Driller were lounging inside along with Backdraft and Lily, and Youngblood – but no Chrissy.

"She's in the bathroom," Youngblood declared when he saw me scan for the lioness of a lawyer.

"Ah," I murmured.

"Grab a seat you three, what's shakin'?" Narcos asked, shoving a chair out from the opposite side of the table with his booted foot.

"Not much, just finished up with some painting. How about you guys? Why's everybody here?" Poe asked.

I let him take my coat and hang it on the back of the plush executive chair that served as the seating around the long glass table in the room. Like someone had plunked a boardroom right in the middle of the restaurant. Given the usual clientele of the place, it was actually fitting.

The longest glass wall looked out over the restaurant's bar area and the shorter glass wall over the short hall to the kitchen. Inside, the opposite short solid wall held a television, while the long wall behind where I was seated held three. All were silently playing some sport or another and were the focus of a few of the guys out by the taller standing tables near the dart boards.

Some of the girls stood talking and laughing around the pool table with their cues at the ready along with a flamboyant drag queen who looked absolutely fabulous in throwback edgy 80s angular makeup. Like they belonged in *Blade Runner* or *Ghost in the Shell* or something.

"I see Pasquale is back from his gay-cation," Poe said with a laugh.

Chrissy walked up and joined them as Youngblood looked back over his shoulder at her, Pasquale, Ally, and Claire around the pool table laughing at something that Pasquale was telling them.

"Yup. Guess he had a grand ol' time on it," Youngblood said.

"I'm so lost," I said laughing.

"Pasquale went on this cruise through the Caribbean over Christmas and New Year; the whole thing catering to an inclusive LGBTQA+ clientele. The whole time leading up to it, he kept calling it his 'gay-cation' and I think it was a thing for a lot of people displaced by family to do during the holidays," Narcos said and Everleigh nodded emphatically and happily beside him.

"I missed his flaming ass around here," Driller said with a grin.

"Is it weird that I did too?" Blaze asked, chuckling and I shook my head no.

"No, he's your friend, isn't he?"

"Let's just say he grew on some of us," Driller said.

"Pasquale can get a little animated," Poe said blushing.

"What I'm hearing is that some fragile male egos may or may not know how to handle all of the wonderfulness out there by the pool table," I said slyly and Everleigh bounded to her feet with one fingertip on her nose and the other excitedly pointing right at me.

I laughed and some of the rest of the guys did too.

"Fair assessment," Youngblood admitted freely, nodding.

"So why *is* everybody here?" Blaze asked.

"Putting together a charity ride," Narcos said coolly.

"Oh yeah? Who's the charity?" Blaze asked, leaning back in his seat.

"Never mind that for now," Youngblood declared, and I had a sneaking suspicion it might be me with the mountain of hospital bills I was likely to have looming and with how cagey everyone was being.

The talk was quashed for the time being with the arrival of the food we hadn't gotten a chance to order. Apparently, it was chef's choice, and I could be on board with that when a deep soup bowl filled with hearty broccoli cheddar soup was set in front of me and alongside it, a rustic thickly stuffed roast beef sandwich.

"This looks amazing," I declared and Reflash sauntered in a moment later wiping his hands on the towel over his shoulder.

"Well, put it in your face and tell a fella how it is!" He made a motion with his hands to hurry it up and laughing we all tried our food and died going straight to heaven.

"Oh, my God, this is so good!" I rolled the slight bite of soup on my tongue.

"Awesome. I'm thinkin' about doin' it as a lunch combo during the week."

"Got us actin' as your guinea pigs, huh?" Blaze asked.

"Shit, you think every meal's free?" Reflash demanded. "I gotta get somethin' out of it every now and again otherwise y'all are liable to eat me out of house and home."

We laughed, especially considering I knew for a fact that *everyone* paid their tab more often than not. However, I also learned that when Reflash told you to eat and it was on his dime you had better not refuse it.

I hummed in happiness and wondered aloud, "Do you cater weddings, because I would absolutely *love* if you did."

Silence rang out as everyone stopped and looked at me.

"Something you and Poe maybe want to announce to the rest of the squad? Should I get everybody in here?" Reflash asked.

I looked slowly to Poe who was laughing silently at me.

"Don't look at me, baby. I thought we had a plan."

I felt myself turn crimson and stammered, "Um, well, I guess I fucked *that* up!"

Laughter erupted around the table and Driller asked, "So for real? You guys getting hitched?"

I stared at Poe who grinned and nodded, slowly picking up speed.

"I asked her yesterday, at the hospital, but we didn't want to hurt any feelings and I had planned to get a ring and ask again in front of you guys."

"I am shit at keeping secrets or surprises. I thought you knew that about me – that I mentioned it or something."

Poe couldn't help himself. He threw back his head and laughed long and hard at my expense, but I couldn't be mad about it.

"Wow." Narcos chuckled and asked Blaze, "Did you know?"

Blaze was trying not to laugh too and said, "He told me today in the hardware store. Asked if I would be his best man."

"Alright!" Narcos got up and pumped a fist. Reflash opened up the door to the rest of the bar and hollered out, "Poe's gettin' hitched!"

"What?" Ally demanded and looked up through the glass at me startled. For the longest half a second of my life, I thought protest would go up but instead, a great big whoop went up and everybody started filtering to the fishbowl's door to congratulate us.

Reflash winked over at me. "Welcome to the biggest family you never knew you needed," he said and I smiled.

"You're wrong there," I said. "I've always known I needed it. I just never thought it would be anything I would *have*."

I looked at Poe and he reached over and put a hand on my knee.

"The only family that counts as far as I'm concerned," he said and I bit my bottom lip.

"Your mom and dad? Your sister?"

"Don't get a say. They had their shot at Christmas and they're going to have to do a bit of groveling to come back from that fuckup. I love you. That's it. The end of the story."

I leaned over and he met me halfway, kissing me soundly as everyone filled the room through the bottleneck of its door.

Suddenly, I was drowning in more well wishes than I knew what to do with and I realized that sometimes it was the family that was chosen that meant more than the family you were born to... and I think Poe had that figured out a while ago.

Of course, I was behind on the curve, having no family left myself, but looking around me at the room full of enthusiastic friends and club? I looked forward to learning.

EPILOGUE

*S*aylor...

"You ready?" I looked in the dressing-table mirror to Skids coming up behind me in a fine, deep blue suit. The canvas of the tent surrounding us flapped in the breeze off the bay.

We were set up in Bayside Park and I was in the smaller canvas square tent that sat at the end of the aisle waiting to take my walk. I was nervous, my heart thundering in my chest, and I didn't know why.

Probably because Lilli spent a fortune to make today perfect and you're afraid of face planting in the middle of the aisle like a klutz.

"I think so," I murmured and Skids smiled.

"You look beautiful," he said, holding out a hand to me and I swung my legs around and put my hand in his and stood.

Ally had made my dress. We had found this beautiful gown in a thrift store that was this lovely ivory with a mesh back and a line of buttons from my neck to my butt, except it had these *God-awful* poofy princess sleeves al la the nineties that had to go. So, she had carefully deconstructed and reconstructed the thing into something so incredibly Bohemian chic that I almost couldn't stand it and when I'd looked in the mirror the first time I had tried it on, I had burst into tears I had loved it so much.

The satin of the skirts whispered against my legs now that the awful tulle had been gotten rid of and it draped just beautifully into a train of only a few inches.

Some nineteen-forties era white shoes and a pair of sleek, natural stockings underneath and I was feeling sexy if not confident and almost couldn't wait for Poe to see me.

"Thank you again, for doing this," I said, my throat already trying to close up and Skids chuckled.

"It's my pleasure," he said as the music which had been playing turned to our cue and the flaps on the tent were pulled aside.

It was a long walk, it felt like, from here.

Up front, a trellised arch stood waiting. The officiant standing regal in his robes, our one concession to Poe's mother – that her pastor do the honors – which honestly hadn't been much to ask considering as president it was Skids' usual place but I had already asked him to walk me down the aisle, so…

"Here we go, head high. You're beautiful, Saylor."

I looked up at Skids who winked down at me and we started forward.

On one side, Ally stood furthest from the center, then Claire, then Everleigh, then Lilli, and finally as my maid of honor, Coco.

Then there was the empty space waiting for me, and then Poe. He had a knuckle pressed against his lips, his deep green eyes already starting to mist over at the sight of me. I felt my own eyes grow wet and gave him a meaningful look begging him not to start or I would, and I didn't want to ruin my makeup – even though I was sure waterproof *everything* had been used.

Next to Poe was his best man, Blaze. Then Backdraft, Driller, Golden, and Yale. Angel had agreed along with Narcos to be ushers and they stood in their places as well. Behind their suited figures were dress mannequins, and the idea that the rest of the ladies and I had. On the dress mannequins were their club colors. When they started down the aisle their colors were faced name patches forward, as much to show their place, but also because when they reached their place, they were to turn their headless, armless mannequin, so the back and the club's patch could preside over the wedding as much as the officiant.

I got to the front and Skids handed me off to Poe and I smiled and thanked him, following him to his front-row seat. Except where he was supposed to be seated on the end there was no chair. He went to the next one in, because the seat of honor had my granddad's guitar in it on its stand. His necklace, that I had given to Poe at Christmas, winking bright summer sunlight against its polished silver surface against the strings at the neck of the guitar, the silver chain secured around the tuning pegs.

A photo of my granddad sat on the ground amid a dusting of white rose petals, smiling out of the eight by ten silver frame that also winkled sunlight along its gleaming surface and I felt tears slip over the edges of my lashes and run down my cheeks.

I turned to Poe, and the smile in his eyes told me everything I had needed to know. That yes, this had been his idea and yes, he was so glad that I liked it.

"Dearly beloved, we are gathered here today to witness the union between Saylor Grace Dresden and Jeremy Allen Poe…"

It was a pretty speech from the pastor that didn't amount to a lot considering that to us, it was all bullshit, but we stood and waited for our turns having written our own vows to each other.

Poe got to go first, and I honestly had no idea what he would say. He took the wedding band from Blaze and I held out my hand. He slipped my fingertip just through and paused.

"I've thought over and over what I would say to you, and in front of all of these people and all of it just sounded trite or corny," he said. "Because there literally just aren't any words in any language to express to you just how I feel. There's no word to encompass how much I love you, or how I live for you. How every breath I take, when I exhale, I want it to be in the shape of your name. Or how I felt like only half a man before you looked up at me under a blue moon on what had to be one of the most trying days of your life."

He cleared his throat and glanced away to get it together as another fresh set of tears slid down my face and I couldn't stop smiling if I wanted to.

"I'm glad I was the one. I'm glad I made the choices I did that night and I'm gifted beyond measure to spend the rest of my life with you."

He slid the ring the rest of the way onto my finger and I sniffed.

"I love you," he said. "To that blue moon and back."

There was a titter of laughter and I laughed too and took his ring from Blaze who offered it to me.

I started it along his finger the same way he had mine and cleared my throat.

"You are," I swallowed hard and tried valiantly to get it together, starting again. "You are, quite simply, the best thing to have ever happened to me," I said.

"With nowhere to go, my back against a rock and nothing but hardships in front of me, you took my hand and led me out of the darkness. I can't tell you how grateful I am to have you by my side. You've done what no one has ever done for me. You've loved me, unconditionally, you've stood up for me when there wasn't even a need to do so, but you did, because that's who you are."

I choked up, I admit it.

Taking a deep breath, I continued.

"You give me shelter, you give me life, and I live for waking up with you in the morning. I would die without you at night, and I too don't have the words to express just how much I love you and how much you make me look forward to 'forever' even though I've never had a reason to look past the next few hours my entire life. You give me permission to dream and I want to dream so big with you until the end of time."

I slid the ring the rest of the way onto his finger and we didn't wait for the pastor or whatever to give us permission. Poe's hands gently cupped my face and we kissed. My arms going around his shoulders, my bouquet lovingly crafted by Lys scraping the back of his dove-gray tux jacket.

The wedding party erupted into cheers, camera shudders clicked, and applause swept over the rippling waters of the Chesapeake Bay.

We parted, and I was glad for this Teflon lip color that didn't transfer, as we turned and the preacher announced, "I give you Mr. and Mrs. Jeremy Poe!"

The little band struck up, music played, and we walked down the aisle, the rest of the club, both men and women, and Poe's immediate family following, after the guys had gathered their patched vests from their mannequins, of course.

The preacher directed the rest of our guests to the larger entertainment tent set closer to the water for refreshments while the rest of us were busy getting the marriage license signed and having our photos taken.

We signed the marriage license in front of a judge, hired specifically for this part and had our photos taken, the little table with its three seats behind it decorated in satin and lace, a crown of flowers around its edge.

"Congratulations, you two," the judge murmured, and we kissed once more. This time, now that the papers had been signed, everything somehow felt more official.

We took so many photos with the bay as a backdrop. The bridesmaids in their peach dresses, the groomsmen in their handsome gray tuxes. Poe's family, us with my granddad's guitar setup. I missed him, but by the same token, I knew he was here, and I knew he was oh so proud and pleased that I'd found a man like Poe. A man who wanted to help me be the best me I could be. A man who didn't want to change a thing about me.

Someone like my gran had been to my granddad.

Poe gave me roots, I gave him wings and that was all that mattered.

Still, what I wouldn't give for even a minute alone with him right now.

Reflash catered the wedding and served amazing fare. We ate and drank champagne toasts, and as the sun began to set, we had our first dance to *There Will Be Time* by Mumford & Sons.

I looked up into his eyes and he looked down into mine, and we might as well have been the only two people on the planet.

"I love you, Mrs. Poe," he whispered and kissed my forehead as we swayed. I felt my eyes close as I basked in the warmth of his love and whispered back, "And I love you, Mr. Poe. For the rest of our lives. For all that there is beyond them. I love you."

He pulled me closer and we swayed. Surrounded by love, surrounded by family both chosen and blood, both physical and ethereal.

He gave me roots.

I gave him wings.

We were all that we needed to be.

ALSO BY A.J. DOWNEY

The Sacred Hearts MC

1. Shattered & Scarred

2. Broken & Burned

3. Cracked & Crushed

3.5 Masked & Miserable (a novella)

4. Tattered & Torn

5. Fractured & Formidable

6. Damaged & Dangerous

The Virtues

1. Cutter's Hope

2. Marlin's Faith

3. Charity for Nothing

4. Stoker's Serenity

The Sacred Brotherhood

1. Brother to Brother

2. Her Brother's Keeper

3. Brother In Arms

4. Between Brothers

5. A Brother's Secret

6. A Brother At My Back

7. A Brother's Salvation

ABOUT THE AUTHOR

A.J. Downey specializes in writing real and relatable contemporary romance stories. She's from Seattle, WA and loves the Pacific Northwest. She finds inspiration from her surroundings, through the people she meets, and likely as a byproduct of way too much caffeine. An avid reader all of her life, it's now her turn to try and give back a little, entertaining as she has been entertained.

Stalker Information:

Website
www.ajdowney.com

Sign up for her newsletter at
http://eepurl.com/dkQiIH

Facebook Group - AJ's Sacred Circle
https://www.facebook.com/groups/authorajdowney/

facebook.com/authorajdowney

twitter.com/authorajdowney

instagram.com/ajdowney

bookbub.com/authors/a-j-downey